MARISSA BURT

A SLIVER of STARDUST

HARPER

An Imprint of HarperCollinsPublishers

A Sliver of Stardust

Copyright © 2015 by Marissa Burt
www.harpercollinschildrens.com

Library of Congress Cataloging-in-Publication Data
Burt, Marissa.
  A sliver of stardust / Marissa Burt. — First edition.
    pages cm
  Summary: After a strange encounter at a science competition,
Wren Matthews discovers a secret magical order known as the
Fiddlers, and must learn to use the power of stardust to save them,
herself, and the world from the return of a sinister enemy.
  ISBN 978-0-06-229155-4 (hardcover)
  [1. Fantasy.] I. Title.
PZ7.B94558Si 2015   2014047813
[Fic]—dc23   CIP
                                                             AC

Typography by Alison Klapthor
15 16 17 18 19 CG/RRDH 10 9 8 7 6 5 4 3 2 1

First Edition

For the fearful

ONE

Mary had a little bird,
Its coat was white as snow.
Everywhere that Mary went,
The bird was sure to go.

Wren Matthews was about to lose the Science Olympiad Trivia Challenge. Wren had never lost the challenge, had never come remotely close to losing the challenge, had never even considered the *possibility* of coming close to losing the challenge before this moment. Now, she sat at the exam table in the corner of the gym, her answer sheet mostly blank, oblivious to the seconds on the timer ticking past. She stared at the rafters, where a huge white bird soared over the tables that displayed students' science fair entries. As Wren watched, the bird swooped down, talons extended, and grabbed a live mouse from Bobby Felton's prizewinning project about rodent aggression.

Wren gasped, and her pencil fell to the table with a clatter.

The trivia challenge judge cleared her throat, peering at Wren disapprovingly over her bifocals. "Five minutes remaining, scholars." She shuffled through her thick stack of answer cards and tapped their edges neatly on the tabletop.

Wren snapped her attention back to her paper, trying to block out the annoying sound of Simon Barker's scribbling. Next to her, Simon's red head was bent low over his paper, and his pencil hadn't stopped moving.

Wren hadn't been surprised when Simon tied with her during the speed round of the trivia challenge, where being fast was nearly as important as being smart. In past years, other competitors had been fast, too. And she had expected that he would also be able to recite the first thirty-five digits of pi, which sent them through the second round neck and neck. But now they had reached the final written portion, and if Wren's answer sheet was any indication, things didn't look promising. There wasn't much time before the judge would tally their scores and announce the winner.

Wren tightened her grip on her pencil and read the problem she was working on for the third time. She licked her lips and tried to ignore the ominous sound of rustling feathers overhead. Wren wasn't afraid of birds. After all, being afraid of a harmless animal wasn't logical. No, she merely had a *healthy respect* for flying animals. The day-trip to the zoo, where she had been swarmed by the too-eager kookaburras, had taught her that. But Wren's mouth was dry. Her heart pounded much faster than usual. And no matter how many times she reread the question on the exam in front of her, she couldn't come up with the answer.

"Three minutes left, scholars." The judge's words were nearly blotted out by an unmistakable screech. Wren glanced up, then shrank down into her seat with a strangled scream, barely escaping the white bird as it dive-bombed the table. She could feel the air pressure shift with the thrum of its powerful wings when it swooped off, ruffling her hair in its wake. Wren ran a shaky palm over her bangs, sliding them into place, and glanced uneasily around. No one else seemed to care that a rogue bird had nearly taken her head off. In fact, no one else seemed to be doing much of anything. The judge leaned back in her chair, her index cards frozen midtap. Wren's parents' faces were turned in her direction, but their smiles were oddly fixed in place. The rest of the room stood motionless, as though someone had pressed a giant pause button on all the activity. Or almost all of it. Next to Wren, Simon sighed and reached for another piece of scrap paper without looking up from his work.

Wren scanned the ceiling. Could it be possible that no one else saw the bird? Had she imagined it? But there it was. Perched on the basketball backboard like it owned the place. As Wren watched, the white bird launched off its roost, glided over the crowd of frozen homeschoolers, and landed on the outstretched arm of a woman standing a few feet away from the trivia challenge table.

The woman was the only person moving in the sea of people. She fixed her light-yellow-brown gaze on Wren and pointed to the floor. Wren glanced down and swallowed another scream. At first, she thought the white bird had somehow dropped Bobby's mouse at her feet. But then she saw that it wasn't an animal at all; instead, the bird had delivered a packet of sooty papers. Wren scooped up the bundle. The bird woman gave her a sharp, distinct nod before disappearing into a puff of shimmering blue-green smoke. The instant she was gone, the rest of the room exploded back into motion. The low rumble of milling homeschoolers. The buzz of the timer. The sound of the judge's voice.

"Time's up, scholars."

Wren leaned out of her chair as though getting a better view could somehow convince her that the woman and her bird hadn't vanished into thin air. "Um," Wren managed, shoving the packet of papers into her sweatshirt pocket as the trivia judge reached for the exams. Wren's voice sounded strange to her own ears, like she hadn't used it in forever. Should she do something? Tell the judge about the bird? And say what? *There was a large bird that you somehow didn't notice, and it flew to a woman who looked at me and then disappeared?* The air where the woman had been standing still flared with little dots of aqua light, so bright they sent matching shooting pains through Wren's skull. She rubbed her eyes.

"Let's see what we have here." The judge flipped through her stack of answer cards, comparing them with Simon's and Wren's responses. Her fingers hovered over Wren's half-finished answer sheet, and Wren studied the pebbled tabletop. She used to purposely

miss an answer or two, so she wouldn't make the older
kids feel bad that she was smarter than them, but that
was before Simon began coming to the homeschool
conference. Now all the questions she didn't have time
to finish would cost her the challenge.

Wren glanced over at her biggest competitor to find
that Simon was staring off past her shoulder, his forehead furrowed as though he was still working problems
in his head. Wren could see the red ribbon that went
with this year's biology medal peeking out from under
his collar. Simon's entry describing advances in animal
husbandry had also won him first place in the living
science portion of the competition, and he was up for
the 4-H prize and just about everything else to do with
science. Except astronomy. That was the one subject
Wren would always win.

The judge folded her hands and set them on top of
their exams. "It's been a close competition this year,
and now it's down to you: Simon Barker and Wren
Matthews. I couldn't be more proud." Her voice was
overly cheerful, especially considering the fact that two
eleven-year-olds were the top contenders for the upper
division trivia challenge. "I'm happy to announce that
we have a tie this year. Wren. Simon. Congratulations."

The judge beamed at them as though they had won a trip to Disneyland instead of not winning anything at all. Wren reached for her half-finished exam. How was it possible that her incomplete answers tied with Simon's annoying nonstop pencil scratching?

Next to her, Simon stood. "Nice job."

"You, too." Wren watched him tuck his pencil into his jacket pocket.

Simon was always dressed like he'd been born a hundred years too late. A tailored vest with a matching wool cap. An overcoat in cold weather. Even a pocket watch that he liked to consult whenever a conference session was supposed to end. He sneaked a peek at it, snapping the gold cover open with a click.

"Tied for the win!" Wren's mom said, coming up behind Wren and giving her and Simon high fives. "How perfect is that?"

Wren's dad clasped his hands together first over one shoulder, then the other, like a champion would, and Wren let a tiny laugh escape. They wouldn't care about the tie. Wren's mom and dad weren't like some of the parents at the Science Olympiad, all helicopterish and worried about their kids being the best. Wren's parents were hardcore unschoolers, which meant they pretty much left Wren's education in her own hands.

Four years earlier, the Homeschool Association had started an astronomy track, and for the first time Wren had begged her parents to go to the Science Olympiad, mainly because of the annual stargazing party. They were dubious at first, pasting on smiles and nodding at all the earnest discussions about core classes and home-school methods and arguments over How Children Learn Best. Afterward, Wren and her parents chowed down at the Mexican restaurant around the corner and celebrated not doing any of those things.

Then Wren's dad met Simon's dad, and now the Mexican dinners were Wren's parents and Simon's dad talking a little bit about unschooling but mostly about politics and what books they were reading, and how much they all had in common. It was odd, considering how intelligent Wren's mom and dad were, that they had failed to notice that Simon and Wren had exactly two things in common: 1. They were both the smart-est kids their age. 2. Neither of them could stand being around the other.

TWO

A tisket, a tasket.

Use the dust to mask it.

I wrote a letter to the one,

And on the way I dropped it.

I dropped it. I dropped it.

And on the way I dropped it.

A little girl picked it up

And put it in her pocket.

Iow are things going with cross-country?" Wren's dad asked Simon's dad around a mouthful of enchilada. "You have any good races scheduled for this year?"

"You bet." Mr. Barker reached across the table to pass Wren the salsa. "Simon and I are training for a 10K in July."

Wren scooped a mound of salsa onto her plate.

Running a 10K sounded like a kind of punishment. She was glad Simon was at the opposite end of the table, with their parents sandwiched between them. She crunched into a chip and replayed the scene in the gym over in her head for the millionth time. Was there a special breed of bird that, when threatened, produced a defensive cloud of gas that obliterated people? At least a skunk-bird made more sense than people appearing and disappearing into blue smoke. She wished everyone would hurry up and finish eating so she could get somewhere by herself and examine the packet of papers that the bird had dropped.

"Wren, you could join Simon's cross-country club!" Her mom's voice interrupted her thoughts. "Wouldn't that be fun? Jogging together is a great way to get to know people. *And* maximize your potential."

Wren choked down a laugh. Her mother wouldn't be caught dead running. "Can we not talk about this now?" she asked, hoping that Simon wasn't paying attention to the conversation. "Besides, the Science Olympiad *is* social."

"All the more reason to build off this great foundation, Wren. I just want you to be well-rounded, sweetie." Wren's mom was using her I-mean-business voice, and Wren wasn't ready to find out what voice she'd use if she knew about the bird hallucination or whatever it was. Wren's mom turned to Simon's dad. "Last month I twisted Wren's arm to take a babysitting training class with other girls her age, and this month I've made an agreement with her: a one-hour limit on her computer time until she's found something social to do." She patted Wren's hand. "It's like I always say: No girl is an island. People need one another."

Wren's face flamed with heat, and it wasn't because of the spicy salsa. The babysitting class had been a fail. A whole weekend spent making forced conversation with kids she'd never met before and would never see again. If her mom was hoping for social development, she'd have to aim somewhere else. All Wren walked away with from that class was a hazy understanding of emergency CPR and a sore stomach from where her partner had practiced the Heimlich maneuver.

"Great idea," Simon's dad said. "That's the biggest challenge about unschooling, isn't it? Finding opportunities to meet other kids? Simon has some trouble with that, too."

Wren made herself look at Simon, but he was examining his fajitas as though he'd never seen a tortilla before.

"The college has a bunch of clubs." Wren's dad wiped

his mouth with his napkin. "I could pull some strings and see if they'd let younger students participate." He leaned back and put one arm around Wren's mom's shoulders.

"That's an interesting idea," Simon's dad said. "They could give each other moral support."

"Sure," Wren's mom said. "Simon and Wren could really maximize their potential together."

Wren poked a fork at the remainder of her burrito. *I'd rather go running.* Her parents usually weren't this focused on what she was doing. They were busy with work, and Wren was busy with whatever she was studying, and once in a while they played a board game together. Until a few months ago, when the neighbor who'd lived down the street from Wren her entire life said, "You have a daughter? How come I've never seen her before?" And, while Wren's mom was perfectly content to let her maximize her educational potential on her own, she was now obsessed with Wren's social development.

Wren wished she could make her mom understand that she was happy being by herself, but it seemed like her mom had seen too many movies in which the smart, quiet girl dreamed about being pretty and popular. Sure, Wren spent a lot of time alone, but she never felt like she was missing out. She could read whatever books she wanted. She could stay up late puttering around her favorite astronomy forum. She could watch old sci-fi reruns on TV. Wren had lots of plans for her time, and none of them included clubs at the community college, cross-country running, or Simon Barker.

Wren's napkin slipped off her lap, and when she reached down to retrieve it from under the table, she noticed an odd mark on her sweatshirt. One side of her hoodie was covered with black dirt. She brushed at the stain, but instead of getting better, the spot seemed to grow darker, and even worse, little bits of soot transferred onto her fingers. Wren rubbed her hands together, and in the dimness under the table, the dust flared with blue-green light. Exactly like the cloud around the bird woman.

The papers! They seemed to be giving off the same strange dust that the bird had emitted. Dinner or not, she had to look at them now. Wren snatched her napkin off the floor and slid back up into her seat to find that her parents and Simon's dad had started debating the merits of the new mayoral candidates. She reached a tentative hand into her pocket and discreetly pulled out the bundle, which sparked with little blue lights as she unfolded it.

Keeping it low in her lap so the others wouldn't

notice, Wren began to read the paragraph centered on
the first page:

Once I saw a little bird
Come hop, hop, hop.
So I cried, "Little bird,
Will you stop, stop, stop?"
And was going to the window
To say "How do you do?"
But he shook his little tail,
And far away he flew.

There was nothing else. No explanation, no pictures, nothing but the silly rhyming words. The next
poem was just as bad:

Away, birds, away!
Take a little and leave a little,
And do not come again;
For if you do, I will shoot you through,
And there will be an end of you.

Was it supposed to be poetry? Literature had never
been Wren's strong suit, but even she could tell these
were no good. She skimmed through more rhymes

and was halfway done with the packet when she finally
stumbled across one she recognized:

> *Twinkle, twinkle, little star,*
> *How I wonder what you are.*
> *Up above the world so high,*
> *Like a diamond in the sky.*
> *There your bright and tiny spark*
> *Lights the traveler in the dark,*
> *How I wonder what you are,*
> *Twinkle, twinkle, little star.*

Wren's mom had sung this to her when she was a
little girl. It used to be her favorite. Wren flipped to
the back cover. As if it had been added later, one more
poem was written in shimmery ink:

> *'Twas once upon a time,*
> *When Jenny Wren was young,*
> *How expertly she played and how prettily she sung.*

> *The Ancient and Honorable Guild of the Fiddlers*
> *   invites*
> *Jennifer Wren Matthews*
> *to join their number.*

You are expected at Pippen Hill tomorrow.
Sapiens dominabitur astris.

Wren rubbed her thumb over the embossed letters. Was this some sort of practical joke? Nursery rhymes and a guild of fiddlers? This day kept getting weirder and weirder. Her thumb was black, as though bits of the poems were sticking to her. Wren folded the papers, sending a shower of blue sparks to the floor, and tucked them back in her pocket. That was when she noticed that Simon Barker was staring at her, his gaze flicking between her face and the smudges on her hand.

"You got the poems, too?" Simon said in a near whisper, glancing at the grown-ups, who were distracted by their political debate. Wren's surprise at him speaking directly to her was soon overcome by the sight of his left hand, covered with the same clinging, shimmery dust.

THREE

As I was going up Pippen Hill,
Pippen Hill was steep.
And there I found the truth of it,
All the secrets I would keep.

After Wren woke up the next morning, she stayed in bed for a long time. Her sleep had been plagued by strange dreams, ones where the whole world was black and white and a chorus of voices kept chasing after her. Wren pushed the images from her mind and pulled out the bag she kept in her nightstand drawer. The sky map on her bedroom ceiling was nearly finished, tiny glow-in-the-dark stars marking out the patterns of the Northern Hemisphere. The other walls waited to be transformed into snippets of the Equatorial and Southern Hemispheres.

Wren's dad had gotten her a student pass to the college observatory, and since they lived in the faculty housing on campus, it didn't take much to sweet-talk him into taking her there on clear nights. Wren liked to mark out the constellations she had actually seen with blue stars. Just last week she had finally gotten a good glimpse of Leo.

But replacing Leo's old stars with new blue ones didn't distract her for long. Wren reached under her pillow and pulled out the folded shimmering papers again, as if staring at them would uncover their meaning. Dinner had ended too soon for Wren and Simon to talk more, but they had agreed to meet this morning at a nearby coffee shop.

When Wren arrived in the kitchen, her mom was about to leave for work. "I'm so proud of you, sweetie," her mom said as she poured her tea into a travel mug. "Getting up this morning and taking initiative."

Wren didn't bother to correct her. If her mom thought interrogating Simon about his packet of papers counted as her social interaction, Wren wasn't going to argue.

The sky was surprisingly clear and sunny for early spring, and after biking to the coffee shop, Wren was hot and thirsty. Simon had beaten her there and was sitting at an outdoor table, two bottles of pop in front of him.

Wren parked her bike and grabbed the packet of papers from the white wicker basket.

"Root beer is the best option here," Simon said, sliding one of the bottles toward Wren without looking up from the notebook he was flipping through. "No caffeine. Best value for the price. And"—he smiled in Wren's direction—"it tastes good."

"Can't argue with that logic," Wren said, slipping into the chair across from him. "Did you bring your poems?"

They traded, and Wren sipped her root beer while she read. Simon's back page had a different rhyme about a canary, but the rest were the same. And so was the shimmering dust.

"There's no Pippen Hill anywhere in town." Simon opened a fat folder full of maps he'd printed off the internet. "How can we be expected at Pippen Hill today if there is no such thing?"

Wren stared at the wrinkled edges of one of the maps. Simon must have stayed up all night doing research. "What about similar names?" she said, making it sound as though she'd done more than just think about the poems. "What if there's a location that used to be called Pippen Hill?"

Simon pulled another file out of his backpack. "Historical maps, all the way back to the town's founding in 1851. There's never been a Pippen Hill anywhere around here." He tossed the stack in front of her. "There are, however, plenty of hills that have had apple orchards on them."

"Apples?" Wren echoed. "What do apples have to do with anything?"

"Pippins are a type of apple," Simon said in a lecturing tone. "I'm surprised you didn't know that, Wren."

Wren ignored the barb. Why would he think she was some kind of apple expert? "Okay. But maybe the apples are a coincidence." Wren flipped through the neatly cataloged maps. "What about the town's historical society—"

"Already called them," Simon said. "They've never heard of a Pippen Hill or any kind of fiddling guild." He hunched forward, leaning his elbows on his knees. "I bet it's some kind of a test."

"A test?" Wren handed the files back to Simon. "For what? To see if we can read nonsense poems?"

"Not a test about the poems." Simon looked in her direction. "A test for the fiddler people. Maybe they want to see if we're clever enough to find Pippen Hill by ourselves."

Wren was used to seeing Simon's profile while their parents talked to each other, but now she found it odd that he rarely maintained eye contact, even when speaking directly to her, which made him appear a little shifty.

"I'm sure of it," he continued. "This invitation is a riddle."

"Why would they—"

"Why would they do anything?" Simon interrupted. "Why invite us with nursery rhymes? Why the shimmering dust? Why use a falcon to deliver the papers?"

"You saw the bird?"

"Falcon," Simon said, rummaging around in his backpack. "Long wings. Swift flight. And did you see those talons? Birds of prey are fascinating animals."

"You saw the falcon." Wren didn't care what he called it.

"Of course I saw the falcon." Simon sounded annoyed and started skimming through his notebook again. "Who didn't see the falcon?"

"Um . . . everyone else? I thought I was the only one, or that I was imagining the whole thing, or that the bird was someone's science project or—"

"No live animals are allowed to roam free in the main exhibition hall," he said with a disapproving frown, as though Wren was suggesting they break conference rules.

"Maybe you were too busy scratch-scratch-scratching with your pencil," Wren said, leaning in so Simon would look at her and actually hear what she was saying, "but *no one else* saw the bird." She told him how everything seemed like it had been paused for a moment. And then it hit her. "Except for your pencil. You weren't on pause either. You *did* see it!"

"How else do you think you managed to tie me for the win? With all the commotion, I kept losing my place in the trivia questions. I was lucky to finish the first problem before time was up." He pulled out a pencil and scribbled something in the margin of his notebook. "I must be missing something."

"*I* managed to tie with *you*?" Wren said to the top of his head. "I don't think so. If it hadn't been for the stupid bird, I'd have— Wait, how many years have I won the trivia challenge?" Wren put her finger on her chin as though she had to think hard. "That's right, four. So I'd have a fifth medal. You should thank your lucky stars that bird showed up when it did. I ought to—"

Wren caught her breath as something clicked. "That's it! The stars!" She grabbed her packet of papers and rustled through it, sending aqua sparks ricocheting around their tabletop, until she found the page with the invitation. "*Astris* means 'stars.'" Wren might not have spent the whole night Googling the topography of the town, but she had looked up the Latin phrase. She pointed to it. "*Sapiens dominabitur astris*: 'A wise man can rule the stars.' That's the clue."

"Clue to what?"

"Your riddle!" Wren folded the papers back up. "I know where Pippen Hill is."

Simon had walked to the coffee shop, so Wren wheeled her bike alongside as they made their way across the university campus. "The observatory is surrounded by apple trees," she said, following the familiar path. "My dad told me the whole campus used to be an orchard." She mimicked his teacherish tone from earlier. "I'm surprised you didn't know that, Simon."

But Wren soon forgot to be snarky with him. As they approached the observatory, she noticed something she had never seen before. Something she was certain had never been there before. Situated in a clump of apple trees some distance from the observatory building was a cottage that looked like it belonged in a fairy tale, complete with misshapen bricks, thatched roof, and a tottering second story dotted with chimneys.

Wren propped her bike against a tree, and they picked their way along the uneven stone pathway that led to the front porch. "How could I have never seen this before?"

"You've never seen this house before, and here it is." Simon took the porch steps two at a time. "No one else saw the falcon, yet both you and I saw it. And no one else saw the dust but you and me. Somehow everything is related."

"How do you know no one else saw the dust?"

"My dad didn't." Simon shrugged. "I accidentally dropped my packet in the living room, and he never said a word, even though the carpet was covered with the stuff."

Wren thought of how the papers had stained her pocket. If her mom had noticed that half of Wren's hoodie was covered with ashes, she would have had plenty to say about it.

"Every problem has a logical explanation." Simon rubbed his forehead vigorously, like he could find the answer by sheer willpower. "If we had more data, we could come up with a better hypothesis."

"Well, then, what are we waiting for?" Wren straightened her sweatshirt and knocked on the weathered door.

When it opened, Wren knew that they had indeed found Pippen Hill. Standing in front of them was the mysterious woman who had disappeared at the trivia challenge, and perched on her shoulder was her sleek white falcon.

"I'm Mary," the woman said, giving them a conspiratorial smile. Mary's dreadlocked hair was twisted into a fat knot on the back of her head, and thick strings of beads were looped around her neck. "You are Wren and Simon, the brand-new Fiddler apprentices"—she pulled a small silver hourglass from her skirt pocket and peered at it—"who are right on time. Come in."

FOUR

Ride a cock-horse up to the sky
And see a fine lady who won't tell a lie.
Rings on her fingers and bells on her toes,
She shall have music wherever she goes.

Before Wren knew what was happening, Mary had whisked them through the door into what must have once been the living room of the house. She couldn't be sure, though, because there were plants everywhere. Green vines snaked up the walls and twisted around an ancient-looking chandelier overhead. Wren ducked under the hanging baskets, whose bright red and gold flowers were drowned out by all the gloomy green. An overstuffed leather armchair and matching couch squatted in the center of the room like unsuspecting prey in the middle of a vast jungle.

The bangles on Mary's wrist clinked together as she made her way to the one wall that was lined with books instead of plants. Mary's fingers were covered with rings, but Wren noticed one in particular, a black oval with tiny dots of silver speckling its surface. A ring that looked like the night sky.

"The universe is full of music, isn't it, Wren?" Mary said, noticing how Wren was staring at her jewelry. "If only we have ears to hear." She gave Wren an evaluating look. "I suspect you are a keen listener. Have a seat."

Wren made her way across the room, taking care not to disturb any of the musty knickknacks that crowded every available surface. All of it was coated with a thick layer of dust, as though no one had cleaned the room in years. A silver goblet entwined with ivy rested on a side table, a tarnished hand mirror propped up against it. In one corner, an ancient birdcage hung behind a veil of ferns, and judging by the thick cobwebs on its bars, the falcon that now perched on Mary's shoulder hadn't lived there for a long time. Wren sat on the edge of the chair, which was positioned right next to an old hourglass that was twice its size. A few crystals teetered on the interior funnel.

"What's going on?" Wren said when she realized that no explanation from Mary was forthcoming. "I saw you and your bird at the Olympiad. Why did—"

"Falcon," Simon interrupted, sitting down on a rickety old rocking chair and crossing his ankle over one knee. "She brought her falcon to the Olympiad."

Wren shot Simon a death glare, which, of course, he was oblivious to. "Your falcon, then," she said in a stiff voice. "That delivered the invitation to become part of the fiddling guild. What does that even mean?"

"Excellent creatures, falcons." Mary reached into her pocket and fed the falcon something that sounded crunchy. The bird shifted on its perch, giving Wren a glimpse of the leather shoulder guard Mary wore. "And further confirmation you belong with the Fiddlers. You saw my falcon, and you saw me play the stardust, which means that you, too, can work the stardust's magic." Mary moved over to a cobwebby corner and ran her hand down one shelf. A spiral of blue-green danced in the air, and a low hollow note filled the room. "The magic calls to you, doesn't it?"

Wren sat frozen in place. *Magic?*

The dust formed a tiny column of smoke between Mary's fingers. It soon blossomed into a cloud of shimmering fog that swirled around her, setting her clothes billowing. Mary spoke under her breath, and Wren could only catch a few words—something about secrets and seeing—because the rest was lost in the crooning of an unearthly wind. Mary raised one hand up in the air and swiped it down in front of her in a fluid motion, and the smoke flared with the bright light of a rainbow of colors. The next moment, the room was transformed. The wall behind the bookshelves melted away and revealed a large workroom with a low table centered in front of a crackling fire. Next to it stood racks covered with glass jars and bottles, bunches of herbs and dried flowers hanging between them. In the corners of the room, candlelight flickered from wax-covered sconces, bathing everything in an orange glow.

"What—?" Wren found her voice.

"How did you do that?" Simon asked, his pencil, for once, frozen in his hand.

"Stardust is an element found in all living things, yet it is invisible to most of the world," Mary said. She looked taller somehow, now that the maelstrom around her had stilled. As she continued, she pulled a basket from the collection on the top shelf. "Those who can see the stardust can manipulate it to their own ends.

Here, among ordinary people, I use it to hide my house from those who would ask bothersome questions." She set the basket down on the table with a thump. When she opened the lid, more of the dust drifted out. "But Fiddlers see things as they really are."

Wren couldn't help herself. She drew near the table, one wavering hand reaching for the stardust. Aqua sparkles winked among the ashes. More than anything, Wren wanted to gather it, to run it through her fingers, to toss it up in the air like a smattering of miniature constellations.

"You feel its pull, don't you?" Mary was watching Wren.

Wren nodded wordlessly.

"Two new apprentices from the wild." Mary looked at Wren and Simon fondly, as if they were long-lost relatives. "I can hardly believe my good fortune." Mary reached into the basket and pulled out a bundle of cloth. "You will have many questions, and, when it is right, you will find your answers. All lambs need time. This"—she shook ordinary dust out of a black and gray garment—"is your apprentice uniform. Put it on while I tell you what you need to know."

Wren glanced at Simon, who had tucked his

notebook into his vest pocket and was already wrapping the fabric around his shoulders. The dark folds fell almost to the floor, making it look like Simon belonged on the set of a sci-fi movie. Or in a monastery. He began fastening the long row of buttons that ran up the center of the cloak.

Mary loaded the basket with a collection of bottles and flasks. When she spoke, her voice was so low that the words themselves sounded like secrets. "Since the beginning of time, the world has been full of the unseen. The sun lights the Earth by day, and the moon watches over all like a diamond in the night sky, but it's in the twilight—the moment when the first new stars are born—that all living things are bathed in stardust. And magic."

The fire covered half of Mary's face in shadow. "For a time, we who could work the magic lived in peace with the people around us. They would come to us for small favors: to ease the birth of a baby or enhance a fruitful harvest. Ordinary people called us Fiddlers, because the way we coaxed life from stardust reminded them of the lesser magic of their musicians." She waved one graceful arm through the air, and Wren thought of the spiral of stardust and how it looked like some otherworldly dance.

"But as time passed, people became less accepting of
the Fiddlers and more suspicious of things they could
not explain." Mary's voice hardened, and she leaned
toward Wren. "Their hearts grew cold, and they saw
evil in our good gifts. They began to despise and shun
the Fiddlers, and soon any record of the good we had
done was lost. The world fell into ignorance, and most
people forgot there had been any such thing as Fiddler
magic." Mary's falcon fluttered from her shoulder to a
ledge on the wall that must have been crafted especially
for it. "Scraps of the Fiddler story are still found in
children's rhymes, and hints of our powers are woven
into legends of other lands. What many consider nonsense is really a garbled version of the truth."

"So the poems you sent us . . . They're supposed
to be about the Fiddlers?" Wren pulled the packet of
papers out of her pocket, letting her gaze fall on the
topmost one about a hopping little bird. She couldn't
see the connection between the wild tale that Mary
was spinning and old Mother Goose rhymes.

"The rhymes have their own kind of magic." Mary
nodded at the papers in Wren's hand. "The ones you
have there are instructions for how to weave the stardust.

But there are other rhymes, some that record what happened to Fiddlers long ago, and some that even foretell what may yet come to pass."

"Instructions for weaving the stardust," Simon echoed. "How exactly does one go about doing that?"

Mary laughed at his question. "You won't learn it by taking notes, that's for sure. That's why you're not a student, you're an apprentice. Apprentices learn by doing. You'll learn to be a Fiddler by working the stardust's magic."

Wren's mind whirled. Could it be possible? A small part of her thought the whole thing was some enormous joke, but she had seen the magic with her own eyes. Besides, the rest of her felt connected to what Mary was saying, like a string was stretched between them, pulling her near. "So what next?" she asked. "What kind of spells can you—I mean, *we*—do? I bet you do all sorts of things to help other people and stuff." Her mouth was working to catch up with her thoughts. "I can't wait to tell my parents. My dad is always going on about—"

Mary interrupted her. "Wren, you mustn't. Not yet." She frowned at both of them. "It is a dangerous thing to be a Fiddler in this world. Ordinary people don't understand. You cannot breathe a word of this to anyone." Her gold-flecked eyes seemed to plead with them. "When you are stronger, you may tell whomever you wish and endure the consequences. Until then, you will set your mind to learning everything that I and the others can teach you."

Prickles crawled over Wren's skin. She imagined telling her parents about all of this—from the flying bird to the children's rhymes to the Fiddlers—and wondered what they would say. If they couldn't see the stardust for themselves, would they believe her anyway?

"What others?" Wren swung the cloak around her shoulders and began fastening the buttons. In that moment, she knew that it didn't matter if no one else in the world believed her. It didn't matter if she had to keep the secret forever. If there was magic in the world, she wanted to play it.

FIVE

Wash the dishes, wipe the dishes,
Ring the bell for tea.
Three good apprentices,
I will give to thee.

Mary led them through the workroom to an alcove nestled in the back. There was a circular green door in the center, and Mary knocked on it.

When the door opened, a delicious smell wafted out. It promised pies and cookies and every delicious thing Wren had ever seen in a bakery window. The man standing beyond it looked older than Wren's father. His dark hair was shot through with silver, and the crinkles around his eyes hinted that he often smiled. As if to confirm Wren's suspicion, his face broke into a wide grin.

"Mary," he said in a booming voice as he pecked the air near her cheeks. "You're just in time for supper. Liza will be pleased."

"Liza's back? Where is she? Did she bring the potions I asked for?" Mary brushed past him into the room beyond, which glowed orange from the fire blazing in the stone hearth. Worn-looking furniture sat next to tables crowded with books. Shelves full of glass jars and bottles covered the walls, so that the space felt like a strange blend of an old-fashioned sitting room and an herbalist's shop.

"Allow me to introduce myself," the man in front of her said with a formal bow. "I'm Baxter, and I'd wager you must be the apprentices Mary told us about. Outstanding. I never thought I'd see the day. Two new apprentices from the wild."

"Mary told you about us?" Simon asked, reaching for the pencil behind his ear. What he found note-worthy in that statement, Wren couldn't imagine, but he rifled through the pages of his notebook and began to write.

"I'm Wren," she said. "And this is Simon."

Simon grunted and continued to scribble, talking without looking up. "This stardust," he said. "How does it change the appearance of things?" He frowned down at the page in front of him. "Is there a material alteration? Or more of an optical illusion? Perhaps it might be both, because there's no way the cottage we saw outside was as big as this place—"

"Do you like cake?" Baxter asked, bypassing Simon's interrogation.

Wren opened her mouth, hunting for the thread of the conversation. Was this some secret code for stardust? Was Baxter talking about magic? Then Baxter laughed. "Why am I even asking? Who *doesn't* like cake?"

He ushered them past the musty furniture and into a kitchen nearly the size of the first floor of Wren's house. An iron chandelier filled with flickering candles hung from the ceiling. Two large stone countertops flanked the room, with all manner of cookware spotting their surfaces. Large bowls piled high with red and purple berries crowded next to one another, and a huge butcher block squatted in the center of it all, covered with flour. In one corner of the room, a black falcon perched next to another feathered in deep purple.

Baxter examined a row of tarts that were set out next to a flat circle of dough. "Beautiful!" he exclaimed, kissing his fingertips.

"Those look good," Wren said. "You must like to cook."

Baxter narrowed his eyes at her. "Like to cook? Oh, child," he said, "you have much to learn." He wiped his hands on the long white apron that hung from his waist and reached for the huge oven door. "One doesn't just like to cook. One is born to cook." He slid out a round chocolate cake, inhaling deeply as he set it down on the counter. "Or, as the case may be, to bake. Here, you take care of the whipped cream."

While Wren scooped the perfect white peaks from a mixing bowl into a smaller serving dish, she looked around the kitchen. There was a pot of something steaming on the stove, and Simon had been put to work arranging fruit and cheese on a wide platter. Baxter hoisted a tray of frosted glasses and beckoned Wren to follow. They walked into a dining room where the walls were all windows that looked out on to a tangled green forest.

"Where are we?" Wren stared at the trees. This didn't look like the college campus at all.

"Right where you belong, darling Wren," a throaty female voice said. A woman with dark hair curving around her tanned face came up to Wren and kissed her, first on one cheek, then the other. The woman set the fluted glass she was holding on the nearby table, then lifted a perfectly manicured hand to riffle Wren's bangs. "I could do something with you, I think." She stepped back, examining Wren as though she were something for sale. The woman was dressed in black, her form-fitting clothes drawn together by a wide red belt. "Much potential."

"Good luck," Baxter said under his breath as he passed her with the chocolate cake, and Wren opened her mouth to snap out a retort until she realized he was wishing *her* luck with this woman.

"Leave Wren alone, Liza," Mary said as she helped Baxter set the table. "She needs lessons in stardust, not in fashion."

"Really, Mary, you'd never know we're sisters." Liza began picking at Mary's ratty hair. "There is a most fabulous salon in Paris. If you would only—"

Simon had swapped his notebook for one of the maps he had brought to the coffee shop and was now unfolding it. "There is the observatory," he mumbled from behind the wrinkled page. "And with Main Street running there"—the map jiggled as he poked it—"and the edge of campus here. Aha!" Simon carefully folded

the map. "That must be the forest outside of town."
He looked around triumphantly. "I don't precisely
know how we got here, but it appears that Pippen Hill
stretches underground somehow." He glanced over at
Liza and Mary, seeming to notice for the first time that
there were other people in the room having a different
conversation. "Oh, sorry. Wren asked where we were,
and I . . ." He trailed off.

Liza raised her eyebrows and exchanged a look with
Mary.

"Clever ones, these new apprentices of yours,"
Baxter said as he set down the chocolate cake, now
garnished with a bright red dipping sauce.

"They're not mine," Mary said stiffly and turned to
Simon. "Well done, Simon."

"He's right?" Wren looked out at the forest.

Mary calmly picked up a pitcher of water and began
to fill the glasses. "We were here long before the university, though they, too, found this to be a prime
stargazing spot. The stardust hides the entrance to Pippen Hill. It's how we keep out the nosy non-Fiddlers.
They have no more idea that we're here than you did."
The ice cubes in the glasses clinked together as she
poured.

"But I've come to the observatory hundreds of times. How is it that I've never seen anything?"

"Because I didn't yet want you to see anything. Now that you've awoken to the reality of stardust, you will find that many things are different than you've always perceived them to be." Mary nudged her to a seat at the table. "Don't look so distraught, Wren. The ability to do things unseen by non-Fiddlers is one of the perks of stardust. You can count on there being many others."

She and Liza shared a laugh, obviously enjoying Wren's confusion, and found their seats. They looked as much like sisters as the sun and the moon. Mary was fair, her long strings of beads trailing over her ruffled dress like some waifish hippie. Liza was swarthy and mysterious, her glamour straight out of the pages of a runway magazine.

"Decadent as ever, *mi amor*," Liza said to Baxter as he set one of the perfectly baked tarts before her. It was shaped like a heart, and Wren could tell by the way Baxter winked at Liza that they were a couple.

Wren took a seat, her mind spinning. Hiding a whole house in plain sight? What else was possible with stardust? The mouth-watering smell of the cake Baxter slid onto the plate in front of her was irresistible.

She felt a laugh bubbling up from somewhere down below. Magic was real. And she was going to learn how to use it.

"What do you think of our little feast, Wren?" Baxter was watching her carefully. "Good?"

"Perfect," Wren said.

SIX

There was a Crooked Man,
And he walked a crooked mile.
He found a crooked sixpence
Against a crooked stile.
He bought a crooked cat,
Which caught a crooked mouse,
And they all lived together in an ancient Crooked House.

And when will Wren come train with me?" Liza sipped her coffee. She and Mary were bartering, dividing up days and skills and setting out a course for the apprentices' Fiddler training. "I think I'll take both of them at once." She winked at Wren. "Perhaps they can stay at my villa on the Mediterranean. Young people should enjoy themselves." She raised a hand at Mary's protest. "There are other things besides stardust, you know."

"And of course," Baxter chimed in, "I must teach them to bake."

Mary scoffed, and Baxter cut her off. "You've always undervalued the ways in which our natural skills influence our Fiddler talents." He looked at Wren and Simon. "Capitalizing on their strengths can only enhance their training. What are you good at, Wren?"

Wren's mind froze. No one had ever asked her that. They'd just always known. "I'm pretty smart," she finally said. She hoped they could tell she wasn't bragging. "With science and stuff."

Baxter waved this away. "Of course you are. All Fiddlers are smart. If you weren't, you'd never have seen the stardust. Instead, you'd be all wrapped up in whatever foolish thing is popular these days. What is it now, the motorcar?"

Liza laughed at him.

"What I mean"—Baxter waved Liza's mockery away with a grin—"is what are you *good* at? What is it that it seems you alone were made to do?" He trailed a finger through the whipped cream and licked it off the tip. "Perfect." He took another swipe and continued. "I couldn't live without baking." He nodded toward the women. "Liza is a healer. Like a goddess of old."

Liza gave him a slow smile, and Wren could tell his comments pleased her.

"Mary grows things," Baxter said. "Plants and animals, and"—he raised his eyebrows at Wren and Simon—"young people, apparently. This year, she's single-handedly found three new apprentices in the wild. That's unheard of these days."

"I like animals," Simon said, setting his notebook aside. His face went pink. "My dad says I have a way with them. That I'd be a good veterinarian or zookeeper."

Wren watched him fidget with his pocket watch chain. His voice had lost the lecturing tone.

"I sensed that connection in you." Mary looked at him fondly. "I greatly anticipate seeing how the falcons respond to you."

"Kinship with the animals." Liza tapped a fingertip on her lip. "Very interesting."

Simon smiled shyly back. "Do you really think so?" Wren listened while he talked about how a species of moth was being destroyed by disease, which turned into a tutorial about dying habitats due to overpopulation by humans and ended with a hypothesis that stardust might save the day for the entire moth world. Even the grown-ups' eyes looked glazed over by the time he was finished.

"And you, Wren?" Baxter jumped in, while Simon paused to search his notebook for a fact on moth recovery. "Where do your strengths lie?"

Wren didn't know how to answer. She wasn't into theater like her mom or running like her dad. She had a feeling spending time on the computer or babysitting didn't fall into the special skill category either. "Astronomy, I guess?" She said it like a question, because she doubted that someone could technically be good at stargazing. "That's kind of my thing."

"Interesting." Baxter pounced on it. "Perhaps you can interpret the prophecies."

"A skill in traveling, maybe?" Mary said, peering at Wren as though seeing her for the first time.

"Astronomy," Liza said. "After all these years."

The room grew quiet. Mary cleared her throat. "A long time ago—two hundred years or so now—I found another Fiddler apprentice who was especially gifted in astronomy. He was so strong, in fact, that his knowledge of the stars gave him unusual insight into the properties of stardust. He is gone now, but your strength in astronomy speaks well for your potential,

Wren." Her smile looked forced. "The Fiddler Council will be very interested in you."

Liza snorted at this, and Mary gave her a dirty look.

"What?" Liza raised her eyebrows. "Do you expect me to let that remark go unchecked? Cole and the rest of the Council may be interested, but why send the girl off to a pack of fools?"

"Cole," Mary said, her voice stiff, "is not the fool you make him out to be." When Liza gave her a look, Mary cracked a tiny smile. "At least not all of the time."

While the grown-ups talked about the Fiddler Council, Simon started to clear the plates, and Wren moved to help him.

"Two hundred years?" Wren asked once they were out of earshot. "She found another apprentice two centuries ago?" Baxter's comments about motorcars ran through her mind. They looked like average grown-ups, but . . . "How old do you think they are, anyway?"

Simon stacked the dishes in the sink. "Three hundred? Four, tops."

"What?" Wren nearly yelled, then dropped her voice as the conversation in the other room paused. "What do you mean?"

"Of course they're long-lived." Simon scraped some leftover tart into the garbage. "Every legend about magicians talks about prolonging life. Besides, some species of turtle live for two hundred years easily. And that's without stardust. It's a perfectly natural conclusion."

Wren sniffed. Perfectly creepy, more like, but there was no way she was going to let Simon know that if he was so matter-of-fact about it all. Mary had said something earlier about stardust changing the way she perceived the world, but this was beyond anything she could have imagined. What else could be true?

Wren rearranged the silverware to make a tottering stack of plates next to the sink. "You know, some of the earliest astronomers were certain that, if you learned the secret, you could wield the Earth's elements and do magical things. Maybe they were looking for the Fiddlers all this time." She squirted some soap on a sponge and turned on the faucet.

"Well said. Bravo, bravo, whoever you are," a voice spoke from behind them, and Wren spun around to see a boy who was only a little taller than Simon standing in the doorway. His apprentice cloak hung open, revealing a thick cable-knit sweater that hugged his neck.

"And who are you exactly?" the boy said.

"I'm Simon," Simon said as the boy moved to clasp his arm like they were in a secret club.

"Good to meet you, Simon." He moved toward Wren, nodding in the direction of the dining room. "Mary and Liza in the same room and no one's yelling yet? Is it a holiday or something?" The newest arrival looked at her with his uncommonly bright blue eyes. He had closely cropped black hair, and the way it was cut made his face look all angles.

"My friends call me Jack," he said, and his smile made Wren feel like she was going to be one of his friends, too.

"I'm Wren," she said, holding out her hand. He clasped her arm, the same way he had done with Simon. Just then, the sound of breaking glass came from the other room.

"Let the catfights begin," Jack said, and Wren and Simon followed him to rejoin the grown-ups. Liza stood by the fireplace, staring at the shards of glass littering the floor at her feet. Mary's eyes were ringed with red, as though she'd been crying, and Baxter was standing between them, hands raised midspeech.

"—let the past stay in the past," he was saying.

The tension in the room evaporated as soon as the grown-ups saw Jack.

"Jack!" Mary scrubbed a hand across her eyes, giving

him a watery smile and a motherly hug. "Where have you been?"

"What uncommon timing you have, Jack," Baxter said. He ignored Jack's secret handshake thing and patted him on the back instead. "As always, the welcome of my house is yours."

"Thanks, Bax," Jack said. He seemed to belong with the others, like he was a real Fiddler, too, even though he didn't look any older than Wren and Simon. Maybe it was because he talked to Baxter like he was his friend rather than a grown-up. "I would have sent you a text or something, but that would mean you'd need to have this crazy little thing we call a"—Jack held his hand up to his mouth theatrically—"phone."

Baxter laughed. "Nonsense. It all changes too quickly for me to stay current. Keep your newfangled gadgets to yourself."

"I will." Jack reached into his apprentice coat. "But I've brought something very old with me tonight. In fact, it's why I was late." He drew out a stone the size of his palm, its surface worn glossy smooth. "My grandfather found it in an antique shop that was closing down. I think it has something to do with the Fiddlers. Look." He pointed to a symbol on the bottom that looked like a flame dancing over a circle.

The grown-ups crowded closer. "This stone is from the old days, when there was fighting among us," Baxter said, clearing a space on the table so Jack could set the stone on top of it. "Fiddlers hid messages in them during the war."

Liza's eyes grew wide. "It's a dangerous thing, to travel with anything that carries this mark," she said, her hand roving over the flame without touching it. "The Fiddler Council would punish you for less."

"Don't be silly, Liza." Mary's eyes were shining, and she touched the stone almost reverently. "Cole isn't vengeful. He leads the Council well."

"I was thinking this might be something important to share with the other Fiddlers. Maybe we could all go to the Crooked House together." Jack gave them a winsome smile. "C'mon, don't you miss seeing more Fiddlers than just one another? Mary said she hasn't been there since last year. Aren't you even a little bit homesick?" He shook his head. "Hanging out with other apprentices sounds nice to me."

"Well, if it sounds *nice* to you"—Baxter's voice was icy cool—"then you must ignore our years of experience. You've been a Fiddler for, what, a couple of months?

Surely you are prepared for the politics of the Crooked House." His words were thick with sarcasm.

"Mary! You went back last year?" Liza's forehead was creased with displeasure. "And you didn't tell us?"

"You don't tell me everything either, Liza." Mary sounded offended. "I had my reasons"—she held up a forestalling hand—"which, I might add, are no one else's business."

"Trying to appeal to the Council again, Mary?" Baxter clicked his tongue disapprovingly. "They won't rewrite history on your word alone. The Crooked House is closed to you. And I, for one, am glad to be rid of the whole lot of them."

Mary clenched her jaw. "The Council didn't know I was there. I went only to the repository, and I slipped out unseen." She glared at Jack. "I understand now I should have kept the whole thing to myself."

"Did you notice the rhyme on the back of the stone?" Jack asked. "It's in a different language."

"Where did you find this?" Baxter's voice sounded hard. "Tell us the truth, boy."

"Grandpa bought it on his last trip to London. Said he got it in some shop that was going out of business." Jack spread his hands wide. "That's all I know, honest.

He's always bringing junk back, but this seemed special, you know? With the Fiddler marks and all?"

"It is special," Baxter said, looking up at Mary. "It was written by Boggen himself." He pointed to some words that the other grown-ups seemed able to read. "It predates his demise."

"You know what this means, don't you?" Mary knelt in front of the table and peered at the stone. "Perhaps we can finally access some of his research." Her voice was soft. "Perhaps it isn't gone."

Liza and Baxter exchanged weary looks. "Let's see what it says first."

Wren leaned in toward Jack, who had come to sit between her and Simon. "What is she talking about? What's going on?"

"Pretty much every time they get together, they fight about the Fiddler Council and the guy who runs it—Cole." Jack shrugged. "Best I can tell, Mary loved him, but for some reason he exiled her from the Crooked House a long time ago. It's the first they've said of this Boggen and his research, but fat chance I'm going to ask for more details." He nodded toward Mary, whose face was hard, her words aimed like darts at Liza and Baxter.

"You don't believe me either, do you? I'm telling you the truth; I've always told you the truth." Mary slapped her hands on the table and pushed herself to her feet. "I didn't know what Boggen was doing. I wasn't part of it back then, whatever the Council says, whatever false evidence against me Boggen planted for them to find." She stepped forward, snatching the stone and holding it aloft. She was nearly yelling now. "Don't you see? This stone, forgotten for centuries, might hold the truth of Boggen's dealings. It might prove my innocence once and for all."

"Come now, Mary." Baxter raised both hands in a placating gesture. "We are your friends. And we were Cole's and Boggen's friends as well." He laid a gentle hand on her shoulder. "It is not we who you are angry with."

"I tire of this same old argument." Liza crunched some of the broken glass under her heel. "We are not the Council at the Crooked House. You don't need to constantly convince us of your innocence. What are you going to do? Take it to the Council?" She pointed at the stone, pinching her lips together as if she smelled something horrible. "And what if it confirms your guilt?"

Mary flinched at Liza's words. "Impossible."

"Are you so sure?" Liza said. "Once the Council opens it and finds Boggen's message, there is no undoing it." She wrapped her arms around Mary in a gentle hug. "It is ancient history now, Mary, whatever you did back then. We don't have to do anything with this stone. We don't have to go to the Crooked House."

"You don't," Mary said, pushing her sister away. "You weren't falsely accused. You weren't branded a traitor. All your years of research weren't stolen from you and given to others." Her voice broke, and there was an awful pause. "I am going to the Crooked House, and I'm taking the apprentices with me. They'll have to at least give me credit for that." She beckoned to Wren and Simon. "We'd go now if I didn't need to settle things with your parents." She gave Liza a stiff hug good-bye. "If you decide to join us, we leave tomorrow at dusk."

SEVEN

Mary, Mary quite contrary,
How does your garden grow?
Silver bells and cockleshells,
And apprentices all in a row.

I didn't know they allowed falcons within town limits, even on an urban farm," Wren's dad said after Mary had left. "Another reason I love this city." Mary had come home with Wren and wielded a different kind of magic with her parents. She had told them all about the falcons she cared for at the university and how she was short of help and asked if they would mind terribly if she took Wren on as an apprentice with Simon, since they were such good friends. Wren could have her own room there, Mary had said, since the falcons needed constant attention, and would there be any way Wren could start right away, that very evening? It was masterfully done because, excluding the bit about Simon and Wren being good friends, Wren couldn't catch her in a single lie. Mary simply left out the whole part about magic and Fiddlers and all the rest.

Wren flopped a big cheesy piece of pizza onto her plate.

"Mary's program sounds interesting," Wren's mom said. "And I want you to know I'm so proud of you for trying something outside of your comfort zone, Wren. But falcons? Really?" She fidgeted with the edge of her napkin. "Are you sure you want to spend a whole month there? I mean, you could at least wait a few days, think it over."

"I'm sure, and I want to start now." Wren worked hard not to roll her eyes. First her mom worried about Wren not doing enough social things. Now she was worried Wren would do too many. "It's not like you get days off when you're taking care of animals anyway." Wren swallowed hard. Her parents wouldn't say no, would they? What if Mary started apprenticing Simon without her? He would be light-years ahead of her. "Look," Wren said in her most grown-up-sounding voice. "I'll be less than a mile away. Dad is on the campus almost every day, and I can come home if I want to. Besides, it's not like anyone will be here anyway. Dad has classes to prep for, and you'll be busy with the play."

"You're right about that. I thought I'd never get out of the theater, and I have yet another meeting tonight," Wren's mom said as she poured a big glass of water. "There are some copyright issues—can you believe that?—and now I have to either come up with an original script or find a different project. It's going to be a massive undertaking to finish it all in time for Springfest."

Wren made a noncommittal sound. Every year her mom swore she wouldn't direct the outdoor performance that ushered in the beginning of summer, and every year she ended up doing it anyway. Wren could count on it like clockwork: April was the month that her mom turned into a stressed-out director who would make the best actor cringe. Wren listened to her mom talk about how she was going to start allotting thirty minutes a day for meditation, and told herself that was why she wasn't talking to her parents about the Fiddlers. *It's for their own good.* Untangling Wren's new reality would be too much for them right now.

She would wait until May, long after the Springfest performance was done, and then she would tell them everything. She forced the bite of pizza down, but there was a knot in her stomach. Wren had never lied to her parents like this. Even if she was technically telling the truth—or, rather, postponing it—she felt horrible.

"It would be great to find something unconventional. Something we could turn on its head and wow the audience with." Wren's mom rubbed her temples the way she did when a migraine was coming on. "Fairy tale retellings are so popular these days. Maybe I should do one of those."

"Or Mother Goose," Wren said, half under her breath. "Some of those old rhymes are pretty weird."

"Wren!" Her mom pressed both hands flat against the table. "That's a brilliant idea! And I don't think anyone's done anything like it. All the material is public domain, and we could do a mishmash of things." She flipped open her laptop and began typing madly. "Think of the costumes!"

"I was only joking," Wren said, wondering if her suggestion counted as spilling some of the Fiddlers' secrets. "Nursery rhymes? Really, Mom?"

"I won't tell anyone you came up with it," her mom

said, giving Wren's shoulder a quick squeeze. "Though you may change your mind when it's a smash hit. We're performing at the stage in the park this year. I'm picturing sheep. And cows. Aren't there a lot of animals in those rhymes?"

Wren's mom was opening tabs faster than she could talk. Wikipedia entries on Mother Goose and photo collages of nursery-themed parties. Wren peered at her screen, wondering if anyone anywhere had any inkling what the rhymes were really about.

Her dad was talking about the midterm grading he had to do for his classes. "You know, Wren, you still could join one of the college clubs if you'd rather. I know nothing ruffles your feathers, Little Bird, but farm chores—even on an urban farm—are awfully hard work."

Wren ignored her dad's pet name for her. "I want to do the apprenticeship with Simon," she snapped, and then immediately regretted it when she saw his expression. He should have been looking cross. Instead, he and Wren's mom were sharing a tiny knowing smile. *Shoot.*

"Okay, okay." Wren's dad spread his hands out in front of him. "I knew this day was coming, when other guys would bump your old dad off your list."

"It's not like that, Dad," Wren said, but she could tell it wasn't any use. "Simon's just a friend." She thought of their history of shared competition and Simon's insufferable tendency to be a know-it-all. "Well, sort of a friend."

"Sure," her mom said as she gave Wren a wink. "We won't say another word about it."

Mary opened the door when Wren and her mom arrived at Pippen Hill that evening. "I know you're short on time," Mary said to Wren's mom, who was trying to inconspicuously check the clock on her phone. "I can have Wren fill out this paperwork here"—she pointed to a rolltop desk over by the wall—"while I give you a quick tour. You can see the falcons another time, but let me show you where Wren will be staying." Mary must have used the stardust to mask things, because neither the plant-filled library nor her workroom were anywhere in sight. Instead, the cottage at Pippen Hill looked like an old, dusty farmhouse in need of remodeling.

"That sounds great," Wren's mom said, the relief showing in her eyes. "I'm usually not this distracted; it's this ridiculous Springfest play, and—" Her phone beeped. "I'm sorry, let me send a quick reply."

"No problem," Mary said pleasantly, leading the way out of the room while Wren's mom punched out a text message.

Wren bent down to the look at the papers on the desk and read the words written in old-fashioned script:

Fiddlers one and Fiddlers all
Are welcome in the Fiddler Hall
Their lips are sealed
Their confidence won
A Fiddler once made
Can ne'er be undone.

Sapiens dominabitur astris

Simon came into the room and moved close enough to read over Wren's shoulder. "What a stellar motto, pun intended."

"Ha-ha." Wren scrawled her signature at the bottom of the page. "So what did your dad say about Mary?"

"He thinks it's a good idea. I've been talking about volunteering at a veterinary clinic anyway, so when I told him about the falcons, he was happy for me. What about your parents?" Simon folded his arms across his chest and leaned one shoulder against the wall.

Wren picked up the paper, letting its edges curl into a scroll. There was no way she was going to tell Simon her parents thought she *liked* him. "You know how they are. With the unschooling and everything. They said I could do what I want." She twirled the rolled-up paper in her hands. "I felt bad not telling them everything, though. Like I was lying or something."

"Yeah." Simon looked down at his arms. "But what else are we supposed to do? Give up the stardust?" He shook his head. "Mary did say we could tell them someday."

Wren nodded. She just wished someday didn't feel like another word for maybe never.

"Excellent." Mary's voice drifted from somewhere down the hallway, and soon she and Wren's mom appeared. "So Wren will be able to pop home if she needs to, but we'll take good care of her. Not to worry."

"Sounds fine to me." Wren's mom came over to her. Her phone was back in her pocket, and she was channeling normal, non-stressed-out Mom. "If you need anything, we're just a few minutes away, okay?" She laughed. "You know my phone will always be on.

Text me. Every day, all right?" She gave Wren a hug. "It looks like a great opportunity, Wren. I'm proud of you."

Wren returned the hug, tighter than she would have otherwise, wondering if her mom would still be proud of her when Wren finally told her why she'd really been at Mary's. For a moment, she wondered what would happen if she just blurted it all out now. What Mary would say and if they could somehow make Wren's mom understand. But then her mom's phone buzzed again, this time with an incoming call, and she gave Wren a quick peck on the cheek.

"It's the costumer. I've got to take this one. Thanks so much, Mary. Bye, Wren. Simon." And then she was gone.

"I thought that went well," Mary said, a pleased smile playing about her lips. "I'm a little rusty on my interaction with contemporary families, but I'd say that was a success."

EIGHT

I am a gold lock.
I am a gold key.
However high and low you hunt,
You'll never find me.

Mary opened the door to Wren's room, which looked like it belonged in a turn-of-the-century novel. There was a big tiled fireplace in the center of one wall with a rocking chair situated in front of it. Across from that, a four-poster bed, complete with velvet curtains that hung from the canopy, took up most of the remaining space on the hardwood floor.

Wren set her suitcase on the window seat and, after bidding Mary good night, slipped into her pajamas. She was too tired to brush her teeth or to feel nervous about sleeping in a new place. She lay down on the massive bed, positioning the pillow so that she could see out the window. The sky was only partially clear, but she could still spot a corner of the Big Dipper.

Wren pulled the covers up to her chin. Even though she was not far from her house, her old life felt a world away. She smiled at the thought. She should be frightened, or homesick, or overwhelmed, shouldn't she? Instead, she felt quiet inside. Everything, all of a sudden, seemed simple and easy. No need for social development or trivia challenges or internet forums. There was only the new idea of stardust. Of Fiddlers and magic and ancient guilds from before the dawn of time. She squirreled deeper under the blankets. Perhaps she wasn't freaking out because she felt like she'd finally come home.

Wren woke to find the curtains around her bed drawn closed. The air had that sharp cold that came with the very early morning, and Wren breathed deeply to shake off the fogginess of sleep. Her chest was tight, as though somewhere deep inside she knew that it would be a Bad Thing if she were to leave her bed. From the other side of the curtains, Wren heard voices. She didn't recognize who was speaking, but she could hear the words very clearly.

"Boggen's had the city searched from top to bottom," a woman was saying. "Three silversmiths have already been executed for claiming ignorance. He'll be after us next."

There was the clattering sound of wood on wood, and then a man's voice. "It's not here. Marley left it behind in the Crooked House and paid for it with his life, but there'll be no convincing Boggen of that fact. Now that he's made contact, he's hungrier than ever to find the golden key."

The Crooked House! Wren got up on her hands and knees, easing herself over to the curtains. She twitched the fabric a fraction of an inch, enough to peek through.

"We waste time talking while Boggen's henchmen might be on their way here." The man was standing at a table, dumping things into a wooden trunk. He wore odd clothes crisscrossed with belts and buckles, and the layers of fabric were covered with a film of dirt that made Wren wonder when they were last washed. "Best make a run for it while we can."

"Robin isn't home yet." The woman looked slightly cleaner, her ratty hair held back with the goggles that were pushed up onto her forehead. "We can't leave without her."

The voices grew less distinct as the man and woman

turned away to gather things from a chest against the wall. Something about messages and candles and sleep. Whatever was going on, their panic transferred over to her, and she felt an icy chill crawl up her spine the more they talked about Boggen and his bloodthirsty hunt for a key. The name tickled at her memory—she had heard it somewhere before.

While they were busy with the chest, Wren tried to gauge the distance to the door, and that was when she realized that the room beyond was nothing like the room she'd gone to sleep in. There was no rocking chair. No window seat. There was a smoky fire where the fireplace should be, but instead of a tiled mantelpiece, Wren saw hammered metal that glinted in the shadows. The walls were covered with the same substance, and a jumble of off-kilter tables and stools were piled where the bedroom door should have been. *Where am I? What is going on?* She sat back on her heels right as a light flashed before her.

"Wait!" The woman must have seen her. "Dreamer! Wait!" Someone ripped aside the curtain around Wren's bed, and she saw the woman standing there, her grubby hand reaching for her, but suddenly a dark silhouette loomed in the doorway behind her, towering up and over. As the shadow expanded, the whole scene disappeared with a thunderclap.

Wren woke in her bed in Pippen Hill, the sheets and blankets a tangle around her ankles, her heart pounding. The curtains hung as she had left them, open, and showed her room at Pippen Hill as it should be. A nightmare. That was all it was. Only a nightmare. Her neck and shoulders were stiff with fear, and she had to breathe deeply to still the racing of her heart. It was dark outside, the few stars now blotted out by heavy cloud cover. The wind set one tree branch tapping against the window, as if to remind her it was all a dream.

Wren leaned back against the pillows. This dream wasn't like other nightmares she'd had, ones where memories of events faded with each passing minute. Instead, every detail seemed clearer to her waking mind. The grainy feel of the scene, almost like it was an old black-and-white film. The smoky look of the room. The tense conversation. The woman's final frantic approach. *Dreamer,* she had called to Wren, as though she knew Wren was asleep and dreaming.

Wren shoved off the covers and switched on a lamp.

The adrenaline rush had chased away any chance of going back to sleep. She slid her feet into her shoes and made her way down to the kitchen. The orange warmth of the old-fashioned stove set off a cozy glow, leaving the farthest corners of the kitchen bathed in shadow. Wren wished that she could rummage in her own familiar refrigerator, maybe find a piece of left-over chocolate cake and pour an ice-cold glass of milk. If she was lucky, her dad might come down, and they could sit together, sharing the cake and talking things over. Maybe he could help her understand what was going on, why she felt haunted by the thought that it was more than a dream.

"You couldn't sleep either?"

Wren jolted, bumping her elbow on the wall, the too-recent feeling of fear returning with a rush.

"Sorry. I didn't mean to startle you," Jack said with an apologetic smile. "I thought you saw me come in." He pointed to a door tucked under the corner staircase. He reached into a cupboard and pulled out a plate of cookies.

"Yeah, I couldn't sleep," Wren said. She took the cookie he handed her. "Though now I'm kind of glad."

"When I visit my grandfather out in the country

and can't sleep, I go outside and stargaze," Jack said, and Wren knew they were going to be friends for sure. "And other nights I don't want to sleep." Jack bit off the edge of a chocolate chip cookie. "Mary says the stardust can affect our dreams. I had the hardest time my first month after touching it. Crazy nightmares. Sleepwalking. You'll get used to it."

"That's a relief." Wren breathed out a sigh and tried to make it into a joke. "I was beginning to think I might be going crazy. I've never had such intense dreams."

"'All that we see or seem is but a dream within a dream.' Didn't Edgar Allen Poe or somebody say that?" Jack pulled up the collar of his sweater against the early morning chill. "It's no surprise, really. Especially with all that you just learned about Fiddlers. Let me guess, you dreamed about magicians or blackbird pies or golden eggs or something."

"A golden key, actually." Wren grinned, sliding onto one of the chairs next to the big kitchen worktable. Now that she was awake she knew where she had heard the name in the dream. "And the Fiddler that Mary and Baxter were talking about—Boggen?—was hunting for it. I guess all the stuff I heard about the Fiddlers got jumbled up in my brain."

"Any clue as to where the key was?" Jack joked. "Maybe we can beat Boggen to it." He winked at her. "Welcome to the Fiddler nuttiness."

Wren supposed her dream made a strange kind of sense, what with her discovering nursery rhymes were tied to magic and stardust and all the talk about the Crooked House. "I think I'm having a little trouble making sense of everything."

"Only a little?" Jack grinned at her. "When I found out that magic was real, my mind was blown for a month. But soon you'll be in what I call magical mode. The impossible won't seem strange anymore."

"How long have you known?" Wren stood and pulled on the sideways chrome handle to open the fridge. Talking to Jack had awakened a whole flood of questions. "When did you become an apprentice? How did Mary find you?" She grabbed the milk and poured them each a glass.

"Thanks." Jack took a big gulp. "Actually, I found Mary about six months ago. My grandpa's kind of a conspiracy theorist. He thinks everyone is working together to pull off some big lie." Jack tipped his chair back so it was balancing on two legs. "He's always thought magic was real, and that the rich and powerful people are hogging it all for themselves. Trying to learn about magic got him all obsessed with alchemists—you know, those old scientists who thought you could use elements to turn rocks into gold and stuff?"

Wren nodded impatiently. She knew that some of the earliest astronomers had been alchemists and had theorized that atomic particles might have had magical properties. "So? What did your grandpa find out?"

"Nothing." Jack smirked at Wren's expression. "*I'm* the one who did the finding. Grandpa had all these faded newspaper clippings and journals full of notes about alchemy clubs. Most of it meant nothing, but one woman's face kept popping up in the newspapers. She was this botanist who exhibited at the world's fair. But she was also a friend of Marie Curie. And then I found copies of her scientific papers and essays on women's suffrage." He let his chair fall to the ground with a thump.

"Who was she?" Wren asked.

"I'll give you three guesses," Jack said, but Wren didn't really need them.

"It was Mary?"

"Sure was. I did some more hunting and found her in some old photos. Shaking hands with Albert Einstein.

Congratulating Feynman when he won the Nobel. In the front row at one of Stephen Hawking's lectures. Of course, at the time, I didn't know it was the same woman." He paused for dramatic effect. "I thought it would be her descendant, and I wanted to talk to her and see if she knew anything about the alchemy stuff." He gulped the rest of his milk and set the glass down, wiping his mouth with his sleeve. "So I did some searching online and found out she was going to be at an herbalist's convention in Manhattan—which isn't that far from where my grandpa lives. When I started asking about alchemy she got all funny, and then she threw stardust at my face. None of the people around us could see it, I guess any non-Fiddler wouldn't, but I started shouting at her, and then she realized I could see it, and, well, the rest is history."

"Wow," Wren said. "I mean, I knew she was old, but hearing about her doing all those historical things makes it so real."

"So your grandfather knows?" Simon's voice took Wren by surprise. He was leaning against the wall at the bottom of the stairway, and Wren wondered how long he'd been listening. "About the Fiddlers?"

"Sure." Jack ran a finger around the neck of his sweater like he was loosening a tie. "I mean, he was right, wasn't he? There *is* a huge conspiracy going on."

"It must be nice to not have to lie," Wren said, her guilt over not telling her parents returning in full force. "To have it all out in the open."

"Sometimes," Jack snorted. "Except he's always pumping me for information and showing me random old Mother Goose rhymes and stuff. But he's not bad for all that."

"Come sit with us," Wren said to Simon, scooting the nearly empty plate toward him. "There're cookies."

"Nah. I'm headed out for an early run," Simon said, and that was when Wren noticed that he was fully dressed, ready for the day.

She groaned. "It's morning already? I barely even slept."

"Sleep is overrated," Jack said, popping the last cookie in his mouth. "Wait for me, Simon, and I'll come with you. Wren? Want to join in?"

"Pass," Wren said, piling the dishes in the sink. Even if she was tempted to go running, which she most definitely wasn't, the night was catching up with her, and she made her way back up to her room, fingers crossed for dreamless sleep.

NINE

Mother Goose, when she wanted to wander,
Would ride through the air on a very fine gander.

Later that afternoon, Mary led Wren, Simon, and Jack through a long tunnel that sprouted from the cellar of Pippen Hill and opened up into a wilderness of trees. They walked for a good while through an orchard in full bloom and beyond into a less tended crush of forest.

"How in the world," Wren said as she pushed her way through the underbrush, "is all this right next to a university campus? How come we've never seen this before?"

Jack gave her a playful look, both eyebrows raised. "And three, two, one . . ."

Wren stared at him. Was he playing some kind of game?

"Come on, Wren. You still can't figure out how a Fiddler could make something appear different than it truly is?"

"Oh," Wren said, feeling sheepish. "The stardust. Of course." They now walked single file behind Mary. Simon first, then Jack, and Wren bringing up the rear.

"Ordinary people can't see the stardust at all." Mary's voice floated back to them. "And you'll find that keeping the effects of stardust hidden reduces unwanted questions. For example, can you imagine the attention my falcon would have drawn if I hadn't used the stardust to mask it at your science convention? Think of the time we would waste coming up with and maintaining a credible reason for Pippen Hill's existence. Using stardust to preserve our privacy saves valuable time for research." The branches crunched under her feet, and she raised her voice. "The Crooked House is isolated enough that you'll find we can wield stardust freely there."

Wren thought this over. She'd probably passed by Pippen Hill countless times on her treks to the observatory. And all the time a whole magical world had been right under her nose.

Jack pushed aside a thorny branch that was blocking the path and held it so Wren could pass through.

"I am so pumped about the falcons. I haven't flown them yet—I can't believe Mary's taking you on your first day."

"The falcons. Right. I forgot," Wren said in what she hoped was a normal voice. Some part of her had hoped that the whole bit about tending the falcons was simply part of keeping Pippen Hill a secret. The only way she wanted to see a bird of prey was through a glass window at the zoo. She wrinkled her nose. "How close do you think we'll have to get to them?"

"What? Afraid of a little falcon?" Jack shot a teasing look at her. "Don't you want to know everything there is to know about stardust?" Jack let the branch twang back into place. "I do. Falcons are part of that. And so is the Crooked House. Apprentice lessons are going to be so much more intense now. First falcons, and then, well, *all* the Fiddler secrets."

"What exactly is the Crooked House?" Wren asked, ignoring the whole topic of falcons and picking at the brambles that were now stuck to her jeans. Mary had been surprisingly closemouthed when Wren and Simon had asked questions at breakfast. All she would say was that it was essential that they go there today, that the discovery of the stone changed everything, and visiting the Crooked House would be good for their apprentice training.

"It's like Fiddler research central," Jack said. "Fiddlers live all over the world, I guess, but most of them report back in at the Crooked House. Some of them even have laboratories there." He turned to look back at her wide-eyed. "Just think about what we could discover about stardust by being there!"

"But Baxter said . . ." Wren began, thinking about how Baxter had flipped out about Jack wanting to go to the Crooked House.

"Baxter is suspicious of telephones." Jack rolled his eyes. "You'll see. Once we get to the Crooked House, it's going to be amazing."

They emerged from the trees to find a field dotted with wooden poles in front of a long barnlike building. On the three foremost poles perched foreboding falcon silhouettes. Wren took a deep breath. There was no way she could ignore them now.

Mary directed each of the apprentices to one of the falcons. Wren stood, arms folded across her apprentice cloak, looking up at the falcon whose fathomless black gaze was locked on her face.

Mary handed her a cloth bundle. Wren unwrapped

it to reveal something that looked like a glove made all of leather, with buckles on one side.

"It's a falconry gauntlet," Mary said, demonstrating how to strap one on her forearm. "To protect you from their talons." She moved over to Wren's left to help Jack.

Wren fumbled with the straps. First the gauntlet hung loosely; then she fastened it too tight. She pressed her wrist up against her thigh to try to stabilize it.

"Awesome," Simon said from Wren's left. He buckled the gauntlet on as though he'd been doing it his whole life and began to edge forward on silent feet.

Wren pulled on a strap but lost her grip as one of the birds gave off an earsplitting screech.

"Stop it, Wren," Simon said. "Don't startle them."

"I'm not doing anything." Wren glared at the bird. "That thing doesn't like me."

The tips of the falcon's tail feathers were bright red, the only spot of color in an otherwise brown coat. *Just like me. Brown hair, brown skin, brown everything.*

Simon stood in the middle of the grassy lawn, his forearm extended. In one soundless swoop, his falcon alit on his arm. On Wren's other side, Jack was whistling at his falcon, which wasn't moving, but still looked much friendlier than the creature glaring down at her.

"All right, bird," Wren said, eyeing the thing. It looked lean and hard, like what it was: a predator. She wondered if falcons were like horses and could sense a person's fear. "I'm not afraid of you," she lied, just in case.

Wren knew the bird couldn't perceive what she was thinking, but she felt certain it was watching her disapprovingly, ready to screech again at her first move.

"Go on then, Wren. Call your bird like Simon has done." Mary gestured at Wren's falcon as though she couldn't see it. "These particular falcons travel the auroras all over the world."

"The auroras?" Wren thought of the breathtaking greens and blues of the aurora borealis. No matter how much she read about it, she was still captivated by the aurora borealis, by the way stargazers had to hunt for the display of colors and yet, once found, it was painted across the sky for everyone to see. "Falcons can fly through an aurora?"

"Falcons can do many amazing things. They are a Fiddler's secret weapon," Mary said. "So it's crucial that you develop a good bond with your bird right from the start. Your falcon will become fiercely loyal." Mary made a gentle clicking noise at Wren's bird. "After all your hours of training, they won't tolerate another human companion."

Simon looked like he was already best friends with his falcon. It roosted on his arm as though it belonged there.

Wren scowled at him. What a show-off.

Jack reached out to his bird and, fast as a viper, the falcon attacked his hand with its beak.

Any reassurance Wren felt at the fact that hers wasn't the only hostile falcon faded when she saw that the bird had actually taken a chunk out of the flesh between Jack's thumb and forefinger. Mary noticed, too, and the next minute she was beside him, stirring up a cloud of stardust like it was the simplest thing in the world. She found some spongy moss, mixed it in with the stardust, and wove a floating spiral of green and gray. She traced an *X* through the stardust, chanting:

Cross patch, draw the latch
Sit by the fire and spin.

The stardust swirled around her fingers, circling the moss. Mary made a little bowl with her palms, letting the element fall.

Take a cup and stir it up
Then smear it on the skin.

"Stardust enhances what is already there," Mary explained. "My mixture merely magnifies the healing property of this herb." She rubbed the newly made ointment onto Jack's wound. In a few heartbeats, the flesh had mended, skin knitting together, blood drying up the way an old cut does after a few hours. With only a small puff of smoke to indicate that there had ever been anything amiss, Jack was healed.

"Liza could probably do a better job." Mary brushed her palms together matter-of-factly. "She is skilled in the healing arts." Her gaze fixed on Jack. "Jack, too, has shown some strength in that area."

Jack stared at his cured hand, eyes wide. "If it means I get to learn how to do that, then I hope you're right. I wonder if stardust can do even more than that," he said, his voice alight with possibility. "Think what this kind of medicine means! No pain.

No suffering. No disease. No dying."

"No one can escape death." Mary wiped the remaining stardust off on her skirt. "Not even the oldest of Fiddlers."

"And when exactly were you born?" Jack demanded.

"Enough." Mary's smile evaporated into a stern look. "It's always the same. Apprentices are fixated on the length of Fiddler life for their first century or two. It will pass. And there are plenty of books you can read to satisfy your curiosity." She pointed at the falcon behind her. "But you'll have a much harder time learning how to ride the aurora from books. So hold your questions and open your ears."

Wren scrubbed the toe of her shoe through the moss while Mary explained how to tend the birds and how to care for their feathers. Her brain was only half listening. The other part was replaying everything she'd learned. What would it be like to live for a "century or two"? What had Mary seen in her years? Wren didn't know whether she was more astonished to think of Fiddlers living through the Black Plague and the discovery of America and the world wars or the implication that she could live just as long.

"Once grown, your falcon will naturally adapt to

the environment of the aurora, enabling you to travel long distances in a short amount of time," Mary was saying, gesturing toward her white falcon as it flew to join the others.

Wren snapped out of her distraction. *Once grown?* She felt an odd sinking sensation in her stomach. It sounded like Mary meant for them to *ride* the falcons.

"If you want to take a short trip through the ordinary sky when the aurora is absent," Mary continued, "you'll need to use the stardust." She handed each of them a small leather pouch and then opened her own and dumped some stardust into her palm. "The stardust must touch the falcon for the rhyme to work." She arranged her feet so that her back foot was planted perpendicular to her front one and began to swirl the stardust in the air, cutting an infinity symbol through it with her fingers. As the light of the stardust built, she chanted:

See, see! What shall I see!
My bird grown tall as it should be.

Even if Simon didn't have a smile plastered on his face, Wren would've been able to tell that he was enjoying this. It was the happiest she'd ever seen him.

He shifted his forearm experimentally, and the falcon obediently flew back over to its original perch.

"How are you doing that?" Wren whispered at him. It was as though Simon had read a secret How to Train a Falcon manual.

Mary paused her lesson and encouraged them to follow her example. Wren sighed and dumped the contents of the pouch into her palm. She could see tiny flickering embers in the mound of ashes. "Here goes nothing," she said, blowing a poof of stardust into the twilight sky. It sparked and shot up in dazzling blue-green swirls, then fell like snowflakes, eventually wrapping gently down around her falcon. She shifted her leg back, mimicking Mary, and traced the pattern in the air. She worked her fingers in a circular movement, saying the rhyme. At first, it seemed a trick of the fading light, as though her eyes were failing her, but then she was sure of it. Her falcon was growing.

Wren stood frozen to the spot. A screeching bird was bad enough. A screeching monster bird, ten times worse. Her falcon stood staring evenly at her with its liquid eyes. Wren couldn't speak. She felt shaky inside, like she might need to sit down that very moment. She tried to breathe slowly, but she barely managed to count to three.

"Excellent," Mary said. "Now wait here while I go into the falcon mews and get the saddles." She disappeared into the building beyond them.

"Our falcons *have* grown tall," Jack said, standing in front of his bird, which was now the size of a small pony.

Wren's laugh came out quiet at first but then morphed into an uncontrollable giggle. Suddenly, Jack's words struck her as the funniest thing she'd heard in a long time. "As tall as they should be," Wren echoed. "See! See! What shall I see?" She unsuccessfully choked back a snort of laughter. "You should see the look on your face!" She laughed harder, wiping at the tears forming in her eyes, and then she was crying, the laughter replaced by difficult-to-hide sobs. *What in the world is going on?*

Jack was watching her, his lips curved up in what might be a smile, the skin around his eyes crinkling in a friendly, amused sort of way, but he wasn't laughing.

Simon, too, had grown his bird. "Instantaneous adaptation on a huge scale. It's mind-boggling."

"It's amazing," Wren said, trying to hide the fact that she was crying. She never cried. "Revolutionary," she sobbed, like the falcons were the saddest creatures in the world.

"Wren?" Simon asked, as if he noticed for the first

time that she was cycling through every possible emotion on warp speed. "Are you okay?"

"I don't think so," Wren said in a wobbly voice. She tried to inhale through her now-congested nose. "I'm laughing. And crying. And I have no idea why. Just give me a minute."

She managed a few deep breaths, while Simon turned back to the falcons, making monotone observations on their intelligent eyes, their deadly talons, and the coloring of their feathers. Wren stopped crying, the tears replaced by the irritation burning hot within her. He was such a know-it-all. Besides, why wasn't Simon more rattled by all of this?

"They're beautiful," he was saying in a worshipful tone.

"How can you say that?" Wren snapped. "Mutant birds are standing in front of us and you think they're *pretty*?"

Simon spun around, his face looking confused. Jack took a cautious step toward Wren. Seeing his friendly countenance look so worried evaporated Wren's anger, and a recklessness swept over her, the wild desire for adventure replacing the fear she felt upon initially seeing the birds. "Let's ride them," she said, her heart quickening at the idea. "Let's do it. Mother Goose rode through the air, right?" She ignored Simon's open-mouthed stare and hurried up to her falcon. "Last one up is a rotten egg."

Wren was close to her bird now, and if a falcon could look angry, this one did. It swiveled its head, screeching right into her face, and then spread its wings wide.

"No! Wait!" Simon yelled. "Don't go!" But the falcon was gone, barreling up and out above the tree canopy and into the sky.

Wren watched it get smaller and smaller until it was a black speck on the gray clouds. She turned around and saw Simon staring at her as though he'd never seen her before. A breeze blew through her hair, taking the sense of adventure with it, leaving Wren feeling like her normal unflappable self again. "I have no idea what just happened," she said in her more normal-sounding voice. "I'm really sorry."

"Don't be," Mary said, coming toward them with her arms full of blankets, several leather contraptions hooked over one shoulder. "It's your first time working the stardust. It's not unusual for there to be an emotional response." She moved on to show Jack how to fasten the saddle, but every so often Wren caught Mary giving her tight, purse-lipped glances.

Simon needed no help, of course, so Mary drew near and gave Wren's shoulder a quick squeeze. "The falcon will come back any moment. All will be well." She patted her own bird, which stood docilely by her side, the tip of its head reaching her shoulder.

"Do you typically find yourself having such strong emotional reactions to new scenarios?" Mary asked Wren casually as she pulled the strap against her falcon's underbelly.

"Absolutely not. The last time I flipped out like that was when I was four and lost my favorite stuffed animal." Wren smiled at the memory. It had taken the whole afternoon for her dad to calm her down. "My dad says nothing can ruffle my feathers. You know, because my name is Wren, like a bird?" Wren winced as the unsuitability of it hit her. Could her parents have picked a worse name? She shrugged. "I have no idea what happened just now." Her analytical mind began to kick in. "Maybe it was the falcons. Like an allergic reaction or something." *Or a phobic one.*

But Mary didn't give her opinion. While they'd been talking, Jack and Simon had kept busy with their birds. And now Jack was astride his, and the giant falcon set off with a jerky run, spreading its wings wide, and then took to the air.

"Jack!" Mary shouted up at the sky. "Jack! Are you all right?"

Jack soared past them, steering his falcon up and over the woods. He waved his arms and whooped.

Mary clapped one hand over her mouth and laughed. "There's nothing like a Fiddler's first flight," Mary said, watching Jack crouch low over his bird. "You'll see soon enough, when your falcon comes back."

"Right," Wren said, feeling sick to her stomach as the reality of what Jack was doing sank in. Not only did she have to be close to the falcon, have to talk to it, and even have to take care of it, but she had to actually ride the thing. They watched Jack do another loop around the mews. "I can't wait."

TEN

Old King Cole was a wise old soul.
A wise old soul was he.
He called for the stone, and he called for his bowl,
And he called for his Council three.

Wren stood, looking up at Mary's fully grown falcon. Her own hadn't returned, and now that the last lingering daylight had faded into shadowy dusk, Mary had decided they would leave for the Crooked House without it.

"My falcon is strong," Mary said, adjusting the strap on her saddlebag. "It can carry both of us."

Jack was still circling overhead, and Wren could tell Simon was itching to join him. He moved toward his falcon, which instantly offered him its tan back. In one smooth motion, as though he'd been doing it his entire life, Simon was up on the creature, knees tucked behind its wings.

"Excellent, Simon." Mary whispered something to Simon's bird, and Wren thought she saw the creature nod its head in response. "Remember to hold the neck feathers and lean low."

Mary reached out a hand, beckoning for Wren to join her on the white falcon. Wren wished the feeling of adventure was back. Or something that might make it possible for her to get up on the thing. She shut her eyes and clasped Mary's hand. Mary pulled hard, and Wren scrabbled at the slick feathers, and then she was up, seated behind Mary. Her knees tingled. The falcon hadn't even moved, and the ground still seemed a long way down. The bird stretched its wings and then bounced forward into a choppy run. Wren could feel powerful flapping beneath her, and then they were gaining ground, higher and higher, until they were past the treetops, the dark trail of the road dwindling away below them.

Wren tightened her hold around Mary's waist. Next to them, Simon was laughing, hands straight up in the air. "I'm flying!"

Wren managed a weak answering cheer and peeked

down. Her ears heard Simon's words and her eyes saw the way the landscape changed below them, but her mind couldn't actually process what was happening. *Flying. In the sky.* The air was icy cold, and Wren's cheeks prickled numb as the falcon found an airstream and began to glide. The roar of wind in her ears soon overtook the muffled rhythmic thump of wings. The falcon skimmed the countryside, coasting above silvery trails of water and up over a mountain, and then beyond to the wide expanse of the sea.

Wren's hands were beginning to cramp from their death grip around Mary's middle. She had been so fixated on not falling off that the glimmering flecks surrounded her for some time before she recognized that they were flying in a glowing cloud. In front of her, Mary was singing a rhyme and weaving the stardust so that webs of light swirled around them.

Wren couldn't be sure how long they stayed like that, wrapped in a great trail of twinkling light, but she sensed the warmth fading. Something in her fought the cold, wanted to draw more of the sensation into herself, but she let it go. She felt the chill of the night air, and the dust evaporated enough that she saw the falcon's feathers again, and beyond the falcon, a shadowed mountain coming closer and closer, impossibly fast, and she yelled that they were crashing, but the bird plummeted onward, at the last moment swooping onto a rocky ledge, and they were back on the ground once more.

Or at least near the ground. The falcon had landed on a rough ledge that jutted out of the mountainside, forming a rocky grotto that flickered in the light of two torches wedged between stones. Jack had arrived first, and he was sliding easily off his falcon. Mary tugged on Wren's shoulder, and Wren half fell, half flopped down the side of the bird after her. Her legs wobbled, and her heart raced wild.

"Here I come!" Simon yelled from behind her. She whirled around to see Simon's bird plummeting toward them, diving in to land nearby, the rush of its wings blowing Wren off-balance. Simon easily dismounted, giving his falcon's side a friendly pat. Beyond him, Wren could see a valley sprawling below them, a shimmering river snaking its way through the shadows and emptying into a choppy ocean that stretched off into the distance. Overhead, the stars shone brightly, dimmed only by the swirls of turquoise and yellow that remained from the aurora. The broad outcropping they had landed on led inward to a natural cavern, but the shadowed cliff face itself stretched up and out of sight, marked only by the twinkling lights of what might be other falcon-landing ledges and the few stone stairways that connected them.

"Well done, Wren and Simon." Mary scooped some kind of food for her falcon from a barrel near the wall. She had returned her bird to regular size, and Wren saw that while she'd been stargazing, the boys had been busy doing the same.

Wren joined them in time to watch Mary weave a pinch of stardust with a hurried whispered rhyme. The next moment she held up her palm, and a glowing ball of light cast shadows about her face.

"How did you do that?" Wren asked.

"So many questions. You must contain them. Fiddlers don't like nuisances."

"Hey!" Wren didn't like being called names.

"Of course I don't mean that you are a nuisance, Wren." Mary darted an alarmed look at the wide black archway behind them. It was covered with thick reams of cobwebby dust that shone in the moonlight. "Look, Baxter and Liza and I. There's more than one reason we take extra care at the Crooked House."

"Doesn't make any sense, if you ask me." Jack folded

his arms across his chest. "All the other Fiddlers come here, don't they?"

"No one's asking you, Jack," Mary snapped. "And all those other Fiddlers will eat you alive for less than arguing if you cause trouble. Apprentices spend years in the kitchens before they even touch the stardust, and you want to waltz in there and befriend them?"

"There are other apprentices?" Simon asked, setting down the bucket he had been using to feed his falcon.

"You think you three are the only Fiddler apprentices ever?" Mary's eyes looked tight. "I've told you again and again, Jack, but you refuse to listen. Apprentices aren't coddled here; they work hard for every scrap of knowledge they learn. I know you're excited, but the Crooked House is not a vacation spot."

"Meaning?" Wren didn't like the sound of that.

"Meaning that you'd best be on your guard. Do only as I say." Mary looked first into Wren's face, then Simon's, and finally Jack's. Wren couldn't tell what she was hoping to see. She counted her heartbeats, willing away the tiny pricks of fear that threatened to balloon into panic. It felt like an eternity, ending only with a strange shiver that rippled through her from the cold night air.

"Speak only when spoken to," Mary said. "Answer

respectfully"—she gave Jack a pointed look—"and apprentices must always use the title 'Fiddler.' You will call me Fiddler Mary. Under no condition are you to approach a full Fiddler on your own." She took a deep breath. "This first hour will be the hardest, and then we will see."

Wren looked at Simon, who was nodding thoughtfully. For once, she wished he had been taking notes—how were they supposed to remember all of that? Jack seemed to bristle with excitement, as though he hadn't heard any of the threat underlying Mary's words.

Wren and the others followed Mary through the door and up winding stone steps that curled around on themselves, circling higher into the mountainside. Soon, the stairs beneath them turned slippery with moisture, and the walls on either side shone thick with water and sparkling veins. Mica, perhaps, or some kind of silver, but Wren didn't stop to investigate. They walked single file, so there was little space for conversation. Instead, Wren watched Mary's shoulders in front of her and heard Simon's and Jack's soft footfalls behind her. Mary was setting a quick pace.

Up, up, up they went, until it felt like they were miles above where they'd started. Suddenly, Mary came to a stop, and Wren stumbled into her back with a muffled apology. They were standing on a small landing that opened out into a giant cavern. Mary's tiny ball of light was lost in the iridescent glow of the space in front of them. The walls and ceiling looked as though they were made of blue ice, pulsing with some unseen energy, and their uneven surface gave the effect of a giant off-kilter crystal cathedral.

The natural formation had obviously been modified by man-made improvements. The farther they walked, the more Wren saw evidence of synthetic alterations. The icy walls were coated with some kind of varnish and polished to a marble-like smoothness. The walkway under them was similarly finished except for places where boardwalks bridged particularly uneven stones. Staircases dotted the walls, climbing to upper levels marked by wooden balconies and green doors. But it wasn't only this that made Wren want to stop and stare.

Wren couldn't tell if they'd walked into a science laboratory or a historical documentary. A woman in a long corseted dress passed by them, holding a lantern high in one hand and a thick stack of books balanced in the other. She nearly dropped both when she saw them approaching.

"Jane," Mary said in a hard voice and breezed by, leaving the woman standing and staring after them.

A man wearing a white lab coat and goggles pushed up over his forehead leaned against one wall, his face flickering in the light of a tablet.

On the balcony above him, two men with their shirt sleeves rolled up were hunched over a table covered with papers, arguing about whether Darwin might have perceived stardust when he visited the Galapagos. They stopped short as they caught sight of Mary.

Wren glanced behind her and saw that clusters of people were gathering in their wake, whispering and not bothering to hide scornful looks.

"Fiddlers," Mary said over her shoulder, "as you can tell, are a very diverse group of people."

"Who obviously aren't pleased to see us," Wren said as she passed an ordinary-looking woman who was carrying a crate full of lab rats. "What are they all doing here anyway?"

"Some live here. Even those who make their homes elsewhere return to the Crooked House for research materials. All come to uncover old rhymes, debate hypotheses, hone their craft, and spy on one another. Everything is about power here. Assume that no one is trustworthy, and you'll be fine. Better yet, don't assume anything. Stick close to me, and keep your mouth shut.

That goes for you too, Simon," Mary said.

Simon had fallen behind, where he stood examining some kind of fungus growing on the rock wall and making vigorous notations in his book.

"Keep your wits about you, and don't you dare ask questions, even to satisfy your curiosity," Mary continued with a pointed look. "Draw no unnecessary attention to yourselves."

They followed Mary onto a bridge that appeared to be floating on a cloudy pool of turquoise water. On the other side, soft waves lapped the edges. A man with his nose buried in a book shuffled past, bumping into Simon and somehow navigating the bridge without looking up. He seemed to be the only one who hadn't noticed their entrance. Everyone else trailed behind at a safe distance until Wren had the eerie feeling that they were foremost in a bizarre parade.

Wren looked across the water to see a girl a little older than she wearing an apprentice cloak. When the girl saw Wren noticing her, she ducked her head and hurried onward, moving from green door to green door, depositing something in front of each. Soon, she disappeared from view, making her way into the farther reaches of the cavern.

After the bridge came a large circular room that had once opened to the outside. Now, the opening was covered with glass, letting in a panoramic view of the bejeweled night sky and the distant waves below. On either side, the sloped cavern walls rose gently, stretching up into a natural amphitheater with rows of seating.

Opposite the window, four figures sat on throne-like seats carved into the rock wall. As Mary led them onward, one figure rose, holding out a hand.

"Of course it would have to be her," Mary said with a formal little bow for the woman who beckoned to them. She turned to Wren and the others as they crossed the amphitheater. "Say nothing."

"We got it. No questions. No talking. Blah, blah, blah," Jack said, with a half grin for Wren.

"Well, remember it," Mary snapped. "Keep your head bowed and eyes on the floor." And then they were standing before the group of important-looking Fiddlers.

"Mary," the woman said. "You are not welcome here."

ELEVEN

Rain, rain go away.
Come again another day,
When the Fiddler dares to play.

Wren had no difficulty following Mary's advice. From the moment they had entered the Council Chamber, she could tell that Mary hadn't exaggerated. The Crooked House indeed seemed to be a tricky place, and the woman who had first unwelcomed them seemed to have a special antipathy for Mary, taking the past quarter of an hour to complain about Mary's character and demanding that the other members of the Council throw them all out. The Fiddlers who had followed them in hovered on the fringes, providing an audience for a most unpleasant performance.

"Mary gave up her place on the Council long ago,"

the hostile woman was saying, "and I am Mistress of Apprentices now." Her profile was all points—from the tip of her nose to the jutting chin and bony arms folded across her front. Next to her a woman in a white lab coat, who looked like she could be in a commercial for a prescription drug, took notes in a thick book.

"And yet you have found no new apprentices in the wild, Elsa," a tall man with white hair said, running his too-long and very pale fingers through his matching beard. "Whereas Mary here brings us three."

The last Fiddler on the Council sat silently wrapped up in a rumpled knit sweater, his dark hair an uncombed mass on the top of his head. He hunched in his seat as though the thick black frames on his glasses weighed his whole head down. A falcon perched on his right shoulder, swiveling its gray-spackled head to glare at Mary and her apprentices in turn.

"Mary." Elsa's voice echoed in the space. She wore a long hooded cape that billowed as she moved toward Mary, raising an incriminating pointing finger. "You found the Fiddler who betrayed us all. Boggen was *your* apprentice"—Wren could feel Mary stiffen next to her—"and yet you still gather other apprentices. You would dare to train them despite Cole's express command?" She flung a hand back at the man with the falcon. "You overreach yourself."

Wren's eyes widened. *He* was Cole? She looked questioningly at Simon, who must have been thinking the same thing, because he gave her the slightest shrug. Simon was standing with his hands clenched in fists, probably to keep from scribbling in his notebook. Jack for once was dumbstruck, the smile gone from his face, as though the awe of being in the presence of so many Fiddlers finally made him speechless.

"Girl, are you deaf? Answer me," Elsa was saying, and it took Wren a minute to realize that Elsa was actually speaking to her. Wren pointed a thumb to her chest and gaped.

"Yes, you. Apprentice. Has Fiddler Mary been teaching you?" The way she asked the question made it sound like Wren had committed a crime.

Wren licked her lips. "Um," Wren began, and then remembered Mary's warning. "I just met Fiddler Mary yesterday, Fiddler." Wren sketched a bow and then immediately felt stupid. The Fiddler Council might seem to be royalty sitting on stone thrones, but they didn't act like it.

"Is it all right?" the man with the white beard asked,

peering at Wren, as if she were a fascinating kind of insect. "Is it convulsing? I hope you didn't bring a faulty apprentice to us, Mary. We have no time for extra work."

"Wild apprentices or not," the woman with the book said, and the words didn't sound pleasant, "I'd never thought to see Mary in the Council Chamber again."

"I have not come to fan into flame old feuds," Mary said, her face stoic. "Nor have I come to beg pardon"— she looked directly at Cole then—"from any of you. I can assure you that I am here with good reason."

"We have heard your reasons before," Elsa snorted, as if she had made a big joke. "And lived with the results for hundreds of years. You were nothing more than Boggen's pawn." She cackled. "Don't tell me you've come with more stories about how brilliant that traitor's research was. Or is it simply to bribe your way back on to the Council with three apprentices?" She sneered at Jack. "That one looks sickly. So pale and skinny." Her eyes skimmed over Wren and then on to Simon. "Hmph. Too cheap a payment by far."

Wren glanced at Mary, whose gaze was fixed straight ahead as though she no more noticed Wren and the others than the stone beneath her feet.

"I've come with the apprentices, yes, but also with an urgent need to seek audience with the Council." Mary's face held an indifferent, almost bored expression. "Though much has changed since Cole and I began it, the Council still governs the Fiddlers, does it not?" Her pointed reminder seemed directed at Elsa, who pursed her lips into a thin line.

"You may approach," Cole finally spoke. His voice was low and deep and commanding. "No Fiddler who seeks an audience with the Council will be denied."

The woman in the lab coat marked something down on the paper in front of her. "Let the Council note that Fiddler Mary has returned to the Crooked House, and her presence before the Council is in immediate conflict with her forced exile from the Council in 1871, tendered at the trial to investigate Boggen's forbidden use of stardust during the Fiddler Civil War of 1869."

"I remember the trial well," said Mary in short, clipped tones. "Perhaps it will please the Council to also remember how I was the first to bring the truth of Boggen's transgressions into the light." She put up a hand to forestall what was obviously going to be an objection by Elsa. "I have never contested the wrongness of Boggen's forbidden rhymework. Using the stardust to consume life is and always has been a horrible evil. But that does not make all his discoveries evil. Boggen was a brilliant Fiddler"—she looked pointedly at Elsa—"which is something I cannot say for all of my former apprentices."

Elsa shifted slightly under Mary's gaze but still held her head high enough to look down her nose. "My how the mighty have fallen. Are you sure it's wise to remind us of your glory days, Mary? I remember very well what happened then—how the heroic Mistress of Apprentices flaunted Boggen as the most promising Fiddler in centuries." She slapped her forehead as though recalling an important fact. "Oh, but I forgot, that was before he gathered his army of Magicians bent on consuming all life on Earth."

Wren gulped and looked over at Jack and Simon, who were eyeing Mary warily. She wondered if Jack still felt excited at all they could learn at the Crooked House. Wren was beginning to think they would have been better off never leaving Pippen Hill.

Elsa moved sideways between the other Council members and Mary, as though she were a lawyer presenting her case. "Who was it, Mary, who said that living stardust could cure anything, even the gravest of illnesses? Boggen? Or was that you?" She furrowed her forehead dramatically. "It's so hard to separate the two of you." Her words grew sharp. "But then it really doesn't matter. Once Boggen and his Magicians died in their final catastrophe, only you were left to pick up the pieces. How convenient." She waved a hand to dismiss Mary. "Oh, you can call it *restoring order* if you like, but it's been a century and a half and the Fiddlers are still reeling from the fallout. You're fooling yourself if you think anyone here is interested in anything you have to say."

Wren glanced up at Mary, whose face had lost all its color, but from the look in her eyes, it was from anger, not fear. "And is this the opinion of the entire Crooked House? Or just of Elsa?"

The woman with the clipboard didn't look up from her notes, and Old White-Beard merely spread out one hand, as if to ward off Mary's questions.

"You come in difficult times, Mary." Cole stood. His falcon spread its wings and then resettled onto the leather strap that covered Cole's shoulder. "Tempers are high. Patience is in short supply. And there have been strange doings." He looked at the apprentices then, and Wren felt that his eyes were remarkably like the depthless gaze of his falcon. "Stranger even than the arrival of three wild apprentices."

"And you think I disagree?" Mary moved forward, covering the space to the Council chairs, and Wren took the opportunity to slink closer to Jack and Simon. "The grains in my hourglass are nearly empty. The end of the age nears, and all we have to show for it is wasted time." Her voice sounded brittle, like it might snap. "You should have let me continue researching alternate sources of stardust."

The Council members all began talking at once: Elsa with pointed fingers and accusations; Cole, whose falcon somehow remained unflappable; and even White-Beard, whose face looked angry. The woman with the record book was writing furiously, trying to capture what they were all saying, though how she kept it straight, Wren couldn't imagine.

The Council members were so occupied, Wren felt it might be safe to risk a whispered question.

"What do you know about Mary's research?" she asked Jack.

He shrugged. "As much as you, I'd guess. She's never told me about any of this stuff."

"They said Boggen used living stardust," Simon

mused. "I wonder what that means."

"All living things are made up of stardust," Wren said absently. "You and me, even. We're made from it, too." It was one of the first things that had fascinated her about astronomy. That all life actually originated in the stars. She looked over at Simon, whose hand was twitching by his side. He reached for his pencil.

"Shh," Jack hushed them. "Something's happening."

"Whatever you thought back then," Mary was saying, "you will have to change your conclusions now." She pulled the stone Jack had found from beneath her cloak. "It contains a message from Boggen. You can decide for yourselves whether an ally of his would bring it to you. "

Elsa gasped. The lab coat woman dropped her pencil. And White-Beard fell back into his chair. Only Cole stayed unmoved, his magnified unblinking eyes studying the table from behind his glasses.

"You've brought something that once belonged to Boggen?" Cole's voice was dangerously quiet.

"Nearly a hundred and fifty years have passed," Mary said, as though it were a fact of little interest, but Wren could see how taut her fingers were around the stone. "And still you stand as you did so long ago.

Frightened. And close-minded." She lifted her palm, as if to offer the Council the stone. "Whether you believe that I supported Boggen or not, you must study what is surely one of his last messages." The strange flame-like etching at the bottom seemed to flare with light at her words. "See his mark? Whatever message is inside, it comes from Boggen himself."

"Boggen is nothing to us." Elsa had found her voice. "A power-hungry fool who deserved death. And the Magicians with him."

"We lost half our strength with Boggen and much of our knowledge. Have you forgotten that the Magicians excelled in making new rhymes?" Mary scowled at Elsa. "And what of the Alchemists who died trying to stop Boggen?" She shook her hand for emphasis. "This can tell us what they died for."

Elsa's laugh was shrill. "Don't pretend to care about the fallen. You brought this to us for one reason only: to prove your innocence." She grinned in a satisfied way as Mary flinched at her words. "You're a fool, Mary. Whatever Boggen's message is—if it is, in fact, authentic and not some fake you've concocted—it won't change the fact that you are a traitor."

"I agree with Mary," Cole said. "Difficult times lie

ahead, and we cannot afford the luxury of arguing."

"Of course you would agree with her," Elsa hissed. "Cole, you are a fool. How can you let a broken heart rule your mind?"

The room fell silent. Wren didn't dare say anything to Simon or Jack. The air around them was fraught with tension. Mary's cheeks were flushed, but Cole seemed unruffled by Elsa's accusation. "That stone was marked by Boggen's hand, and no one can fabricate his spell-writing. It is his message." He ran one hand lightly over his falcon's back. "Put the stone in the oracle-wall, Mary. I will open it."

Elsa looked like she might choke as Mary ascended the few steps. Between the middle two throne-like chairs a space was carved in the wall, and she placed the stone into it.

Cole threw some stardust into the air and began to play it. Already, Wren had become accustomed to the sight of the magic, and her mind filed away the patterns Cole used. His movements were quick and sure, very different from Mary's graceful motions. He manipulated the stardust as though he were in a swordfight, his deep voice singing a rhyme that was hard for Wren to make out. Some of the words were

English—she caught *fire* and *pyre*, *foretell* and *once more*—but the rest were unfamiliar, filled with *thee*s and *thou*s and the archaic sound of a forgotten dialect. The gray of the stone flared with colors. Beneath his ministrations, the stardust sparkled like jewels, the air glowing in a mysterious light.

Cole bent forward, reading the magical words of the message. It was unlike any language Wren had ever heard. Hard guttural sounds danced with the smooth slurred vowels that were more familiar. She watched as the stardust grew more agitated with the cadence of his words. Then there was a resounding crack that split the stone open like an egg. A funnel of cloudy ash spun up to the ceiling, and Wren saw it forming images she could recognize. Lines of writing on a page, glimmering in moonlight. A figure flying on a giant bird and holding aloft something that glowed golden. Dark creatures with shimmering wings. The shadow of a huge mountain, shot through with a dart of lightning. A blue pendulum swinging in a luminescent arc. And a web stretching through the sky up to a flame made of stars.

The images played over and over again as Cole read, imprinting themselves on Wren's memory. After a time, he stopped speaking, and the stardust pictures faded into a swirl of unrecognizable flickers. Soon, everyone was left in silence.

"It is difficult to see what it means," White-Beard finally said. "A lost rhyme, obviously. And a key and a map. But the gateway and the pendulum? What can that signify?"

"A gateway," Mary said, and her eyes looked like burnt-out hollows in her pale face. She turned to Cole. "I didn't know."

"I did," Cole said. "I've known for some time. I feel his oily touch in my nightmares." He stood, studying the now-still stone for what seemed like a long time, and the air grew heavy with expectation. Then, he spoke to the others. "Boggen didn't die." He held up a hand to stop Elsa's cry of alarm. "His last spell didn't kill him and his Magicians. He created a gateway!" He pointed to the windowed wall that revealed the starry night sky. "A gateway leading somewhere out there." The Fiddlers all began talking at once: Elsa firing angry accusations at Mary, the white-bearded man interrogating Cole, and the woman with the clipboard recording it all.

"But that's good, isn't it?" Jack asked Wren. "Not

dead is better than dead, right?" But he wasn't quiet enough, and, despite their arguing, the Council noticed.

"It speaks," White-Beard said, frowning at Jack. "The apprentice dares to interrupt Council business."

Elsa seemed all too eager to replace worry about the unknown threat of the Magicians' existence with railing at Jack's breach of protocol, and discussion about Boggen ceased immediately. "You train your apprentices ill, Mary," Elsa gloated. "And you insist on breaking every rule we have."

"Not every rule," Mary said, shooting Jack a death glare. "I see I will have to discipline them more thoroughly."

"I am the Mistress of Apprentices now, not you, Mary," Elsa said, drawing herself up to her full height. "I will see to his discipline." She wrapped her cloak around her and folded her arms over her chest. "And he will never speak out of turn again."

Wren felt a chill run through her—not at Elsa's dramatic words, but at the cold glint in her eye that made Wren think she was exactly what she appeared to be: a medieval witch contemplating medieval punishments.

Jack must have been feeling something similar. He looked like a scolded puppy, his head bowed and gaze locked on the floor.

"Truly, it *is* odd, this new way of interrupting one's betters," Cole said, "but perhaps you are being too severe, Elsa." He frowned, his fingers tugging on the falcon's tail. "He knows nothing of Boggen's atrocities. Or of what this means. Indeed, we have much to learn ourselves." He pointed to the now-silent cluster of onlookers. "Gather the rest of the Fiddlers. Begin the summoning." At his words, the relative stillness of the cave was split with a loud gonging noise, as though there was a clock tower somewhere underground that was marking time.

"The summoning has begun." Elsa looked down her very long nose at Mary and her apprentices. "Full Fiddlers only, I'm afraid, which means I'll have to deal with your children later." The way she said *children* made it sound like a dirty word.

Footfalls sounded on the bridge behind them, as the people they'd seen earlier entered the amphitheater. The men in their old-fashioned clothes quickly found seats. The man with the goggles, too, was hurrying past. And the woman with all the books.

"*My* apprentices, Elsa," Mary said, without looking at them. "I found them in the wild."

More people were appearing from behind the green

doors, spilling into the center area and moving past Wren, the sound of their voices echoing off the smooth walls. Some had obviously been woken from sleep. She saw flannel pajamas, old-fashioned nightgowns complete with hats, and even long underwear as the Fiddlers filed into the amphitheater seats.

"So you said. From the wild." Elsa stared at them as though *the wild* equaled a garbage dump.

Wren stared right back, fixated on her thick eyebrows that blended into one above her remarkable nose.

"I'll foster them," Elsa said in a greedy voice. "I can always use an extra pair of hands." She came over and pinched one of Wren's between two fingers as though she meant to snatch it off her body, leaving two stardust thumbprints that looked like bruises.

"Don't touch me," Wren said, and Mary gave her a warning look. Wren crossed her arms and glared at Elsa. Fiddler or not, she wasn't going to answer respectfully to this witch.

"Perhaps you are right, Elsa," Mary said. "They are of no further use to me now."

"They do need training," Elsa said. "A good flogging will make her more pliable. Double lashes for the boys. That one looks like he might not be right in the head," she said with barely a glance at Simon.

Wren brushed Elsa's stardust off, sending little glimmers in the air around her hands. She took in Jack's downcast eyes and the look of shame Simon wore, his shoulders slumping. Her veins pulsed with emotion. Embarrassment for Jack. Outrage at Elsa's cruel words for Simon. Shock at Mary's casual dismissal. Frustration that none of what they had just witnessed made any sense and that no one had bothered to explain anything, let alone treat them like actual human beings. Fury that she had not asked any questions, that she had followed Mary's stupid orders exactly. Her heartbeat quickened, matching the throbbing pain in her head, and her cheeks burned hot. *It's happening again, just like it did back with the falcons.* She looked down at the stardust prints on her arms. Too late, Wren realized that she had touched stardust. The emotions boiled within her, anger and fear and shame blistering up to the surface beyond her control.

"Who do you think you are?" Wren's voice was rising so that she was nearly shouting, but she couldn't hold it back. "Calling me an *it*. Talking about who we *belong* to? And how dare you say such things about Simon? That's his name—*Simon*. Not it. Not apprentice.

Simon." She was yelling now, beyond the possibility of moderation, her volume matching the pounding in her skull. "And what exactly do you mean by *a good flogging*? A *flogging*? Are you insane?"

Mary placed both hands on Wren's shoulders, as if to calm her, and Wren shoved them off. "And you? You would sell us to that *witch*?" A low rumble of thunder cracked the sky outside, and the cool scent of rain gusted through the arch on the far side of the room. A moment later, lightning cut through the clouds, flashing through the darkness of the cave.

The room was utterly silent after Wren's outburst, and in the intervening seconds she felt all her emotions, even her anger at Elsa, slip away. Everything except embarrassment. *What is wrong with me?*

"Um. I mean. We should talk about this." She could feel the eyes of all the gathering Fiddlers on her. She started backpedaling, talking about legal ramifications and child protective services, but Wren could see from Mary's expression that her damage control was only making it worse. Simon was staring at his hands. Jack's mouth hung open, like he was a surprised cartoon character. Elsa's gaze was cool, as though she was considering what might be worse than a flogging.

White-Beard was dictating something excitedly to the woman with the record book, and, from the looks he kept giving Wren, it had something to do with her. And Cole was studying Boggen's stone, a little smile playing about his mouth, but his falcon had locked its piercing gaze on Wren.

Wren's forced laugh sounded more like a gasp for air. "I'm not myself right now."

"Falcon travel can have odd side effects, you know that. It was Wren's first time today." Mary's usually unruffled voice sounded uneasy. "And sometimes I find that apprentices have surprising reactions to the northern climate." She grabbed Wren by both shoulders and spun her around. "Perhaps I should take them somewhere to rest." They had taken two steps back toward the bridge when Cole's voice rang out.

"A Weather Changer, Mary?" he said. "Did you plan to hide this from us? Especially now?"

Mary closed her eyes, wincing. "So close," she muttered, turning back around.

All four Council members were staring at them. At Wren, actually. The Weather Changer.

"There hasn't been a Weather Changer since the Magicians left," Cole said, and Wren shifted under the heaviness of his magnified gaze. "Odd that one should appear now." He tapped his fingers against his chin, no smile this time.

"And such a powerful Weather Changer." The man with the white beard rubbed his hands together in a way that made the hairs on the back of Wren's neck stand up. "She must be studied."

"Well," Mary said in a strained voice that showed this was not the outcome she wanted. "What will be will be." She changed her tone. "But such conduct is unacceptable from my apprentices. Permit me a moment to reprimand her myself."

Elsa raised her unibrow at Mary. "You flog them in public?"

"Ah," Mary said. "Too simple. Won't you excuse us?"

She piloted Simon, Jack, and Wren over toward the wall.

"I told you to leave it to me," she hissed. "What were you thinking, Wren?"

"I don't know! It's like something came over me. I couldn't help myself, and, oh, that woman is awful."

"Who is she?" Simon asked in a dull voice. His face looked as though someone had wiped all the life out of it.

"She is the one who will make you miserable if you can't keep your mouth shut," Mary snapped. "Elsa is only interested in you because I am. If she thought I was indifferent to you, she wouldn't have bothered, but now there's no way any of them will let a Weather Changer slip out of their greedy little hands. Did you listen to anything I said about the politics of this place? Nothing is as it seems. And now they'll have you locked up in their apprentice quarters for months, if not years."

"Years?" Wren's eyes felt like they were going to pop out of her head.

Mary ignored her. "When we rejoin the others, you must look properly chastened, as though I've threatened the worst punishment you can think of," she said with stern eyes. "And I'm not so certain I don't want to. For the life of all that you hold dear, Wren, say nothing else. I wasn't sure when I felt the wind after your first outburst with the falcon, but now there's no doubting it. You are a Weather Changer, that is clear enough to everyone, but let's not remind them of that again, okay?" She gave Wren an encouraging look. "I will have to remain here for the summoning, and you will be sent to the apprentice quarters. Stay out of trouble, do as you're told, and everything should be fine." Her voice was back to being cool and collected, as though she wasn't informing them that she was abandoning them in this crazy place.

"And Elsa's flogging?" Wren could see Elsa pacing beyond them, and the girl Wren had noticed by the bridge was hovering nearby.

"She won't dare touch my apprentices," Mary said. "Another thing you should know. In the Crooked House apprentices belong to their training Fiddler. They're kind of like"—she smiled apologetically even as she said it—"servants that the Fiddlers own."

"Belong to them? Like slaves?" Simon said. "That's crazy!"

The amphitheater was full now, and the buzz of talking Fiddlers filled the room. Some, probably the ones who had witnessed Wren's outburst, stared at the group in the corner, but most had their attention fixed on the four stone chairs, where Cole was preparing to speak.

Elsa moved toward them then, rubbing her hands together eagerly, as though she was enjoying the thought of Mary's apprentices getting punished.

Mary glanced back over her shoulder and then turned to them with a stern expression on her face. "And I won't have my apprentices ever doing that again," she said, loud enough for Elsa to hear, before dropping her voice back to a whisper. "Stay out of her way. I'll come find you as soon as I can."

"What are you going to be doing?" Jack asked.

"Oh, only the same thing I've been trying to do for the past hundred years." Mary blew out a breath. "Prove that I'm innocent."

Before she could say more, Elsa dragged the girl Wren had spotted earlier by the ear and shoved her in their direction. The girl's curly hair frizzed out over her ears, and wide brown eyes stared at Wren with a perfectly emotionless expression.

"Take them to the apprentice quarters, Jill," Elsa commanded.

"Go with Jill. I'll find you later." Mary gave Wren's hands a quick squeeze. "Wish me luck. We're all going to need it."

TWELVE

Little Bo Peep has lost her sheep
And doesn't know where to find them.
Leave them alone, and they'll come home,
Bringing their tails behind them.

Jill took Wren, Simon, and Jack to the kitchens, which were filled with bustling apprentices. Jill served them bowls of hot soup and then disappeared without a word.

"Well, that wasn't very nice." Jack spread a thick layer of butter on his bread. "No 'Welcome to the Crooked House. We're so pleased to meet you.'" He licked the crumbs off his fingers. "But, nothing ventured, nothing gained. We're here now, and I bet we'll find out all kinds of cool things."

Wren shook her head. "You amaze me, Jack. You're

still excited to be here after what we went through up there?"

Jack slurped a spoonful of soup. "Gotta stay positive."

"I bet it's hard for Mary to stay positive," Simon said in an even voice, but he stayed focused on his food. "Seems like she's in a lot of trouble."

Jack set his bread down. "Maybe. But she can hold her own. And what do you think about that message?" He looked at Wren. "And the weather-changing thing! That was awesome!"

"You mean the thing that was the same thing the horrible Magicians did?" Wren let her spoon fall back against the bowl. "It was the opposite of awesome, Jack. It was awful. I don't even know what I did. It just happened." Simon and Jack must have read her mood, because they focused on their food and didn't ask any more questions.

Wren took a sip of the hot sweet drink the apprentice-cook had brought her and looked around at all the activity. The kitchen was similar to the rooms she'd already seen in the Crooked House. Rough walls hewn from carved stone surrounded a workspace covered with wooden tables. In every corner, thick, wax-covered candelabra sconces lit the room. There was an arched doorway

that led out to one of the falcon ledges, where Wren
could see the clear night sky. The aurora they had
flown through was fading now, and only a thin stream
of pale blue was visible along the horizon.

Inside, there was a constant flow of apprentices
coming and going. Kids their age were filling dinner
plates. Some older ones prepared trays for delivery. A
couple of boys were scrubbing huge pots on one side of
the room, and opposite them other apprentices scraped
leftovers into a bucket. Unlike the serious-faced Fiddlers they had passed on their way down, most of the
apprentices were laughing and talking. Apparently,
they hadn't yet heard about Boggen, or if they had,
they didn't care. Wren felt herself relaxing. Away from
that horrible amphitheater and all the Fiddlers who
now probably thought Wren was an evil Magician
come again or something, the Crooked House didn't
seem that bad.

When they were finished eating, Jill reappeared to
escort them to a different level of the Crooked House.
"This is the apprentice wing," she said as they wove
between a pair of whispering girls who seemed to
size them up as they passed. Most of the apprentices
appeared to be in their teens or twenties. Some of them

looked completely grown up, though they still wore the telltale black-and-gray apprentice cloak.

The apprentice quarters were somewhere between the lower-level kitchen and the amphitheater. The boys' rooms came first, and Wren told them good-night a little wistfully. She wished she could somehow bunk with them. Being alone in the Crooked House felt awfully intimidating.

The room Jill showed her to wasn't much bigger than her walk-in closet at home. A single twin bed took up most of the space, with a simple table holding a pitcher of water and a shallow bowl situated to the left of it. A few pegs on the wall behind the door where she could hang her cloak and a hard wooden chair made up the rest of the furnishings.

"Thanks! This is great," Wren said, mostly because she couldn't really think of a non-complaining adjective to describe the sparse accommodations. Besides that, no matter how Wren phrased what she said, Jill only responded with monosyllabic replies. Wren had learned nothing. Not where Jill was from. Nor when she became an apprentice. Nothing.

Jill's head bob was barely discernable over the blankets she'd been carrying.

"So, maybe I'll see you around?" Wren tried again, but Jill only dropped the blankets on the bed and turned to go. Wren smiled in what she hoped was a friendly way. "Thanks again."

"Now is when you should sleep," Jill said before she shut the door, which Wren took as her way of saying good-night.

Wren stared at her cell phone for a long time after she had climbed into bed. She had been surprised to easily get a signal, and now her mom's latest text blinked at her: *Miss you already. Love you so much! xoxo Mom.* Wren should send a reply—she wanted to, in fact—but anything she thought of sounded stupid, not to mention vastly incomplete. It felt like a whole year—no, a whole lifetime—had passed since she had last been in her old home. She finally settled on a brief reply: *Turning in for the night. Love you, too!*

There was a small skylight cut into the rock ceiling, and Wren looked out to see a smattering of constellations glimmering like a sea of jewels flung across the sky. Wren thought of the night before, when her mom had dropped her off at Pippen Hill, and wondered if things could get any crazier. If the past twenty-four hours were any indication, she was betting they could.

★ ★ ★

When Wren woke, the sun was full-on blazing through the window. Her room was hot but not uncomfortably so. She sat up and poured some water from her pitcher into the bowl, slurping a sip to quench her dry throat. In the harsh daylight, she noticed what she must have overlooked the night before: a rounded door tucked in the far corner of the room. She put on her cloak and her shoes and made her way outside.

The world was bathed in a bright light that set her head pounding and cast everything in a palette of grainy gray and white and black. She wasn't two steps outside when she heard the door slam behind her. When she turned back, the door was gone, replaced by the jagged exterior wall of the Crooked House.

Heart pounding, she ran her hands along the place where it should have been, feeling for some kind of latch, but there was nothing. She would have to go forward. She set off on the path in front of her that wound down an exterior stairway toward an outbuilding planted in the middle of the valley floor. She shaded her eyes against the light, but she couldn't see if anyone was there.

Up close, the shed was weathered gray, with strips of

paint curling up in disrepair. The twin doors hung ajar, flanked on either side by intertwined cogs and gears that were rusted from disuse. The stillness of the morning let Wren know the building was empty, and she didn't think there had been anyone there in a long time. She took a few steps into the dark interior to make sure, and as she moved back outside, she caught a familiar metallic smell. She tried to place it—something like chemicals and lab experiments and—she froze in the doorway as recognition crashed into her mind. *Blood.* Just beyond the barn, there was a black tree, barren of leaves and made out of some kind of metal. Below it shone a puddle of dark liquid. The blood was fresh, not yet congealed, and she could see drops falling from the things hanging over the empty branches, spaced every foot or so.

Wren moved closer, burying her nose in the crook of her elbow to hide the smell. She couldn't be sure, but it looked like animal pelts had been set out to dry. Wren had seen taxidermy exhibits before, but even so, her empty stomach turned. She moved closer, noting that there wasn't a whole animal hanging, only a woolen mass. Now she was near enough to see that each one was nailed to the tree. Tails of some kind.

Sheep, perhaps? She scoured the ground for a stick and poked at the furry blob closest to her. Wisps of black wool clung to the stick. Then, as she watched in horror, the wool began to change and grow, creeping up toward her hand. She threw the stick down, but there was no releasing it. She watched powerlessly as her skin was drenched with the bright red liquid, the only color in a world framed with shadows of black, white, and gray.

She tried to scream, but her voice was muffled as though someone had put a pillow over her face or trapped her words in a cramped little box. She heard a sound from somewhere near the edge of the woods and saw a girl about her own age, a shepherd's crook raised high above her head. Wren couldn't tell if she was frightened or excited. Her mouth was open, and she was shouting something at Wren, waving her crook, as she ran toward her.

Wren held out her hand, her voice still paralyzed with fear. She wanted to warn the girl to stay away. That something horrible was going on here. That there was blood and sheep's tails, and the nightmare of not being able to speak. The girl was closer now, and Wren could see that she was indeed a shepherdess, because her flock was following her from the cover of the trees. Behind them was a shadowy shape that tickled Wren's memory.

"A Dreamer," the shape said, and Wren heard a man's voice that was full of surprise. "Come closer, Dreamer, so that I can have a look at you."

Wren's feet were rooted in the ground, but even if they weren't, she would never come closer. He seemed made of shadows, despite the contrasting landscape, and his words sounded almost robotic.

"Dreamer!" he said, much louder this time. Wren tried to speak, but her voice was trapped inside, her chest squeezed with the pressure of it. She couldn't look away. Couldn't run or move. He had her in some strange spell, and even though he hadn't moved from the forest's edge, she knew he was coming for her. Wren fought against it. If she could tear her gaze away, perhaps the rest of her would follow.

"Dreamer!" It was the girl's voice this time, and it was what Wren needed. She wrenched her thoughts away from the man, reaching for some protective wall, and she saw his look of astonishment as she eluded his control. Wren's limbs were free now, and she moved toward the girl.

The shepherdess was almost to the tree, her mouth open, wailing at the sight of the tails hanging there, and then she turned to Wren, her dark eyes wet with tears. "Dreamer," she said. "You have to help us."

The shepherdess didn't see the man behind her, didn't see how he clapped his hands in delight at the sight of her dismay, didn't see how he looked over the top of her head at Wren, his soulless black eyes piercing her skull. "You will be mine, Dreamer."

THIRTEEN

Twinkle, twinkle, little star,
How I wonder what you are.

When Jill came to find her the next morning, Wren had been sitting on her bed for what felt like a long time. She couldn't shake the memory of her dream, but she tried to hide her unease from Jill.

Jill brought a note from Mary saying they were to begin their apprentice studies and "stay out of trouble."

Jill waited until Wren read the note, then said, "The library is two floors up—cross the bridge over the Opal Sea. You can't miss it." She prepared to leave.

"Wait." Wren grabbed her apprentice cloak off its peg. "We can go together."

"Today isn't a group lesson," Jill said, explaining that apprentices spent most days with their mentoring

Fiddler. A few times a week, they gathered to study as a group. Her face fell flat. "I belong to Elsa, so I need to go find her."

Wren pounded on Jack and Simon's door, eager to get to the library and finally ask Mary some questions. The boys were ready and waiting, and soon they were following the same route they had taken the night before, up the spiraling stone steps and out through the cavern with the turquoise pool of water.

As they moved farther into the cave, Wren saw signs of Fiddler life. A grated fire pit with wooden benches situated around it. A wagon laden with glass jars and beakers. Several deserted kiosks looked like they belonged at old-fashioned county fairs but were each fitted with electrical outlets. Wren made a mental note to return there when she needed to charge her phone. Green doors dotted the wall nearest them, most flanked by signs with faded letters.

Wren hurried past the amphitheater. If she didn't look at it, maybe she could avoid the embarrassing memory of how she had lost control and become labeled a Weather Changer. She had a lot of questions for Mary.

Soon they were in what seemed to be a more inhabited part of the Crooked House. They began to see other people who looked as if they actually belonged in the present century, even if their skin was a bit sallow looking. A man in a dirty white lab coat nudged a woman with her hair pulled back in a smooth bun, and both stared at them as they walked by. A cluster of men, who looked like they went shopping at vintage thrift stores, were leaning around one of the green kiosks, sipping coffee. Wren could feel their gazes trailing her. A boy a little older than them and wearing an apprentice cloak was pushing a cart loaded with baked goods, selling them to hungry Fiddlers. He stopped and gawked at them outright.

"Does *everyone* know?" Wren tried to slink down into her cloak.

"Hmm?" Simon said in an absent voice. He had been covering the distance in fits and starts, stopping to look for evidence of subterranean animal life at every turn.

"Haven't you noticed?" Jack said with a laugh. "Wren's famous." He nudged her with an elbow. "A Weather Changer. You should have told us."

"Stop it." Wren wasn't in the mood for Jack's teasing. "It's not funny. I wish I'd never said anything to the Council. I wish I'd never come here. I wish—"

Wren broke off what she had been about to say, because it wasn't true. She didn't really wish she'd never even heard of the Fiddlers.

"You're not the only weirdo here," Jack said in what Wren guessed was a consoling voice. "Most of the Fiddlers look like they are the ones in their rhymes. That must be Jack Sprat himself," he said, pointing to a rail-thin man who towered over his companion, a stout woman who overflowed her corseted dress. "Or maybe Peter the Pumpkin Eater."

"Don't be mean," Wren said, choking back a giggle that became a laugh when he started reciting "Little Miss Muffet" as they passed an old woman sitting by herself and scowling at everyone.

Soon they arrived at a gothic-looking double door. Even if Wren hadn't seen the neatly painted sign marked LIBRARY, there was a shingle hanging above it with a picture of a stack of books.

If any two spaces were the opposite of each other, it would be the Crooked House and the library. Instead of the soaring blue ice-cathedral, they were in a small round room that looked like it belonged back at Pippen Hill. Wood-framed bookcases attached to the rocky walls were lined with tomes that could have been centuries old. There was no table, though. Instead, a large flat stone about waist-high took up most of the floor space. Perfect for standing at while flipping through books. They roamed about the room, but only for a moment, because the door behind them opened and Liza poked her perfectly coiffed head in.

"Hello, darlings," she said. "Surprised to see me?"

"Liza!" Wren gave her a hug, while Liza air-kissed both of her cheeks. She turned to greet Jack and Simon, and when she moved, Wren spotted Baxter waiting beyond.

"You came! What happened to you never visiting the Crooked House again?" Wren ran over to give Baxter a hug. "Not that we aren't glad to see you." She felt a rush of relief at the sight of friends.

Baxter clasped arms with Simon and Jack. "Even we couldn't ignore the summoning. It required all Fiddlers—even estranged ones—to return to the Crooked House immediately. We came right away, and I'm sure others will be trickling in for weeks. The Crooked House won't know where to put us all." He smiled but it didn't quite reach his eyes. "And we arrive to find you all at the heart of it."

"Mary told us what the stone revealed. How Boggen

isn't dead." Liza rubbed her hands together and avoided looking at Wren. "But that's no reason your apprentice lessons should stop. Mary is busy with the Council, and if we don't step in, the Mistress of Apprentices will."

Wren couldn't tell if they had heard about the Weather Changer thing. She would've thought not, except for the occasional moments where Liza's glance lingered on her a second too long, or when Baxter's eyes looked sad. She tried to stop guessing what that might mean and focus on her first official Fiddler lesson.

Liza rummaged in her handbag and pulled out a pair of chic glasses. She put them on and began to jot something down in a little jeweled notebook. "Now, let's find you some basic Fiddler texts. The Mother Goose codex, I think—all the volumes, please, Baxter, and *The Legends of Nod*. Those will give them a good start."

"Excellent choices, *mi amor*." Baxter splayed his palm along the shelves nearest Wren. "You apprentices can choose from any of these. I'll give you a few minutes to make your selections, and then we'll begin the practical lesson."

Wren crowded closer with Jack and Simon. It was almost humorous to see the dark, faded leather of the spell books labeled *Mother Goose* at the top. Simon wasted no time and grabbed two that had subtitles having to do with animals. Wren skimmed over the faded spines until she came across one titled *Fiddler Talents through the Ages*. She slipped it out, pulling another one at random, leaving Jack still hunting.

She set her choices on the stone table with a thunk, opening the first to carefully lettered words, some using such an archaic spelling that Wren could barely make them out. Embellished pictures in the margins showed figures in motion, some accompanied by animals or detailed drawings of plants. It seemed to be arranged alphabetically, and Wren flipped the pages until she came to the *W*s.

And there it was. A whole chapter on Weather Changers. There was a rhyme demonstrating how a Fiddler who also had a talent for gardening could pair the two and increase a harvest. And another having to do with turning a sprinkle into a downpour. She skimmed more rhymes, which seemed mostly to center around plants and agriculture. Apparently, Weather Changers were quite useful in times of drought and famine.

She stopped at the part that detailed historical uses of weather-changing, which was topped with a definition of sorts. *An inherent strength at manipulating the weather can have other collateral effects.* She ran her forefinger down the words, skimming the list of symptoms. *Sleep disturbances, geological changes, foretelling visions, climate control, and emotional manipulation of others. Great care must be taken for these Fiddlers to learn to identify and accept their response to the stardust in order to avoid unintended consequences.*

Wren read the paragraph again. She'd already bought the reality that there was magic in the world, and that she, Simon, and Jack were some of the few who could play it. Accepting that her abilities might have other bizarre consequences didn't seem like that much of a leap. At least, that's what her head told her. Inside, she was terrified.

She read the rest of the page, but most of it had to do with recorded instances of geological phenomena attributed to Weather Changers. A big earthquake back in the 1500s. And a flood shortly thereafter. Wren only read that bit through once. It was hard enough to deal with this new reality without worrying about what horrible thing she might accidentally do. But no matter how many instances of disastrous weather she could ignore, she couldn't wipe out of her mind that one nagging phrase: *sleep disturbances.*

The nightmarish dreams that she'd been somewhat successful in pushing to the edges of her mind came crashing back in. She skimmed faster. Were the dreams connected to being a Weather Changer? She found a rhyme about the phases of the moon and how that might increase the dream cycle in nighttime sleep. And how a Fiddler could induce a dreamless sleep by lighting a certain herb or cause someone to have extra-vivid dreams with another. She bent closer, hunting for clues, and then saw that someone had ripped out several pages from that section. The book went from talking about sleep disturbed by something called *dreamopathy* to how the cycle of the moon could help a woman give birth to a baby. Wren glanced through the rest of the pages, but they all felt irrelevant, information to help people who'd lived hundreds of years ago. She sighed. No doubt the answers she was looking for were somewhere in the missing pages, and judging from the weathered appearance of the book, those pages were long gone.

"If that one's boring," Jack said, misinterpreting her sigh, "try this one. It's all about love potions." He snickered.

"That's nothing." Simon barely looked up from his

books. "This volume catalogs other species besides falcons that have adapted to a regular use of stardust." His
ever-present notebook lay flat next to the spell books,
and he was carefully copying down what he read.

"Not boring." Wren leaned back and rubbed her
eyes. "Just confusing. I mean, were Fiddlers like witch
doctors or something? Good harvests. Medicine. That's
what we have irrigation and vaccinations for. What's
the use of some of this stuff?"

She picked a rhyme at random and read it out loud:

As soft as silk, as white as milk
As bitter as gall, a strong wall,
And a green coat covers me all.

"What does that even mean?"

"It's your job to find out," Baxter said, bringing
over an armload of books to set in front of them. "You
didn't think Fiddlers from the Dark Ages would be
writing about cellular biology, did you? They were
medieval people, and so their science reads more, well,
medievally."

"Like alchemists," Jack said.

Simon leaned close to read over Wren's shoulder. "I

wonder if it was cow's milk."

"Alchemists," Wren said, ignoring Simon. "Or Magicians."

"Exactly," Baxter said. "But don't say the *M*-word around the Crooked House if you know what's good for you." He pretended to wipe at some nonexistent dust on his sweater.

"What do you mean?" Wren asked. "You've been telling us that stardust is magic since the beginning."

Baxter and Liza exchanged glances.

"We said that so you would understand," Liza said. "But if you talk like that here, they'll think you're talking about Boggen and his Magicians."

"The Magicians," Wren said as evenly as she could manage, looking at Liza. Cole had said there hadn't been a Weather Changer since the Magicians. "I thought you all were Magicians."

"We are in the sense that we all can work stardust. But a long time ago, two groups formed among the Fiddlers: the Alchemists and the Magicians." Liza grabbed a piece of paper and began to sketch. "It might help to think of what Fiddlers do as two equal and yet codependent forces: alchemy and magic. Alchemy, like science"—she drew a diamond shape—"enables us to understand and, in certain ways, manipulate the properties of all living things. Magic"—she drew something that resembled a flame—"does the same thing on a metaphysical level. You know, the unseen realm of thoughts and emotions." She circled both markings. "As Fiddlers, we work together to unite the two forces. Those of us who were stronger in what you might call the scientific part became Alchemists. This is our mark." Her pencil point touched the diamond. "Those who were stronger in, well, the rest of it, became Magicians." She let her fingers rest on the flame.

"That's the same symbol that was on Boggen's stone," Wren said.

"That's right." Baxter sighed. "The problems started when the ordinary world began to suspect and despise us. The Alchemists and the Magicians disagreed on how to respond."

"Disagreed!" Liza snorted. "A civil war is more than a disagreement."

Baxter continued. "The Magicians wanted to take over, to rule the ordinary world. They increased their power by consuming the lives of others."

"Living stardust." Simon's voice was agitated. He

flipped back several pages in his notebook. "That's what the Council called it yesterday. Living stardust."

"You're right." Baxter's voice cracked. "It was disgusting. They thought that stealing life from another would somehow enrich their own. But they were wrong. Death begets death." He shook his head. "Sad as we were at their demise, we were glad when the Magicians failed. Their dying brought an end to the civil war."

"I don't understand," Wren said, her words spilling faster at the thought of what she'd overheard the day before. "The Council was talking about the Magicians. About how they weren't dead after all."

"So we heard," Liza said, taking off her glasses and folding them up. "They told us at the summoning, but I still can't believe it. Not dead? What can it mean?"

"We will find out. All the Fiddlers have been summoned, and with this new development, the Council will certainly give Mary access to the rest of Boggen's research." Baxter squeezed Wren's shoulder and looked at the rest of them in turn. "The important thing to remember is that there are centuries of conflicts and alliances that you know next to nothing about. Better not to speak to any full Fiddler in the Crooked House. Best of all not to mention magic or Magicians or Boggen's name. Understood? Now, back to our lesson. We must begin the practical portion. The starlamp first, I think."

Baxter and Liza led them through one of the library doors and into a space three times its size and completely empty. Wren soon saw why. "Put one foot behind the other, here." Baxter pressed on Simon's chest. "And lean your torso back like this. Good form. Now, say the rhyme, and I'll show you what to do with your hands." Baxter pinched some stardust and tossed it into the air, stirring up a cloud of silvery blue around Simon. Baxter chanted the lines and then instructed Simon to repeat after him:

Twinkle, twinkle, little star
How I wonder what you are.

"Cup one palm like this," Baxter said, letting some of the dust settle. "And use the fingers of the other hand to cut this pattern in the remaining dust as it falls."

Up above the world so high,
Like a diamond in the sky.

Simon's fingers traced a diamond through the stardust.

"Now, raise your hand up here," Baxter said, "toward the ceiling. And sing the rest of the rhyme."

There your bright and tiny spark
Lights the traveler in the dark.

As Simon chanted, the stardust began to come together, the different strands of blue light tightening up and coalescing into a pulsing mass.

How I wonder what you are,
Twinkle, twinkle, little star.

By the time Simon was finished, a ball of light hovered above his palm.

"Excellent!" Liza said with enthusiasm. "You're a natural."

Simon was staring at the ball of stardust light, his face aglow with the wonder of it. "This feels amazing. Wren, you've got to try it."

"Useful, no?" Baxter said. "Especially in dark places. Your turn, Wren."

Wren stood, grateful that Simon went first and that at least she knew the opening part of the rhyme. She copied Baxter's movements, leaning back like she'd been blown by a gust of wind, raising her arms to play the stardust. And then the magic was there, the warmth and energy swirling around her in a shower of aqua light. She reached out to touch it, but it slipped out of her grasp. She cupped her hands as Baxter showed her, but the stardust fell flat.

"Keep practicing," Baxter said with an encouraging smile, and moved on to Jack.

Simon came up on the other side of her. "Don't worry, Wren. It can take a while to get the hang of it."

Wren knew he was trying to be nice, but she still had a hard time returning his smile. "You seemed to get it right away," she said pleasantly. She shut out the sight of Simon creating and snuffing starlamps as if it were as easy as turning a light switch on and off, and tried again.

Baxter had finished instructing Jack how to begin the rhyme. If Simon made it look easy, Jack made it look like he'd been working stardust forever. On his first try, a glowing ball of light flared in his palm.

"Very good," Baxter said, running his thumb over his stubbly jaw. "Very good indeed."

Wren tried again. Jack might have had an extra few

months to work with stardust, but that didn't mean she couldn't catch up with him. When she started to sing the final verse, the strands of stardust quivered, as though they might come together in a ball, but then collapsed into a pile of glimmering dust, the glow of the magic winking out.

Wren clenched her jaw. Her skin prickled with irritation, and she felt like throwing her whole pouch of stardust in Jack's and Simon's faces. Instead, she tossed up another pinch of dust, but this time no sparkling strands appeared. The room around her disappeared in a fog. She felt a jagged surface at her back, pushing her forward to the edge of a rocky cliff.

"Simon?" she called. "Liza?" But there was no answer. She was alone on a ledge with nothing but a perilous drop at her feet. The cave in front of her was all shadows, black and gray, and Wren recognized that she was somehow back in the world of her dreams. A waking dream this time. The stone at her feet crumbled, a few bits breaking off and plummeting into the murky water below. She looked to either side of her, frantic to find another ledge. A bridge. A path. Anything.

"Help!" she screamed, but no sound came out of her mouth. She tried again, fighting hard to say something, to say anything, when the wall behind her gave another massive push, and she was tumbling, falling, hands flailing in desperation before her body hit the water, her scream cut off before it even began.

She braced herself for icy cold liquid, muscles tensed and prepared to fight her way to the surface. But instead, she found herself cocooned in a wooden boat, her panic at falling overcome by a whispered chorus of music. Voices that sounded like flutes and strings and the wind through the pines swirled around her as her boat was swept along the waterway.

"Dreamer," the lovely voices sang. "Dreamer, you must find the way."

"What do you mean?" Wren could actually speak this time, and the sense of terror was gone. Instead, she felt at peace. Like she belonged there with the voices. "Find the way to what?"

But the voices didn't answer. Instead they kept singing:

Winken, Blinken, and Nod one night
Sailed off in a wooden shoe
Sailed off on a river of crystal light,
Into a sea of dew.

"The wings mark the way to find what you wish,"
The old moon told the three.
"Leave your nets and leave your fish,
And dive down beneath the sea, the sea.
You will find the wings that you seek, down beneath
    the sea."

"What wings? The way to where?" Wren asked. "What am I to find?" But the voices only repeated the same chorus in different harmonies as her little vessel rocked its way gently down the stream. Wren looked over the edge, where one of the boat's many propellers whirred below the surface. The water shone like an opal, covered with a thin layer of fog. She reached out a finger and trailed it through the mist, astonished to find that it wasn't liquid at all. Instead, glimmering pinpricks of stardust were carrying her along.

The music around her changed, quickened with urgency. The rhyme came faster now, one verse upon another, so that it was soon hard to distinguish the lyrics, a rising cacophony of sounds that all stopped on one word: *wings.*

"Wren?" Liza's voice cut through the chorus of wings, and with the sound came clarity. The foggy scene evaporated in an instant, and Wren was back in the lesson room, crouched on the floor.

"Wren, is something the matter?" Liza stooped down, putting her glasses on so she could peer into Wren's eyes. "Are you reacting to the stardust?"

"I'm okay," Wren said, conscious of Simon and Jack watching her from across the room. "Really. Just a bit queasy, that's all."

Liza waved away Baxter's concern. "I'll work with Wren. You continue with the boys."

While the others returned to their rhymework, Liza sat Wren down on the floor and produced a bottle of water from her bag. "Drink this."

She watched as Wren drank the cool liquid, her face full of concern. "Self-discipline is important for anyone using stardust, of course," Liza finally said. "But it will be especially crucial to your ability to mature as a Fiddler, Wren. I know you didn't intend to cause trouble yesterday, but that's just the problem. You have got to stay in control. Otherwise the stardust—or your emotions—will get the best of you."

"Control myself?" Wren echoed, thinking of how powerless she had felt when the cauldron of emotions overtook her the day before, of how she had no ability to do anything in the dream world, especially now that it could draw her in even when she was awake. "How am I supposed to do that?"

"Think of the present moment. Let the stardust wash over you like waves from the ocean," Liza said. "You can try breathing slowly. At least, that's what Boggen used to do."

Wren felt a sudden chill, and she didn't think it was from the water. "Boggen?"

"He was the last Weather Changer we have record of, and he was very private about it. I remember him being extraordinarily focused. Deep breaths in and out when he worked the stardust." Her eyes grew wide at Wren's expression. "You didn't know, did you? That Boggen was a Weather Changer?"

"No," Wren said, and sat in the silence that followed. *Boggen* was the last Weather Changer?

Liza sighed. "One way or another, you're going to have to control it, Wren. More outbursts like the one from yesterday will get you in serious trouble in the Crooked House."

And will remind everyone that I'm like Boggen. Wren filled in the missing pieces. No wonder all the Fiddlers had reacted that way in the Council meeting. No wonder even Mary had been surprised. What would

Liza say if Wren told her it was worse than just out-bursts? That she'd been having strange dreams, too? She opened her mouth to admit the truth when something bright whizzed by her ear.

Liza turned in a flash, stardust spinning in front of her as though she was going to throw it at someone.

"Sorry about that!" Simon said, giving her a sheepish smile. "I didn't know you could throw a starlamp."

"Nice shot." Jack elbowed Simon in the ribs and began to ball up another starlamp. "I wonder if I could hit Wren."

"You'll do no such thing," Liza said, marching over to them and cuffing Baxter on the shoulder. "What are you teaching them, anyway? Basic rhymework, Baxter. That's what we need to focus on."

"Fine. I'll teach them the *proper* way to throw things with stardust." Baxter smirked at Liza and began demonstrating the next rhyme. "As round as an apple," he said, curving his palms like a bowl. "As deep as a cup. Work the stardust"—he jerked his hands back suddenly—"to pull it up." The room filled with glowing light. Wren watched Jack execute the rhyme perfectly, sending the book on the floor in front of him spinning through the air.

Was it only a few minutes before that she had cared that Jack and Simon were better than her at using the stardust? It felt like longer than that. Simon sent his book flying across the room, and Wren managed a weak smile, but her heart wasn't in it. All she could think about was what she had just learned. Why was she having those dreams? The fact that she was awake for this one hinted that the dreams were more than just her subconscious popping up in weird ways, but she didn't want the dreams to mean something. She pushed them out of her mind in the same way she did the significance of being a Weather Changer, as if by not thinking about it she could erase the fact that all the Fiddlers now suspected she was somehow connected to the Magicians. And Boggen.

FOURTEEN

In marble walls as white as milk,
Lined with skin as soft as silk,
Mysteries manifold do appear,
For those who seek them, crystal clear.

Between stardust lessons with Liza and Baxter, apprentice chores in the kitchen, and exploring the Crooked House with Jack and Simon, Wren's days were busy. Every night she faithfully texted her parents something vaguely related to what she had actually done that day, and their replies gave her fleeting stabs of homesickness. It was hard for her to imagine that her old life was spinning along as usual—her mom was wrapped up in the annual Springfest play and her dad busy teaching courses at the college. How could all that stay the same when her whole world had changed?

Wren wondered what her mom and dad would say if they could see her now. She stood on a balcony that overlooked the Opal Sea and pulled the rope to one of the dumbwaiters that connected the kitchens to the rest of the Crooked House. All apprentices were given a daily job assignment, and Elsa had saddled Wren with the midmorning hot cross bun delivery. Most Fiddlers ate in their rooms or in their laboratories. Baxter had clicked his tongue over the lack of culinary interest, and Wren was beginning to see what he meant. Oatmeal for breakfast, some kind of soup for lunch, and dinner was always a variation on meat and vegetables. Hot cross buns midmorning and midafternoon, like clockwork.

Wren carefully transferred the baskets to her small handcart. Over the years Fiddlers had claimed the natural caverns that pigeonholed the walls of the Crooked House, and an impressive latticework of wooden balconies and staircases connected the labs. Wren steadied the cart with one hand as it tipped its way over the rough planks. "Don't speak to the full Fiddlers," Elsa had commanded her that first day. Wren needn't have worried about breaking that rule. But for the sound of the one rumbling wheel, Wren was surrounded with silence. She wondered what was behind the green doors that lined the wall. Some were marked with cryptic abbreviations and numbers. A few held only a title that seemed connected with a rhyme.

She checked her clipboard. The door marked WILLIAM BLUE was to receive three orders. Her cart was laden with baskets of fresh-made rolls, each expertly twisted into a neat knot and marked with an *X* on top. Wren prepared the trays and stacked them by the door. Mary had warned her to be careful near the laboratories. She said some of the Fiddlers spent weeks at a time immersed in their research, coming out into daylight surprised to find a whole season had passed. Like Mary could talk. Wren hadn't seen her for more than a few stolen moments each week, when Mary left her meetings with the Council to give them some odd task. One time it had been to find all the library books having to do with moonlight. Later, Mary had changed her mind and wanted anything referencing Jupiter's moons. And then she had wanted to speak to Simon alone about the state of the falcon mews. The last time they'd seen her she had quizzed Jack on where exactly he had found Boggen's stone. Mary was working her way through Boggen's old research logs, but she wouldn't tell them anything more than what she needed them to do.

Wren had given up hope that she would ever be able to talk to Mary about her dreams. At first it had been because there never seemed to be time. Mary appeared and disappeared before any of them could say much at all. But the more Wren dreamed, the more she became uncertain. She strongly suspected that her dreams were somehow connected to being a Weather Changer. She was learning to control her emotional response when she worked the stardust, and sometimes she could even get through a whole lesson without freaking out. But when the deep breaths didn't work and she failed to rein things in, one of the waking dreams was usually the result. If the Council had gotten all weird about her being a Weather Changer, what would they do if she told them the rest of it?

Wren pushed the cart around the curving corner for the next delivery and then came to a sudden stop, scrambling to make sure she didn't lose her remaining baskets. The door in front of her was unlike all the others. It was wide open. NUMBER 3 was hand-lettered on the sign just outside, and a faint humming sound came from within. Her pulse quickened. She knew what she should do. She should unload the trays and move on, exactly as she had been instructed. *Don't disturb the Fiddlers*. But this might be her only chance to get a peek at a real honest-to-goodness Fiddler lab. She tiptoed closer to the door, and she was almost to it—she could even see the whitewashed walls inside—when the humming sound stopped. Everything went still, and the silence of the hallway seemed almost deafening. She set the trays down noiselessly and crept back to her cart. Wren eased it forward, mentally cursing the telltale wheel, when she heard the click of what sounded like dress shoes on stone.

"Ah, an apprentice." The voice from behind froze her into place. "And just the one I was hoping to speak with. You're one of the new ones who belongs to Mary, aren't you? The Weather Changer?"

Wren turned around to see Cole, the leader of the Council, standing in the open doorway. He was wearing the same rumpled sweater she had seen before, but this time no falcon perched on his shoulder.

"Won't you come in?" Cole said without a smile.

Everything in the Crooked House was a strange mixture of old and new. Kiosks with power outlets and Wi-Fi hubs next door to the library full of ancient books. The kitchen where modern appliances hummed beside old-fashioned cast-iron stoves and spits turning over the fire. But nothing had prepared Wren for what she saw in Cole's lab.

Once she followed him through the door, it was as if she'd left the Crooked House behind altogether. Gleaming stainless steel tables filled the room, marking stations where white-cloaked Fiddlers bent over microscopes. The Fiddler nearest her stood in front of a huge touch screen adding data to a hovering 3D strand of DNA. The humming sound she had heard earlier came from a robotic laser that someone was using on what looked like an animal pelt. Hanging fluorescent lights replaced the sconces she had become used to. Only the stone floor below her feet reminded her that she was still inside a mountain.

"What is this place?" Wren gasped, taking it all in.

"My laboratory," Cole said pleasantly, leading her past the maze of tables to a glassed-in cubicle that stood in the center of it all. He gestured to the metal desk with a chair on each side. "Won't you have a seat?"

Behind him, she could see a Fiddler carefully measuring a steaming liquid from an eyedropper into a glass petri dish. The Fiddler conjured some stardust, and while Wren watched, the liquid flared red and then a bright neon green.

"What are you researching?" Wren managed as she sat down. She couldn't think what DNA and neon liquid and animal skins had to do with one another.

"Anything and everything. Surely even in your short time as an apprentice, you've thought of the potential for stardust." Cole waved his hand to point to different stations. "Improving technology. Finding cures for terminal diseases. Unlocking the mystery of genetic sequencing. Any new scientific discoveries made in the ordinary world likely have an Alchemist behind them." He folded his hands flat on the table, interlocking his fingers. "I've had to pause my own research, because of this new crisis—this message you've discovered from Boggen."

"I didn't discover it," Wren said, distracted by the sight of a stardust explosion on the far side of the room. The woman at that station was now covered in the neon liquid, rescued only by the Fiddler next to her, who wove a rhyme that somehow quenched the glowing fire. "Mary's the one you should be talking to."

"*Fiddler* Mary, you mean? You can be sure that I've learned everything she has to tell. Odd, isn't it, that Boggen was the last Weather Changer before you?" Cole's voice was low and soothing. "And that you and your friends arrive just after we learn he's touching our world again. In fact, we believe Boggen has been communicating with someone here at the Crooked House, and we think he meant for that someone to find his message."

That got Wren's undivided attention. She snapped her head back around.

Cole's smile was still in place, but there was a hard look in his eyes. "Or perhaps it's that someone *here* is trying to find *him*?"

Wren's heart started to pound. Her thoughts felt muddy. What did Cole mean? Why was he asking her these questions? He was saying more now, something about suspecting that Boggen was in another dimension or on another planet and wanted someone from the Crooked House to help him. Someone Boggen had special access to. Her mind whirled at the idea. Cole was talking about space travel and other dimensions. And then things began to come into focus. He wasn't just filling her in on the latest Boggen research. He was interrogating her. Cole thought *she* knew something about Boggen.

"But my particular research interest," Cole was saying, "is in sleep disorders and the psychology of dreams." His thick-rimmed glasses made his eyebrows look extra sharp as they furrowed down disapprovingly.

"Boggen was a Weather Changer and a Dreamer, you know. The two often go hand in hand. Wren, how have you been sleeping lately?"

"Fine," she lied. One part of her brain was screaming at her to tell the truth. This was proof that the dreams meant something, and Cole could probably tell her exactly what. But the other part instinctively knew that would be dangerous. Here she was, already suspect as the first Weather Changer. There was no way she was going to tell Cole, with his frowning eyebrows and incriminating gaze, that she, coincidentally, was also a Dreamer who couldn't control her dreams.

"Elsa keeps us so busy, you know?" Wren babbled. "I'm exhausted at night and conk out right away. Never slept so well as I do here." But the claim sounded false even to Wren's own ears. Every night was the same. Repeats of the dreams she'd had before, or something very like them. Colorless scenes where strange things happened.

"Fiddler Elsa, you mean" was all Cole said in reply, his frown making two deep lines between his eyes. "Have you wandered anywhere in the Crooked House you shouldn't?"

"No," Wren said, wondering if he thought apprentices were stupid.

He folded his hands and leaned in toward her. "Have you touched any magical object you don't know the purpose of?"

"No." *Seriously?* Did he actually think Wren would own up to it if she had? "No, sir." The creases between his eyes deepened. "I mean, Fiddler. No, Fiddler," she added belatedly.

"What about Fiddler labs? Have you gone into any of them?"

Wren folded her hands to match his. So apparently he did think apprentices were stupid if he thought she would give a different answer to the same question thinly disguised. She ignored his frown. "I already told you," Wren said evenly. "I only go where I'm told and do what I'm told."

"And your dreams." Cole shifted topics without warning. "Fiddler Liza reports you've had some odd moments, when you seem to be somewhere else. Could you explain?"

"I—uh—" Wren hunted for words. *Liza* had told Cole about their lessons? That was unexpected. "It's Simon, you see," Wren said, thinking fast. "I've always been smarter than him, but here"—what had started out as a stalling tactic was becoming genuine—"here, he's better with the stardust. And sometimes having lessons with him and Jack is"—her voice dropped—"really hard."

Cole sat back in his chair, arms folded across his chest, a look of disappointment in his eyes. "I don't want to hear about your petty rivalries, Apprentice." His voice was hard. "Don't waste my time."

Wren drew herself up. Waste *his* time? He was the one interrogating her! "I'm sorry I can't be more help, Fiddler Cole," she said in her most grown-up voice. "But I really should get back to my rounds. Fiddler Elsa"—she made sure to enunciate *Fiddler*—"will be upset if I'm not back soon." She glanced around the lab, feeling a fleeting sadness that she couldn't learn more of what was going on here, but even that wasn't worth the risk of extending her time under Cole's hawkish gaze. "Thank you for letting me see your laboratory."

Cole eyed her over steepled fingers. "Very well," he said. "If you think of anything else, you know where to find me."

FIFTEEN

One misty moisty morning,
When cloudy was the weather,
I chanced to meet an old man,
Clothed all in leather.

Wren thought about what Cole had told her in the days that followed. She listened carefully in her apprentice lessons for any mention of dreams. She reimagined her past ones and hunted for connections between them. She scoured the library for books that had anything to do with sleep but came up with very little. Either Cole himself had taken them all for research purposes or no one else in the Crooked House cared very much about dreams. Wherever she went, she avoided the main passageways and the piercing gazes of Fiddlers who tracked her movements. She wagered that they, too, thought she was Boggen's ally. Between the suspicious looks of full Fiddlers and the whispered conversations among the apprentices that suddenly dried up when Wren approached, the only times she felt free of the looming thought that she might be somehow connected with Boggen was during her lessons.

It had taken her a lot of practice to get the stardust to come together at all, but now she could gather a pale clump of light to make the starlamp. The more she discovered about its uses, the more she realized how much she had to learn, and that made her want to be the best apprentice in the history of apprentices. But there was one apprentice lesson that she could do without: flying.

It hadn't been a fluke, that day at Pippen Hill when her falcon had abandoned her. If daily flying practice had taught her anything, it was that her falcon definitely hated her. It had arrived at the Crooked House shortly after they did, but not because it wanted to see Wren. Most of the time it wouldn't even come out of the massive thornbush it liked to roost in. Occasionally, it swooped over to Baxter's or Liza's gauntleted arm, but if Wren called it—or she even came near— the flying lesson would be over for the day, because the falcon would fly off and return at its whim.

Today, it was crouched on the farthest possible branch of the thornbush. Wren could see its beady eyes staring at her through the tangle of leaves, and every so often the bird gave out a horrible screech, as if to warn Wren that she had come close enough.

"Perhaps you should leave it for now," Liza said, and Wren could tell that she didn't mean it as a suggestion. "Come over here with the others while I teach you this rhyme, and then you can coax your falcon out."

Wren tossed the handful of dried crickets she'd been using to tempt her falcon onto the ground. "Stupid bird," she muttered, picking her way through the outer branches of the thornbush.

"Let's practice returning your falcon to its ordinary size," Liza was saying to Jack and Simon. "It's quite simple, really, almost the reverse of the first rhyme." Her fingers moved fast, cutting the infinity symbol in the opposite direction that they used to make the bird grow. "Take care to perform this exactly," she said from the middle of the cloud of stardust. "Else the results might be unpredictable." Her voice carried on the air, the pulsing swirl of the stardust matched by the rhythm of the rhyme.

Away, birds, away!
Take a little and leave a little,
And do not come again;
For if you do, I will shoot you through,
And there will be an end of you.

As Liza said the word *little*, her falcon shrank, diminishing in size until it was small enough to fly back up to the leather perch on her shoulder.

"Intriguing," Simon said, moving close to study the bird's tail feathers. The falcon barely twitched at his approach. Wren sighed. As surely as Wren's falcon hated her, Simon's falcon loved him. In fact, all the falcons loved Simon.

"When you're done flying," Liza continued, "you'll need to make sure your falcon has enough to eat. As birds of prey, they hunt on their own, of course, but we also feed them regularly. Now that you are accustomed to life at the Crooked House, you will take on the additional responsibility of daily meals for your bird." She led them over to the falcon mews.

"What do you think?" Jack whispered. "Has Baxter whipped up some gourmet cricket treats for the falcons? Or mouse fondue?"

Wren gave him a weak laugh. Jack didn't have Simon's magical touch with all of the falcons, but he had at least developed the promised Fiddler-falcon relationship with his own bird. Most days, Jack's falcon perched on his shoulder at all times, even while going about his apprentice duties in the Crooked House. Wren kept a wary eye on it now as she followed him around the outbuilding to where Liza introduced them to the ancient-looking Fiddler who manned the falcon mews.

"This is where the mice are kept," he said in a reedy voice. He went on to tell them about the feeding schedule, showing them where to draw water, when the sun came out from behind a cloud, blindingly bright in the sky. Sudden pain shot through Wren's forehead. She rubbed her temples, but the throbbing intensified.

Everything had stopped around her, as though the entire world had been frozen. She couldn't hear the man's steady stream of instruction. Couldn't hear the screeches of the falcons. Couldn't hear Simon's or Jack's friendly voices. Down a rise, near the edge of the woods, was a huge tree, its metal branches stretched like black gashes across the sky. The tree loomed large, as though it was growing, too.

From the wood's edge, a dark shape shuffled into sight, a man bent down by age, leaning on a cane. He made his way to the foot of the tree, hunched over, as if under a great weight, and sat on the roots. It was then that he saw Wren.

"Dreamer!" he said, confirming Wren's suspicions that she was back in the dream world. His voice sounded stronger than he looked. "You there. Weather Changer!"

Wren's body went ice cold at his voice. He was the same one who had called her the day she met the shepherdess. How did he know she was a Weather Changer? Wren turned to run, but her legs were stuck fast.

"I see you," the old man said. "I see everything." A spot on the back of Wren's neck flared hot at his words. She tried to turn her head, but she couldn't. She tried to speak, but her voice wouldn't work. She opened her mouth, but nothing came out.

"You are mine now, Weather Changer," the man said. "You belong to me and will do as I say."

He raised his hand and made a mark in the air, and Wren felt it cut into the burning spot on her neck. What had she done last time to break the spell that held her fast in the dream? Somehow she had shifted things and escaped his clutches. She tried to re-create the sensation, focusing her mental energy on leaving the tree behind. She closed her eyes. *Please let it all disappear.* The air around her seemed to shift, as though she were riding an elevator. An image flashed behind her closed eyelids. The bent old man was not sitting under a tree. In fact, he was not bent at all. He was standing tall and strong in front of a bay window made of black-and-white glass.

"Stop that," the man's voice echoed in her head, and Wren could hear his surprise and displeasure. "Stop changing the dream." Wren opened her eyes, but the man had disappeared. She was standing there, arms reaching out toward nothing but an empty field.

"Wren?" Liza said, her hand cool on Wren's shoulder. Wren turned to look at her, and the blinding headache was gone, the colors of the world back to normal. Wren glanced back to where the man had been, but he was gone. The black-and-white-checked window was gone. The tree was gone. She could speak again, but she found she had nothing to say.

"Wren, are you all right?" Liza's words jolted her back into reality.

"Yeah. I'm okay. Too much sun, maybe." Her heart

was pounding loud with panic. The waking dream had come again. Wren couldn't figure out what triggered it. It was as sporadic as the weather-changing, but this time she had somehow traveled within the dream and surprised the tall man. He seemed to be the same person as the evil bent man, but who was he? And what did he want with Wren? As if in response, the back of her neck flared with heat. She placed a tentative hand up to the spot, but her fingers only met smooth skin. Whatever he had done had been done only in the dream world.

The Fiddler in charge of the falcon mews was still prattling on about how to properly feed and water their birds, so Wren couldn't have been dreaming that long. She ignored Simon's questioning look. Jack's head was cocked, and he was studying her thoughtfully.

The Fiddler finished his lecture with a grave warning not to try and feed any other Fiddler's bird, and Liza took over from there. "Wren, are you ready to try to make your falcon grow? She's returned."

So her falcon was a female. Wren nodded enthusiastically, even though a knot of fear tensed in her chest. Female or male, she didn't want to be stuck with the bird. Just like she didn't want to be stuck with the dreams. She couldn't escape either. And the dream-man, what had he meant by *You are mine*? She followed Liza over to the corner of the mews, where her wretched bird was perched on a knobby ledge, clawed feet gripped around the peeling wood.

Wren was some twenty feet away at least, but the animal responded. The twitching tail feathers. Shifting feet. A warning screech.

"That's right," Liza was saying. "Nice and slow. Very gently. Control your response." Liza's voice was low and steady. "Even breathing, Wren. Remember to breathe."

Wren tiptoed forward, hand stretched out. She practiced the breathing like Liza had taught her. Four counts in through her nose. Seven counts out through her mouth. It didn't do any good. Even though it was cool outside, beads of sweat popped up on her brow. From somewhere in the distance, thunder rumbled. Wren inched closer. A single twig snapped under one ill-placed foot. She froze, but the bird didn't fly away. Ever so carefully, Wren reached into the pouch that hung at her neck and pinched some stardust. Once it flared into light, she began to play it. Planting her back foot firm, she positioned the other perpendicularly, using one hand to cut the infinity symbol through the dust, moving faster to keep the motes dancing, matching the rhythm of her fast-beating heart.

Her falcon kept time with a minuscule shifting of its head to follow her hands. She said the words:

See, see! What shall I see!
My bird grown tall as it should be.

That was when the bird was supposed to come down and start growing. Wren chanted louder. Her falcon angled its claws farther up on the branch, as if it was preparing to jump down.

Wren chanted even louder. She was doing it! The falcon had never let her get this far in the rhyme. Her heart sped up. She was finally going to successfully make her bird grow. And then it was over. Her falcon was not getting down. Instead, it was swiveling around, oh so carefully, so that it was facing the other direction, the crimson of its tail feathers pointed toward Wren. And then it pooped. It pooped right there, and a trickle of bird dropping splattered down to the ground in front of Wren.

All Wren's thoughts of flying snuffed out in one

breath, and the stardust fell limp to the ground. Wren's face grew hot with either rage or embarrassment, she couldn't tell. It was deathly silent behind her. Which was probably good. One single snort or choked-back giggle or witty comment from Jack, and Wren would be done. The falcon screamed a final curse at her and took to the air, leaving nothing but the breeze of its flapping wings in its wake.

"Nice try, Wren." Simon's words stung, even though she could tell he meant to be encouraging. She *had* been trying. And failing. Hot tears burned the back of her eyes, but she willed them away. *What is wrong with me?* It wasn't like she'd never made mistakes before. But levelheaded Wren just picked herself up and tried again. That Wren's feathers never got ruffled. But that Wren was the old Wren, the one she seemed to have left back at home.

She stared up at the sky as though she could still see the falcon, but it had long since become a tiny speck.

"Give it time." Liza came up next to her as a light rain began to fall. The leaves on the nearby trees rustled gently with the weight of the drops.

Give it time? Liza was saying something comforting now, something about how it might take many years to perfect using the stardust. Wren looked over at Simon, whose falcon stood saddled and ready to fly. Simon hadn't needed any extra time. Simon was doing just fine.

Wren didn't like how ugly her jealousy felt, but she couldn't push it away. The wind picked up, sending a frigid gust through the falcon mews. Liza wrapped her cloak about her shoulders, leaning close to laugh at something Jack was saying as he pulled himself up onto his falcon.

Wren's heart pumped hot with envy, her blood pressure rising with frustration. How come she couldn't get her bird to listen? What was she doing wrong? She looked up in the sky, hoping to catch a glimpse of the errant falcon. Perhaps if it came back, she could try again. Instead, she saw dark cloud cover appear almost out of nowhere and unleash a torrent of rain.

"Wren," Liza cautioned. "You can control this."

"And how am I supposed to do that?" Wren's voice sounded plaintive to her own ears. She couldn't control anything. Not her emotions. Not her falcon. Not even her dreams. "I never pretended to be some stardust genius," she burst out. "Being smart in some things doesn't mean I can do everything right." She scrubbed her fists across her eyes to wipe away the angry tears. She felt silly for crying. *This isn't like you, Wren,* she told herself. *Pull it together.* She breathed in from her stomach, but her throat was tight, and she couldn't get to the full four counts. The tears came faster.

A boom of thunder seemed to underscore her mood. Raindrops fell on her bare head, setting off a pounding headache, as if to underscore how weak she was: She wasn't only powerless to fly on her falcon, she was powerless in the face of whatever her dreams meant and whatever truth was hiding there about her being connected to Boggen. Scenes from her dreams flashed through her mind. The black-and-white window and the old man under the tree. The sheep tails and the bright-red blood. Faster and faster. The rowboat and the song of the wings. Her thoughts spiraled until she felt like she might explode if she didn't scream or kick something or run.

Wren sprinted toward the forest, relishing the feel of the hard drops of rain awakening her senses. Lightning flashed on the horizon, followed by a crash of thunder. She ran faster. The wild weather mirrored exactly how she felt. Wren didn't go beyond the tree line, but she raced along the forest's edge, running through the swirling storm until a stitch of pain sliced into her side and her lungs burned from the effort. She stopped then, letting the now-soft raindrops cool her face.

The next moment, Wren heard footfalls and whirled around to see Simon loping across the spongy turf toward her. He moved easily, looking like a natural runner even with his apprentice cloak streaming about his wool vest and trousers.

Wren's anger was spent. Her jealousy, too, and she found herself glad to see Simon. She wondered what she should tell him, when she landed on the truth. "I felt like I had to run, you know?"

"Why do you think I do cross-country?" Simon said, grinning at her. "I had no idea you were so fast."

They walked toward the falcon mews in companionable silence. Liza and Jack were tiny silhouettes in the distance.

"Sorry I ran off like that."

"You've nothing to be sorry about," Simon said matter-of-factly. "You should be happy. Each time you use the stardust, more of your weather-changing capabilities manifest."

Wren's laugh came out like a laugh-sob, and she worked to control her breathing. "Did you ever imagine anything like this, Simon? Back when we were home, I mean?" Somewhere in the distance, a rumble of thunder rolled toward them. "Look at us. Here I am with this weather-changing thing, and here you are all instant best friends with all the falcons. What is happening to us?"

Simon shoved his hands in his pockets. "I think it's pretty cool. Imagine all the good you could do to address climate change. Stopping global warming. Eliminating drought. Predicting tsunamis." He grinned. "You'd be like a walking seismograph."

"I guess so." Wren saw his point, but it wasn't the science stuff she was worried about. Climate change she could deal with. Tectonic shifting—no problem. It was the weird impossible-to-logically-explain dreams. The frightening man who said she belonged to him. How real it all looked. How in that black-and-white world nothing she did seemed to matter: no matter what she said, no matter how deeply she breathed or how hard she worked to control her response to star-dust, she couldn't escape the dreams.

Sixteen

Little King Boggen he built a fine hall,
Smooth words and sly ways, that was his wall;
His rhymes were all made of spells black and white,
And coated with poison—you ne'er saw the like.

It was hard for Wren to remember how overwhelming the Crooked House had seemed back when she first arrived. Now, after many afternoons of work assignments, she found herself quite at home in the twisty passageways. The Crooked House had been created around a network of caves inside the mountain, and it reminded Wren of a giant anthill. Stolen moments spent exploring with Jack and Simon had revealed countless forgotten tunnels, most of which had been blocked off by rocks. The ones still in use spiraled up the cliffside where stone staircases cut into the steepest spots. Some opened up to jagged exterior balconies, and others led to the interior spaces that were the hubs of Fiddler activity. The Opal Sea ran through the biggest cavern, situated about halfway up the cliffside, and the openings above and below housed laboratories or sleeping quarters and far down at the bottom, the kitchens and laundry, where Wren now stood, eyeing the large grandfather clock that showed her Mary was once again late.

Two days a week were designated as full workdays for the apprentices in the Crooked House, and at this point, most of the Fiddlers had already given their apprentices assignments. The workroom was emptying and, as usual, there was no sign of Mary.

Elsa stood in front of the huge open hearth, studying the row of leftover apprentices with obvious malicious glee. "I see your Fiddlers are otherwise occupied," she said, giving Wren a wolfish smile. "I imagine I can come up with some important tasks. You there," she said to a tall thin boy. "You'll be cleaning out the chimneys." She made a note on a long piece of paper spread over the table in front of her.

"But, I . . ." the boy began.

"*But?*" Elsa said, the pen pausing over the paper.

"*But* an argumentative apprentice would like to learn discipline? Scouring the dungeon, perhaps, instead of chimney cleaning?"

"No, Fiddler Elsa," the boy mumbled as he was matched up with another boy who was just as tall as him and twice as wide.

"There's no way we can even get partially inside a chimney," Wren heard the first boy say as they left to begin their assignment.

"Where is Mary?" Wren whispered to Simon. "Have you seen her lately?"

"Not since last workday." Simon stared back over his shoulder as though that would make Mary appear.

"Probably too busy for us," Jack said, his voice hard. Jack had taken a cynical turn toward Mary, for which Wren could hardly blame him. The few minutes they actually saw her, she was either giving them orders or Elsa was hovering nearby, which meant that Mary had only scolding words for them.

"You will clean out the falcon pens," Elsa said to two girls Wren's age who were the only ones who managed to make the apprentice cloaks look glamorous.

"The laundry for you, I think," Elsa said to a slight girl. "Jill can take you." Wren watched the girl and poor, beleaguered Jill make their way out of the kitchen. She could hardly look at Jill without feeling like crying. It was horrible enough to be bossed around by Elsa. It would be ten thousand times worse to be her personal apprentice. No wonder Jill never talked.

Another pair of apprentices got sent to rake the midden heap. An older girl was ordered to sluice the waterspout. Whatever that meant, they looked none too happy about it.

Wren shifted her feet uneasily. There were only six of them left, and Elsa was eyeing Simon, Jack, and Wren as though she'd saved the best for last. Ever since their arrival, Elsa had been watching them closely. Wren had come to the conclusion that Elsa must think the apprentices were idiots, so she didn't need to hide the fact that she was spying on them. Elsa's friends would stop them in the passageways of the Crooked House to interrogate them, and once another apprentice had been skulking around outside her room when Wren returned early from a lesson. Until now, it had been a sort of a game between Jack, Simon, and Wren to see how they could outwit Elsa's maneuvering. But now it seemed that they were out of luck. They would be under Elsa's complete command.

"Ah." Mary's most welcome voice floated into the kitchen. "Elsa, thank you so much for filling in for me, but I see I'm just in time to monitor my apprentices." Mary's countenance was as calm and collected as usual, but there were fine little lines around her eyes.

Elsa looked pointedly at the clock. "The workday assignments were to be given out a quarter of an hour ago."

"Right you are, as always," Mary said brightly, gathering Wren and the boys by the shoulders and sweeping them out in front of her. "I'll make sure to add extra time to their work detail."

"See that you do." Elsa jabbed the pen at her paper. "And *where* will they be working? I need a complete accounting."

"They'll be working in the repository. The research logs there are a horrific mess, and who, I ask you, has time to sort through centuries of scribbling?" She gave Elsa a wink. "Apprentices do, that's who."

Elsa looked slightly placated. "Very well. But keep in mind that hard physical labor tends to be more productive for character formation. Section ten of the apprentice manual."

"Of course," Mary said. "The repository will also

need a good scrubbing, so make sure to note that down on your little sheet."

Mary grinned at Wren as they ducked out of the kitchen and into the main passageway. After they wound down the spiral stone staircase for several levels, she led them out onto one of the exterior balconies.

"I'm afraid I can't stay long with you," she whispered. "The Council is meeting today, and they will no doubt make some foolish decision without me there to help them see sense."

"What has the Council decided so far?" Wren blurted out. "What have they found out about Boggen?" This was the first time they might actually have a real conversation with Mary. No spying Elsa to overhear. Nothing but wide-open air. From where Wren stood, she could see out over the whole landscape, down to where wind-tossed ocean waves met the green valley that housed the falcon mews.

"They're trying to decide what to do about the Magicians." Mary spoke in a low whisper. "The Council knows that some Fiddler, or perhaps a whole contingent of Fiddlers, has been in contact with Boggen."

"What?" Jack said in a too-loud voice.

Simon, too, looked astonished at the news, and

Wren tried to hide the fact that she already knew as much. Apparently, Cole hadn't felt the need to interrogate the boys.

"It seems that after the Civil War, Boggen left Earth altogether," Mary said. "We thought he and his followers died, but we were wrong. We of all people should have known to look for conclusive proof." Mary opened the door a crack and peeked back into the corridor to make sure no one was coming.

"But what is Boggen trying to do?" Wren's mouth felt very dry. "What would these Fiddlers who've contacted him be trying to do?"

"That's the very question," Mary said. "I'm trying to find out, but we only have the things hidden in his message to go on, and those lead in a hundred different directions. The image of the lightning striking the mountain, for instance. Was that a description of something that happened back in the Fiddler Civil War or a prediction of the future? The same with the blue pendulum. It could mean several different things, but no one seems to know anything." She set her lips in a thin line. "At least no one's saying they know anything. I am sure I can trust you three, which is why I need your help."

"Our help?" Simon echoed.

"Yes. I'm trying to find something, something that I think will help us discover where Boggen went, which is the first step toward deciphering what he now intends to do." She urged them closer, and they huddled together against the cold wind that whipped around the ledge. "The Magicians had been planning to leave the Crooked House for ages. As best we can tell, they used the stardust to travel somewhere else, which makes sense given that one of the images in Boggen's message is certainly a gateway. Gateways are referenced everywhere in his notes," she said almost to herself. "But nothing about where one was or how they created it."

"A gateway to where?" Simon frowned.

"Aren't you listening?" Mary said. "We don't know. But according to Boggen's notes, once they used the gateway, they planned to lock it up somehow, so none could follow. They hated the restraints the Alchemists had put on stardust, the way we limited their power. When the tide turned against them in the Civil War, the Magicians came up with another plan. They decided to begin anew, to start a colony somewhere they could be free to do as they pleased with the stardust. It is clear that back then Boggen meant to leave Earth forever. The question is what he intends to do now."

"And you think this gateway is just lying around somewhere, undiscovered for a couple hundred years?" Jack sounded doubtful. "Don't you think a Fiddler would have found it by now?"

"We thought Boggen was dead, and the entire Crooked House rejoiced over it," Mary snapped. Then she sighed and lowered her voice. "I'm sorry, Jack. I'm just frustrated. Boggen was my apprentice; not only did he ruin his own future, but mine as well." She wrapped her cloak around her shoulders.

Wren moved closer. "But what does it do? A gateway, I mean, and what will you do with it once you find it?"

"I won't do anything with it," Mary said. "If the Council is right, and someone in the Crooked House *has* made contact with Boggen, it's possible that he or she is on the hunt for the gateway as well." She chewed her lip, as if deciding whether to go on or not.

"And?" Jack prompted.

"Gateways are portals between places." Mary picked up two stones. "Imagine I am here at the Crooked House." She set the stone down. "And I want a quick and easy way to get back to Pippen Hill." She took two strides and placed the other stone down. "With enough stardust and enough skill, I could make a gateway, a place where time and space is compressed, allowing me to pass from the Crooked House to Pippen Hill as simply as taking a single step." She stood between the two. "In general, gateways are open to anyone who can use stardust, but what if I didn't want a Fiddler to show up uninvited to Pippen Hill?" Mary kicked the farther stone, and it skittered off the ledge.

"Can you hide the gateway?" Simon asked. "Disguise it like you do Pippen Hill?"

"That won't work on other Fiddlers," Mary said.

"What about locking it?" Wren suggested. "So only the people you wanted could pass through."

"And how would they do that?" Mary looked pleased at their deductive work. "How does anyone pass through something that is locked?"

"They need a key," Jack said slowly.

"Exactly." Mary blew on her hands and rubbed them together to fight off the cold. "When Boggen and the others left, they locked the gateway, sealing it from this side so that no one could follow them and, I would imagine, locking it on the other side, so that no one could pass back over. It's how they've escaped detection all these years." Mary let her hands fall to her sides. "The Council believes that something has happened, something dire enough that Boggen is trying to unlock the gateway. While he may be able to open it from his side—"

"He needs someone from here to unlock this side!" Simon finished for her, clearly happy to have solved the puzzle.

"The image we saw in Boggen's message was of someone flying with a golden glowing object. Cole thinks that was the key, and Boggen hid it before he left so none could follow." Mary's face looked drawn and tired. "The question is, if Boggen is indeed desperate enough to reopen the gateway, what does he want?"

"Why don't we try to find out who he's been contacting?" Jack said. He looked more excited than scared, like Mary had invited them to go on a great adventure. "Why not stop it before it even happens? Does the Council have any idea who it is?"

Mary winced. "Right now, Wren's the favorite."

Wren felt a twisting in her stomach, but it wasn't only because Mary had confirmed her suspicions about everyone thinking she was helping Boggen. Wren thought back to her very first dream, the one with the man and the woman talking about someone hunting for a golden key. Was it possible? *I see you,* the man in her dreams had said. Her heart was beating fast, and no amount of deep breathing would quell the cold fist of fear clamping down on the back of her neck. Boggen wasn't just involved with her dreams. Boggen was in them. What if the Council was right? What if she *had* been in contact with Boggen all along? Wren's knees wobbled, and she wondered if she might faint. She took a few steps backward, feeling with one hand for the solid rock wall, and leaned up against it.

Mary was watching her with the same sad expression on her face, but Wren couldn't look in her eyes anymore. What would Mary say if she knew about the dreams?

"So what do we do? Where do we look for this gateway?" Jack said, rubbing his hands. He might not have noticed Wren's response, or he was trying to cover for her. Either way, she was grateful. "It's about time we did something besides fly on falcons or make glowing lights," he continued. "This is going to be awesome!"

"I'm trusting in your instincts especially, Jack,"

Mary said. "You've had uncanny luck in finding old objects—even in finding me—so whatever talent lies in you, use it."

"So are we going to fly through the aurora?" Jack asked. "Travel the world to hunt for the missing gateway?"

"No," Mary said in a businesslike tone. "You'll be cleaning out the repository just as I told Elsa you would be. I don't lie, Jack, whatever the Council says, and you would all do well to remember that. The only way to stay above the politics in the Crooked House is to tell the truth."

"Cleaning?" Simon groaned. "How will that help anything?"

"When the room you're cleaning is full of old Council notes, it can be a *very* helpful thing," Mary said. "The repository is—"

"The repository!" Jack interrupted. "That's the place you visited when you came to the Crooked House last year."

"Something you would do well to keep quiet." Mary gave Jack a stern look. "But you have a good memory, Jack. I sneaked into the Crooked House last year, because the repository is full of valuable information that is often overlooked. You'll be organizing records and scouring them for mentions of a gateway or a key. It's unlikely you'll find anything about Boggen there, but any scrap of information about gateways could prove useful. Any whisper of a Fiddler ever talking about a gateway. Any mention of a lock or a door. Anything that resembles a treasure map or chart with a portal. Anything that you even suspect might be relevant: you copy it down in these books." She handed each of them little leather notebooks.

"Why us?" Simon asked. "If this is so important, why are you having apprentices do it?"

"Because whatever everyone else thinks about Wren," Mary said, giving her a tight smile, "I know it's impossible." She had a shrewd look in her eyes "The only people I know for sure aren't helping Boggen are the ones who have arrived at the Crooked House after he was already gone."

"The apprentices," Jack said with a slow nod.

"Exactly," Mary said. "Any other Fiddler is suspect."

"Even Cole?" Wren asked, wondering if she should tell Mary about his interrogation.

A flicker of something crossed Mary's face, and then she tightened her jaw. "Even Cole. And that's why I've given you this task. As important as it would be to find any forgotten knowledge about gateways, it is even more important to know who else might have been interested in them. Perhaps tugging on that thread will lead us to Boggen's new friend." She pointed to the notebooks in their hands. "You're also looking for a rhyme. Gateways can only be opened with a unique rhyme crafted by their creator. So search any rhymes you find for mention of gateways or maps or travel or golden keys." She then produced a pail from a cupboard near the door, full of scrub brushes and old rags. "Do some cleaning while you're at it." She held up a hand to forestall their groans. "Or not, if you choose, but you'll have Elsa to answer to. Don't think she won't check up on you three."

Judging from the cobwebs that coated everything, the room Mary left them in hadn't been used much in the past fifty years. A few faint shoe-prints marked the dust on the floor, probably made by Mary herself the last time she was there. The space was like most of the nonmodernized ones in the Crooked House. A large wooden table with candelabras situated to provide light as needed. Bookshelves stacked high with sheaves of paper, ledgers, and books. Glass cabinets with little drawers full of tiny notecards covered with a thin spidery script.

"It'll take us ten years to go through all of these!" Jack complained as he pulled out a drawer and set it down on the table with a thump, sending up clouds of dust.

"But think what we'll get to"—Simon covered his mouth with his elbow, coughing—"read about while we do it." His eyes shone in the candlelight as he began skimming the cards.

"Simon is right," Wren said. "We'll probably learn more than even Baxter or Liza could teach us." She looked down at the nearly full page she'd already copied. She hadn't found anything about Boggen or gateways, but she found a few rhymes that mentioned sleeping. One about an old woman scraping the sky for dreams. Another about nightmares and the land of the fairies. And more detailed notes about whether experiences in dreams could be reality playing out in a different plane. She had put a star by that one, because it made her think of the times she had somehow moved within the dream and, despite the feeling of powerlessness, controlled her surroundings. If only she could learn how to do that all the time. The three sleep rhymes were from Council meetings where Cole had shared his latest research. Wren wondered if she should have told him about the dreams back when he first asked her. If Cole was the dream expert, he at least would have answers. But now it was too late. Now anything she told him would only further link her with Boggen.

Wren copied down another rhyme about birds and their feathers. That seemed more like something the Fiddler that oversaw the falcons would want to see than Mary. One of her hands was cramped from writing with a pencil, and the other was smudged with flakes from the ancient book.

Jack stood and stretched, pushing one fist on the small of his back.

"Not exactly the most comfortable place to sit, is it?" He slipped a pencil behind his ear. He'd spent most of the last hour copying things down from a slim blue volume.

A flash of heat grazed Wren's ear, and she whirled around. "Simon! Will you cut that out?"

"Sorry, Wren." Simon reached out a hand to catch the starlamp. He had spent the first hour copying things down and then decided to try to use stardust to clean the repository. In the course of the morning, he had figured out not only how to create several starlamps at once but also how to send them flying like boomerangs around the room. The next one skimmed the tabletop, knocking Jack's notebook to the floor.

Wren scooped it up for him and couldn't help but see what he'd been working on. A diagram, with numbers and arrows and equations. Nothing at all like the list of rhymes she'd compiled.

"Did you find something?" she asked as Jack smoothly slipped his notebook out of her hands.

"I wish." He laughed. "The book I've been reading is full of old Fiddler math. I'm hoping that if I stare at the equations long enough, I'll figure out what they mean." He shrugged, looking sheepish. "But math isn't really my thing. Did you make any interesting discoveries?" He turned to flip through Wren's book that she'd left sitting on the table.

Wren snatched it out of his hands, causing him to pull back in surprise. "I found lots of interesting things." She slipped her leather-bound book into her cloak pocket. "But nothing about gateways."

SEVENTEEN

Birds of a feather flock together,
And so will pigs and swine.
Rats and mice will have their choice,
And so will I have mine.

At first, Wren thought the group lessons that included all the apprentices would be nice, an opportunity to make new friends. But she soon saw what Mary meant about the Crooked House being political. Except for a few apprentices who, like she, Simon, and Jack, had arrived relatively recently, the others stood clustered according to their Fiddler mentor. Pockets of whispering kids eyed one another across the amphitheater. A lot of the time, the whispering was directed at her. Two girls giggled and pointed as Jill came in and sat alone against the wall.

Most full Fiddlers had two or three apprentices. The white-bearded Fiddler on the Council even had five. But Jill was the only apprentice who had to endure Elsa.

Wren moved over to the wall and sat down next to her. "Hey, Jill."

Jill looked up at Wren with dull eyes.

"You okay?"

"Fine." Jill's gaze darted over to the entranceway, as though she expected Elsa to show up any minute.

"Hope things go better than last time," Wren said. During the previous group lesson they had spent about five minutes learning a new multiplication rhyme when the snooty girl next to Wren overdid it with the stardust and let loose an exponentially expanding waterfall of butterflies. Afterward, Wren still didn't know how to multiply objects, but she did learn that the easiest way to catch and trap a butterfly was by standing perfectly still until one landed close enough to pinch its wings. "Did you see the look on the butterfly girl's face?"

"I guess," Jill said.

Wren sighed. That should have at least gotten a smile. The track record for the all-apprentice lessons wasn't that great so far. There had been another that was supposed to teach them how to read the traces of stardust left behind after a rhyme. But two apprentices ended up having to take sick leave, because somehow instead of looking at the stardust they managed to magnify it and coat their eyes with it. Temporary blindness was not on the list of things Wren wanted to experience. Now she sat waiting for the next lesson with a sour taste in her mouth and a nervous feeling in her stomach. "I suppose butterflies are better than being stuck in the sickroom, though."

"It's healing this time," Jill said tonelessly. "The lesson is on healing."

"Oh." Wren proceeded cautiously. It was the first time Jill had volunteered information. "Who teaches healing?"

Jill shrugged.

Wren gave up and sat next to her in silence until a woman wearing jeans and a button-down shirt came through the doorway. The other apprentices didn't seem to notice her until she made her way to the center of the floor and cleared her throat.

"If you're here for a healing lesson, you'd better pay attention," she said.

It took Wren a minute to register that this woman

was a full Fiddler. She looked like she might be a college student out in the real world. Her dark skin complemented her hair, which was cut close to her head. She wore glasses that glittered with rhinestones at their sharp points, and she adjusted them on her nose while she waited for the last apprentices to settle into their seats.

Then the instructor moved to a shelf on the wall and pulled out a small potted tree. "Watch." She sprinkled stardust over the top of the sapling's thin branches. "A Fiddler cannot always predict how manipulating the stardust will change the world. Perhaps it will make something more of what is already there." As she strummed the dust in the air, murmuring a rhyme under her breath, a dissonant note echoed through the room. Wren could see the tree stretching and changing. The branches pulsed and grew, reaching out like knobby claws. The trunk glowed bright red, and its wood split, curving out in sharp ribbons. The tip of one branch blossomed into a serpentine head that opened its jaws and unleashed a growl.

The instructor didn't even flinch. "Or perhaps it will become an altogether different—and potentially unmanageable—beast." The tree bent toward the apprentices, and Wren's skin crawled at the animal look of its branches.

"Even with centuries of practice," the Fiddler continued, "stardust is unpredictable. Wielding magic recklessly will damage the harmony of all living things on Earth." She frowned down at the mutant tree. "When you learn the healing arts, you learn something held in a sacred trust. Something to be used only with respect for the nature of all living things." She murmured a rhyme and with a wave of her hand, the tree returned to its former appearance. "A wise Fiddler is careful to practice only known spells, calculating the cost as best she can, and restraining from magic outside the Fiddlers' ken: Kill no living thing. Create no unknown thing. Cause no undue harm." She examined the sapling and pinched off a dead cluster of leaves with her fingers before turning to face the apprentices. "Find a spot for the lab, please." She pointed to the long tables situated at the opposite end of the room, where trees were evenly spaced above each bench seat.

By the time Wren got to the table, Simon and Jack were already sitting next to each other, and the spaces around them were filled. She slid into the bench across from them, and Jill slipped in next to her.

The sapling at Wren's spot was wilted, one branch split. Looking around, Wren saw that the other trees were much the same. Each one had a torn leaf or a broken branch. Something for the apprentices to heal.

The instructor recited the first part of the rhyme they would use.

Intery, mintery, cutery-corn.

"You'll need to play the stardust like this." The instructor held her long fingers up so that the thumb, middle, and pinky touched their counterparts on the opposite hand.

Apple seed and apple thorn.

"Then twist to the right on the word *limber-lock*."

Across the way, Simon was practically crooning at his plant, even though nothing seemed to be happening. Jack, too, was midrhyme, but he must have done something wrong. His tree looked like a drooping weeping willow. The first time Wren tried the rhyme, her fingers got tangled up and the stardust fell flat on the table.

"That's all right," the instructor's voice came from behind her shoulder. "Scoop it up and try again." And then she left, circling the table to offer pointers to a student who had managed to twist his tree into a pretzel shape.

"She's got to be crazy," Wren said to Jill. "To be the only full Fiddler monitoring all of this."

When Jill didn't answer, Wren looked over to see that she was midrhyme, and whatever she was doing, it looked like she had doused her sapling in Miracle-Gro. The little tree was stretching up, broken branches knitting together and leaves growing an even brighter green.

"That's amazing!" Wren said.

Two spots of color appeared on Jill's white cheeks. "Thanks." It was the most animated Wren had ever seen her.

"Wait! Stop!" the instructor said from the other side of the table, rushing to the end to counteract an apprentice who had accidentally lit a tree on fire.

The stardust fire was unnaturally bright, not like the kind lit by a match. Blue and green flames shot in little arcs over the tree, dancing around a blindingly white center.

In a flash, the walls of the Crooked House melted away, and Wren was back in the gray dream world. A familiar bay window with its cut-glass black-and-white squares filled her vision, but there was no figure standing in front of it this time. The window took up almost a whole side of what appeared to be some kind of important room. Maps lined the wall on either side of the window. The shelf below it was full of tools that Wren didn't recognize. A contraption that resembled a weighted scale. Sundials. Gyroscopes. Invention blueprints.

Wren moved over to look at a messy pile of papers. Graphs and angles and words and numbers covered the pages. She thumbed through some, pausing to note the few that reminded her of star maps, but with no constellations she recognized. A sheaf of rhymes that Wren hadn't read before. Poems full of odd jewels and gems. And ashes. All of them had something to do with ashes.

Wren heard footsteps, the sound of people talking, and then the two tall doors opposite swung open.

"Dreamer!" the foremost man said. It was the tall man she had seen once before, his dark hair slicked back into a knot on the top of his head and his lean form cloaked all in leather. He was flanked by others, but their faces were blurred, and Wren couldn't make them out. "How dare you come here unsummoned?" the man said. His words sounded hard as ice.

Wren tightened her muscles, hunting for what she had done before, the way she had altered the dream, and then she felt it. Something shifted inside, the resistance that she'd tried before in the visions, and the scene changed. She wasn't sure what it was that she was doing, but it was the only way to move in the bizarre dream world. She opened her eyes again, and this time she was standing at the edge of a wide circular space, a shallow bowl carved into the earth like a crater. There was no sound. No wind stirring the dusty ground.

Wren stood very still, repeating the shifting trick, but with more focus this time. She let the land around her shiver, then waver, and then she was on the opposite side of the bowl, looking down over a vast wasteland where trees twisted in on themselves to cover a barren ground stripped of all other vegetation. Stumps and jagged tree trunks rested on one another between the remains of what must have once been houses.

The air was unnaturally close, like a heavy blanket on her skin. Something horrible had happened here, Wren was sure of it. Movement flickered against the horizon, growing as it came closer until it was the shape of a bird, winging its way toward Wren. The animal landed on the closest branch, and although the shape was bird-like, something wasn't quite right. The lines were off, as though the creature was disjointed somehow. It cocked its head, locking its one-eyed gaze on Wren's face.

"Mer-ter," it said. "Mer-ter." It fluttered its wings out and then resettled them.

"Can you talk?" Wren said, surprised that her tongue was loose in the dream world. "What happened here?"

"Mer-ter," it repeated, as though it was a parrot asking for a cracker.

Wren heard a large boom in the distance, strong enough that it startled the bird, which immediately took to the air. The rumbling sound came again. And then again, as if someone was shooting a cannon. Wren looked to the horizon, but everything seemed the same monotonous gray, broken only by the black silhouettes of trees. And then someone was shaking her, tugging on her shoulder and pulling her awake.

"Wren?" It was Jill's voice, and her face bent over Wren's. "Wren, are you okay?"

"I'm fine." Wren shook her head. Jill must think she was a complete idiot. Staring off into space for who knew how long. "Daydreaming, I guess." Something had triggered the waking dream again—the bright light of the stardust, she supposed—but this was the first time she had intentionally tried to travel within the dream and succeeded, the first time she had actually gone somewhere in the dream world. What could it mean? And what had she seen?

"The lesson is over," Jill said, and Wren could see the table was emptying around them. The Fiddler instructor was at the other end, cleaning up a glowing neon liquid that had come from somewhere. Simon and Jack were adding their newly mended trees to the long row positioned on the ledge above. And the rest of the apprentices were disappearing.

Jill's tree was perfectly restored, the very image of health. And Wren was shocked to see that hers was equally pristine.

"I didn't do that," Wren said, shaking her head. The last she had looked, her tree was in bad shape, and Wren hadn't even been able to gather the stardust to work the rhyme.

"I didn't think you'd want any unnecessary attention," Jill said matter-of-factly. "I hope you don't mind." The two spots of color were back in her cheeks.

"Mind?" Wren was exceedingly thankful that Jill had kept the instructor from noticing. If word got back to Cole that she was having more problems with focusing during lessons, she didn't know what she would do. It didn't feel like the I-want-to-beat-Simon excuse would work a second time. "I don't mind. Thank you. How long was I spaced out for?" Wren asked Jill, who was watching her intently.

"A long time," Jill said, without breaking her gaze. "You know, Wren, you are kind of an odd person."

Wren slid off the bench and picked up her tree. "It takes one to know one, Jill."

EIGHTEEN

Pease porridge hot,
Pease porridge cold,
Pease porridge in the pot
Nine days old.

Making pease porridge takes precision and focus," Baxter said, hoisting a cauldron onto a worktable and then using a long spoon to stir the thin layer of stardust inside.

They were in a room that looked like a medieval apothecary. Cabinets full of haphazardly arranged jars and bottles lined the walls. Dried herbs hung from beams that ran along the cavern ceiling. Flames flickered in the fireplace, and Baxter occasionally fanned them with a pair of old bellows.

Baxter pulled down several glass beakers from a

corner cabinet, each labeled in his illegible script.

"So crude stardust needs to be refined before working magic?" Simon asked. He had his notebook out and was detailing every move Baxter made.

"Yes." Baxter measured out a pale liquid into the bottle. "The first Fiddlers explored the magical properties of stardust, but only when it had gone through a process of refining. In its raw state, it looks like a plain old meteorite."

Wren didn't think there was anything plain about meteorites. "I wonder how they knew to try heating it."

"How else does a scientist learn anything?" Jack uncorked a bottle and shook out tiny dried flowers into his palm. "Experimentation."

Wren pinched a few of the flowers between her thumb and forefinger. They looked like snowflakes that someone had dried out and captured forever. Their minuscule geometric patterns were embossed with the iridescent dust that coated the edges.

"Random experimentation with stardust is risky." Baxter wiped his hands on the front of his apron. "If you don't perform the rhyme exactly as intended, you can get strange results. One time Mary ended up losing all the hair on her head, including her eyebrows, when she tried to grow her falcon a thicker layer of feathers for the winter." Baxter winked at them. "Don't tell her I told you."

He continued talking as he chopped some dried herbs into bits. "There are recipe books that give detailed instructions for making pease porridge. You would do well to study them." He nodded toward a tottering pile of books perched on top of the cabinets and then used the flat edge of his knife to expertly scoop up the remnants and slide them into the pot on the table in front of him. He sprinkled a tiny bit of refined stardust on top, grabbed a spoon, and stirred it all together.

Piping hot, smoking hot.
What I've got you have not.
Hot gray pease, hot, hot, hot;
Hot gray pease, hot.

While he sang, something was happening in the pot. Sparks shot up from the interior even though there was no flame and no heat source. The familiar glow of stardust filled the room, but this time a burnt smell came with it.

"Scalding hot," Baxter said in response to Wren's wrinkled nose. "Now we let it steep." He turned back to the shelf, sending glass bottles tinkling together, while he rummaged around inside. He finally came up with an empty jar. "Rats. Out of astrid petals. You three wait here." He gave them each a cutting board and a sheaf of dried herbs. "Chop these. Tiny cuts, just like this, and I'll be back in a minute." He bustled out of the room, leaving them alone with the bubbling cauldron.

Wren sniffed the plant in front of her. Catnip, maybe. Or spearmint. "I thought that with, well, modern scientific methods, medicine and chemistry and all the rest, Fiddlers might be beyond the herb thing."

"Where do you think modern medicines come from?" Simon set down his notebook and unplugged one of the beakers. "Nature. Even synthetic medicines are made up of compounds of natural ingredients." He reached for his knife and cutting board. "You're just not used to this kind of laboratory."

"And you are?" Wren said, looking around the room. "You do have to admit, it's all kind of strange."

"What isn't strange around here?" Jack shrugged. "Think of all we've gotten used to already." He cut at the pile of herbs in front of him, but for once he was not able to do something expertly.

Wren snorted. Jack had no idea what she had to get used to. She'd had another of the dreams the night before, a return to the same desolate landscape of trees and stumps. The heaviness of the place lingered in her memory. The more dreams she had, the more significant she felt they might be. Like they were messages, somehow. Or warnings. She tried to push away the thought that they were most certainly connected to Boggen. That those who called her Dreamer might somehow be part of Boggen's world or possibly even be Boggen himself. Was she seeing things that had already happened or were her dreams giving her a glimpse into wherever Boggen and the Magicians had gone?

Wren finished chopping her pile of herbs and meandered over to the stack of rhyme books, pulling them down, blinking against the cloud of dust that accompanied them. Their thick covers were warped with age and the pages wrinkly from spills and stains. None of the books had titles. They seemed to be more observation logs than actual books, but each had a Fiddler name etched into the front cover. Wren flipped through the first volume, skipping over the parts stained with unidentifiable blotches, and moved on to the second. It seemed that a hundred years ago a team of Fiddlers had worked together to come up with a new rhyme that helped speed recovery from the measles. Notes had been written in several hands. Together, they had used stardust to create something that probably saved many lives and was the forerunner of the modern vaccination.

Wren ran a hand over the various Fiddlers' notes. Perhaps part of her problem was that she was trying to solve the mystery of the dreams alone. She wondered what would happen if she told Baxter everything. Would he help her? Or would he hand her right over to Cole and the Fiddler Council? No, telling Baxter and the other grown-ups was out of the question. But what about Jack and Simon? Would they laugh and call her crazy? Would they accuse her of being the one who was contacting Boggen? She watched Simon's messed-up hair bouncing as he chopped the diminishing pile of leaves in front of him. Not Simon. Simon wouldn't think she was crazy.

Wren took a deep breath. "There's something I need to tell you guys," she said in a quiet voice. "About these weird dreams I've been having."

"Dreams?" Simon's gaze fixed on her like a hawk's.

"What do you mean, *dreams*?"

"Dreams," Wren said, hardly knowing how to begin. "Or maybe messages." In that moment, her idea of the dreams being something more seemed silly, the result of an overactive imagination. And as she told the boys about them—first the woman and the man who were so frightened about something, then the old man and the shepherdess, then the boat on the Opal Sea, and the bizarre crow in the desolate wasteland—it all seemed even sillier.

"Do you think they could be important? I mean, what if they're messages or something?" She picked at her thumbnail. "From the Magicians," she finished weakly.

"I don't know." Simon's eyebrows knitted together thoughtfully. "Weird dreams could just be a side effect of using stardust. Or being a Weather Changer." He chewed on his pencil eraser. "But you say they talked to you. And the one with the window—you're sure he was surprised to see you?"

Wren thought back on her different dreams. "I'm sure. They all kept calling me 'Dreamer,' like they recognized me or something."

"But what did you say to him? The scary man who

marked your neck." Jack separated out a few stalks of the herbs. His voice sounded oddly intent until Wren realized he was about to make another joke. "Did he hop over a candlestick, perhaps? Or maybe he lived in a shoe. Or, wait, I bet he's really a merry old soul." He gave Wren a crooked half smile. "I told you before, Wren. Your subconscious is probably just connecting what you know from old rhymes with what's actually happening here. Weird dreams aren't anything to worry about."

"We've got to know more." Simon shut his notebook and tucked it into his pocket. "Next time, Wren, don't run in the dream. Don't try to hide. Talk to them and see what they want."

Wren licked her lips. That was easy for Simon to say. He'd never felt the heart-pounding terror of it. The horror of not being able to speak. "Okay," she said, but she didn't feel okay. Not because Simon's idea wasn't a good one, but because of the hidden assumptions in it: They were messages, and there was going to be a next time.

"Oh, good," Baxter said, bustling back into the room. "You're still here." He moved over to the cauldron and gave it a quick stir.

"Don't. Tell. Him," Wren mouthed to the others. Jack shrugged and Simon gave her a sharp nod. Wren hoped she hadn't made a mistake trusting them.

"I ran into some other Fiddlers in the garden. Charles is out of crude stardust," Baxter said. "And so is Hester. I need you to run over and gather some fresh."

"*Fresh* stardust?" Wren said.

"Well, relatively fresh. Only a million years old or so," Baxter said as he puffed the billows to fan the flames of the fire. He laughed at their astonished faces. "Off the meteorite. What better place to gather it than from a fallen shooting star? Come now, there's lots to learn, and no time like the present." He stooped to pull some tools out of a low cupboard. "Simply chip it off with this." Baxter gave each of them a small pickax and what appeared to be a paintbrush. "I can't go with you, because the porridge is getting to the tricky part. Needs constant stirring." He dumped a handful of the leaves Simon had crushed into the cauldron. "Grab some of the buckets near the doorway. Off you go, now."

NINETEEN

"The wings mark the way to find what you wish,"
The old moon told the three.
"Leave your nets and leave your fish,
And dive down beneath the sea, the sea.
You will find the wings that you seek, down beneath the sea."

"Baxter said to go through the green door right past the bridge," Jack said as they made their way across the glowing opal water.

"I wonder what a meteorite looks like up close," Simon mused. "Examining the source of stardust should be illuminating. Pun intended."

Two Fiddlers approached, but if they were Elsa's or Cole's spies, they were more subtle than the usual ones. Neither spared Wren and the boys a glance.

Wren eyed the opal stream as they crossed the bridge,

the vivid memory of her dreams fresh in her mind. What would happen if she jumped into that liquid?

"Just a second," she said to the boys, making sure no one else was in sight. Then she leaned down and stretched out a finger. Ice-cold liquid. *Definitely water.* Nothing like the warm stardust of her dreams.

She got to her feet, and there, coming toward the end of the bridge, was an unwelcome but familiar shape. Elsa's tall form moved in their direction, her cape billowing out behind her. Wren didn't think she'd spotted them yet. She was too busy shouting orders to poor Jill, who skulked at her side.

"We've got to get out of sight," Wren hissed, grabbing Simon and Jack by their elbows and shoving them toward the end of the bridge. It wouldn't matter that Baxter had sent them on an errand. Elsa didn't care that Baxter and Liza were helping to teach Mary's apprentices; in fact, it only made her more quick to accuse them of doing something wrong.

Wren hurried off the bridge toward the right, dashing through the green door. Elsa was still engrossed in berating Jill.

"Just in time," Jack said, bending over to catch his breath.

"Poor Jill," Wren said with a sigh. She wished they could somehow snatch her away from Elsa's grasp.

"Interesting." Simon wasn't even winded. He was examining the mosslike substance that covered one wall. "This resembles an aquatic moss, yet we find it here in the mountain." He whipped out his notebook and began scribbling. "Very interesting." With a flourish he dotted the paper with his pencil. "If sea life actually exists here, perhaps your dream isn't so outlandish, Wren. Maybe we really could dive underneath the sea."

The dreams. Wren hurried over and looked at the moss, which seemed to her like every other kind of moss she'd ever seen. "This came from the sea?"

"Seriously, Simon? Dreams are dreams." Jack laughed, but he sounded a little annoyed.

"Obviously, dreams are dreams," Simon said stiffly. "But that doesn't mean they can't be messages as well."

Jack only harrumphed at this, but Wren thought about Simon's theory as they walked along. What if the dreams were symbolic? What were they trying to tell her? And, more important, who was the one trying to tell her something? The tunnel was worn smooth with use, and they followed it for some time until the blue ceiling sloped down, and ice and dirt crystalized to form iridescent columns.

"Hmm," Simon said, examining the base of the arch. "I wonder if these are man-made or natural."

"Fiddler-made, more like," Wren muttered as she pushed past him to the crossroads, where jagged archways stretched off into the distance in three different directions.

The first smelled earthy and the walls fairly glowed with a thick coating of luminescent vegetation. The second was pitch-black, with only the slightest light reflecting from the white of the columns, and the third lay directly in front of them, painted a pinkish red with the colors of a brilliant sunset.

They followed the directions Baxter had given them and chose the third, and Wren was pleased to find the air grew fresher the farther they went, hinting at an external opening somewhere nearby. Soon, the path connected to a wide cavern, and way up overhead, Wren could see the promise of blue sky. The ground dipped down into a shallow bowl where the cave walls had long ago been pushed aside by a powerful force. Chunks of rock lay scattered across the floor around what at first appeared to be a wall of the cavern. It took Wren a moment to register what she was looking at. "A meteorite," she breathed. "A piece of living astronomy, buried down here." She moved over to what wasn't a wall at all and ran her hand over the massive side of the meteorite.

"This rock was actually once in outer space," she said to the boys, but they were staring up at the crack of daylight. "Think of it," Wren went on. "Thousands, maybe millions of years ago, it barreled its way through Earth's atmosphere and changed things forever." Wren didn't know how long she stood there, tracing the pockmarked surface with her palms.

"Look. You can see how it's been mined for stardust." Simon had come up behind her and now used the paintbrush tool to poke at the dull aqua color shimmering in a crack.

The surface appeared to be an ordinary Earth rock, except for the ashy substance that hid in the craters. Empty crevices showed places where stardust had already been excavated. Wren took her pick and painstakingly dug at what seemed to be a particularly rich lode and then brushed out the stardust, which fell dully into her pail. "It doesn't glow at all," she said.

"Of course not," Simon said. "It hasn't been refined." He examined some lichen growing on the rock formation next to them. "Hey, this plant is covered with stardust as well." His voice was full of excitement. "Fungi, perhaps." Simon paused to pull out a specimen bag, but as he tried to collect the substance, it evaporated like steam off a hot drink.

"Very strange," he said, after trying another time. "Definitely not plant matter."

"Maybe it's a chemical reaction," Wren said as together they examined the substance. "Something in the atmosphere producing a gaseous response."

"Or maybe it's just a plant." Jack sounded bored from where he sat on a crumbling remnant of meteorite. "C'mon, you guys, we shouldn't be wasting time in this place. Let's harvest the stardust and go."

"Just another minute." Wren moved back toward the meteorite and, in her haste, she stumbled on the uneven path, falling onto her hands and knees. She rubbed her scraped palms on her pants and took a deep breath.

"Are you okay?" Simon was at her side, but she didn't answer him. From her position on the floor she saw something she hadn't noticed before. There, carved on one corner of the reddish wall, was an unmistakable pair of wings.

She crawled forward, ignoring the burning on her hands, and began brushing at the wall.

"Wren? What's wrong?" Jack stood with his hands on his hips, looking at Wren like she'd gone mad.

"The wings," she said. "The wings from the dream."

"You've got to be kidding me," Jack said, moving closer, and then his voice grew tense as he saw the etchings. "Are you sure?"

Wren scrambled to her feet, scouring the wall for clues. More wings appeared, leading them up and over the side of the meteorite. She jogged forward, brushing the small stones out of her cut palms, and then braced herself to climb up. Wedging one foot on a small outcropping, she was able to hoist her body over the top, scraping her stomach as she went. And then she was on the other side, following the trail of wings into what seemed a maze of rock formations. She squeezed between lichen-covered towers and scrambled over flat ones, slid through slim openings and balanced on narrow ledges, hunting for the wings all the while. If she hadn't been following them, she would have never found the way. But after she crawled through another gap and dropped down to the other side, she knew the wings had led her to the right spot. Ahead, a narrow sliver of stardust covered an opening that seemed to be cut between two giant stones. Delicate webs of gossamer floated around the edges, glistening white against the black of the crack.

"I found something!" she yelled over her shoulder to the sound of the boys' labored breathing and scraping shoes. They'd had no trouble climbing over the formations but were having a harder time with the slender passageways.

Something drew Wren forward, closer and closer, until she stood before the opening. She knew all the way through her bones that it was important that she continue on, that she follow the way of the wings. She hesitated for barely a moment, but the driving impulse pushed away her uncertainty. She couldn't wait any longer. "I'm going on!" Wren shouted to the boys. "Stay here if you want. I'll be right back."

She slid sideways, edging her body through the narrow space, holding her breath as she eased forward into darkness. Then, with a sigh of relief, she found that the gap widened as she continued on. Real cobwebs mingled with the shreds of stardust. Certainly no one had come this way in a long time.

There was a flare of light from somewhere behind her. Wren paused, watching it grow brighter, and then Simon was next to her, a perfectly made starlamp hovering over his palm. Jack soon joined them, mumbling something about tight spaces.

"Look," Wren gasped. Simon's starlamp illuminated the walls to reveal that the same silver mineral that pocked the meteorite was worked into a pattern here, the repeated imprint of hundreds of wings. Wren moved forward, the boys close behind, and as she went, the wing marks grew thicker, pressing in on top of one another as though they were passing through a whole flock of birds in flight.

And then the wind came. First it was the faintest hint of a breeze. Despite the dampness of the passageway, the current was warm. Wren smelled something like cinnamon, and more scents she didn't recognize, but the whole effect was of the delicious rich spicy smells of autumn and winter baking. She took another step, and the wind blew harder, pressing her clothes against her and tossing her hair about her eyes. It reminded Wren of that first wild ride on the falcon—the warm breath of stardust filling her completely. She laughed out loud and stretched her hands to either side, welcoming the wind.

"Whoa," Jack said. "This is weird."

"An updraft," Wren said. "Warm air blown up from the Earth's hot crust. Isn't it amazing?"

Jack grunted in reply as the wind accompanied them, carrying Wren on toward the sound of running water. The tunnel bent round to one side and then spilled out into a glorious cave, bright with the late-afternoon sun. Wren stood at the tunnel mouth, blinking at the light streaming in from a high opening at the far end of the cave. Stairs had been cut into the rock, leading the way up and out, where Wren could see green foliage covering the entrance.

But it wasn't the outside that left Wren standing speechless. Nor the glistening rainbow of blues and purples that covered the cavern walls. It was the waterfall, spilling down from a rocky ledge near the cavern's roof, falling into a pool that steamed with the opal mist of the Crooked House and rushed merrily out of sight. The path they were on led to a stairway that curved behind the waterfall, where Wren could see the faint outline of an opening, a shape that looked remarkably like the doorways so pervasive in the Crooked House.

She left Simon trying to convince Jack that the plant that coated the walls here was the same as the lichen-like substance near the meteorite and made her way carefully over the slippery stone, the words of the dream rhyme echoing through her head. *You'll find the wings that you seek down beneath the sea.* She slipped

under the waterfall, the icy spray cold against her skin
after the warm wind. There was no weathered green
paint on this door. Instead, it was charred black with
the remnants of a carefully lettered sign that had two
lines of text. Wren worked hard to make out a *c* and
an *a, n* and then some barely legible scratches before
the archaic English letter that looked like a cursive *f.*
"Cana? Candi?" she murmured. The sign said Can-
something or other. The word on the first line was
hard to decipher, but there was no doubt about the
second line. Wren read the clear unmistakable letters
out loud: "Boggen."

She took a deep breath and stepped through the
rough doorway. Scraps of what must have once been
rugs covered the stony floor, and other clues to human
existence dotted the room: a few pieces of splintered
wood, some tottering chairs and empty barrels.

Near one wall, a tarnished pan hung above the
remains of long-cold ashes, and next to it, some rusted
pots that must have once held coal. Wren poked
through them, surprised to find a large intact piece
amid the dusty remnants. It was difficult to see anything in the fading daylight that filtered through the
open door behind her. She pinched some stardust and

wove a wobbly starlamp that revealed a stash of fat squatty candles. *Candles!* That must be what the sign had said. Wren held one up, squinting. It seemed to be made of a dark purple wax that had withstood the wear of time and elements.

Wren took one and tucked it into her pocket. Maybe it was nothing, but if this was in fact a room Boggen had used, she guessed Mary would want to see it. She raised her head and scanned the room. A sheen of stardust caught her eye and she went over to what appeared to be a workspace carved into the stone walls with a mural painted above it. She moved closer. It wasn't a piece of artwork at all. It was a star map.

Wren stood breathless before it, the familiar horizon lines crisscrossing over constellations and galaxies she had never seen before. Between each point, someone had drawn what looked like a giant web, tracing a pathway through the atmosphere.

"What's that?" Simon's voice cut through her thoughts as he entered the room, his starlamp sending shadows scurrying over the map.

"It's what Mary's been looking for. Give me your notebook," Wren demanded, rummaging around the candle in her cloak pocket for a pencil. "A star map, remember? This has got to be one of Boggen's labs, and I'd bet anything Mary hasn't seen it yet," she said as she copied down the markings, taking care to write exactly what she saw.

Jack whistled as he joined them. "Well done, Wren. Won't the Council be pleased at what you've found?"

Wren froze. *The Council.* The ones who suspected her of being in contact with Boggen. She glanced up at Simon, who seemed to be thinking the same thing.

"We all found it, Wren. We were right here with you." Simon swallowed nervously. "We don't think you're helping him."

Wren felt better to hear that, but she noticed Jack wasn't agreeing. Instead he made his way around the room, clattering together the pots as he went. "Rusty old pans." Jack dipped his hand into the pot where Wren had found the candles and pulled out the coal. "Old rocks?" He tossed it from one hand to the other and pocketed it. "Boggen really was wicked, wasn't he?"

"That's nothing," Wren said, returning to her notations. "*This* is what we're looking for. It's not just a star map." She scribbled faster, leaning the notebook up against the workspace to draw the lines that encircled the unfamiliar constellations. "It's a guide for space travel."

"Hey, Simon," Jack said, laughter in his voice. "Don't you want to come collect a sample of this?" He pointed at a pile of animal droppings.

"Bats, I'd wager." Simon eyed the pile of poop thoughtfully. "I do have an extra specimen bag."

"Gross, Simon," Wren said, scanning the mural to make sure she hadn't missed anything. She'd covered six pages with markings. They'd have to tape them together to see the full mural, but she'd managed to get it all down.

"Don't forget that," Jack said, coming closer to point at a symbol in the corner.

It was the confirmation Wren didn't really need. She carefully copied the flame in her book, neatly labeling it in capital letters: THE MARK OF THE MAGICIANS.

TWENTY

Jack and Jill went up a hill
To bring a pail of water;
Jack fell down and broke his crown,
And Jill came tumbling after.

"We've got to let Mary know we found a star map
in Boggen's secret lab," Wren told Jack and
Simon as they hurried back the way they had come. It
hadn't taken nearly as long to return through the rock
formations, and now they raced up the tunnel. "Or at
least find Baxter and Liza." Wren led the way across
the bridge over the Opal Sea. She had decided to try
the amphitheater first, and so intent was she on looking
for Mary that she didn't see Elsa beelining toward them
until it was too late.

"Apprentices! Stop!" Elsa's face was creased with

displeasure. "Who gave you permission to leave your work? Why are you in the Council's quarters?" She narrowed her gaze at them. "Alone."

Wren managed a weak "Um," her mind whirling fast to think of a believable reason, while Jack choked out a nervous laugh. Simon said nothing at all, and Wren wondered how long they had before Elsa started talking about floggings.

Instead, Elsa began to list the new rules she was proposing to the Council, limiting apprentice activity even more. "For your own protection, of course." Her mouth creased into an unpleasant smile. "Until I speak to them, why don't you come with me. I'd like to see what these other Fiddlers are teaching you."

"Or we could go talk to the Council now," Wren said desperately. If they were lucky, Mary might be in there.

"Apprentices disturb the Council?" Elsa raised one eyebrow. "I think not. I will take charge of your training this afternoon."

"But you have that meeting." It was Jill who came to their aid, popping out from behind Elsa. "With the cook, remember?"

Elsa scowled at her. "Blast the cook."

"Beg your pardon, Fiddler Elsa," Jill said from Elsa's side, giving a perfect little bow. "But perhaps these apprentices could join my work detail until you are available. I will keep an eye on them."

"Yes," Elsa said thoughtfully. "You could watch them. An excellent idea, and one I can't believe I haven't thought of before." She pinched Wren's ear in one hand and Simon's in the other and pushed them toward Jill, barking at Jack to follow close behind. "The old observatory, Jill. Don't forget the deep-cleaning supplies, and work there until I come for you." She pointed toward a green door. "Well? What are you waiting for?" she hissed. "Only *undisciplined* apprentices take their time."

No one said anything until a whole level was between them and Elsa's furious face. Jill led them to an exterior door and cracked it open, pausing to listen back the way they had come, and then hurried through. "The observatory is at the top of the Crooked House," Jill said. "It's ancient. Hardly anyone goes there now. Not since the new one was built on the other side of the cliff." She hooked the bucket of cleaning supplies she was carrying over one arm and began climbing a rough switchback stairway that cut across the face of the Crooked House. She smiled at Wren, the first genuine smile Wren had ever seen from her. "You can talk freely out here. None of Elsa's spies to overhear what we're saying." She told them how most of the upper floors were abandoned, left over from when Magicians and Alchemists together filled up all the lodgings in the Crooked House. It seemed to Wren that the fresh air had worked some kind of magic on Jill. Her expressionless eyes became animated. Her cheeks flushed with a more healthy-looking color, and that smile kept blossoming across her face.

"Why are you helping us?" Simon's voice was very quiet. "You don't even know us."

"I know Elsa," Jill said. "I know what she's capable of, and I know what she'll do to you if she can get away with it." She paused, her fingers hovering around her collarbone as if she was remembering something that she once wore on her neck. She shook her head. "But that's not why I did it. I want you to help me."

"What can we do to help you?" Jack asked. "We're only apprentices, too."

"Yeah," Jill said, and her voice suddenly sounded brittle. "But you came from out there. You're not from the Crooked House." She clenched her jaw. "I've seen you get flying lessons. I've heard you talking about gateways. Elsa forbids me from knowing anything that I could use to escape. I want you to teach me what you know." She gathered her unruly curls into one thick bundle and tugged on it. "So that I can leave this place and be free in your land."

"We can't promise anything," Jack said, giving Jill a half smile. "All we can do is try."

"We can do more than try." Wren reached out to squeeze Jill's hand. "We'll figure something out. There's no way we'll leave you here with that woman if you want to go. Where did you used to live anyway?"

"Here."

"No, I mean before you came here. Like when you had a family."

"Here," Jill said, and some of the deadness was back in her voice. "I was born here."

"I didn't know that someone could be born a Fiddler," Wren said, carefully picking her way over a crumbling part of the path. Simon stopped to jot something down in his notebook, but Jill picked up the pace, almost as though if she walked faster, she could avoid the questions.

"Well, you can," she said in clipped tones. "Most of us are. I only know one other apprentice who came in from the wild before you three."

"Hmm. So Fiddling has a genetic link?" Simon was somehow able to navigate the narrow path and take notes at the same time. "Is everyone in your family a Fiddler?"

"I don't want to talk about my family," Jill said, and shut her mouth with a snap.

"Hmm." Simon chewed on his pencil eraser. "It must be a recessive gene, because neither my dad nor Wren's parents have any idea what a Fiddler is." He squinted out over the valley. "But my mom? Hmm, I wonder."

"Hmm," Jack said. "I wonder if the sound of all your wondering is getting annoying. Hmm. Oh, wait! No need to wonder. It is."

"What's your problem, Jack?" Wren jumped to Simon's defense. "Don't be a jerk."

"What about your parents?" Simon said as if Jack hadn't been rude. "Either of them Fiddlers?"

"Don't know, don't care." Jack stumbled and reached out for the cliffside to catch his balance. "And before you get all wondering about them, don't bother. I sure don't."

Wren chose her words carefully. Jack hadn't ever

talked about his parents before. Maybe that was why
he was being so snappish with Simon. "Wouldn't your
relatives have told you, though?" Wren asked, making sure she stepped around the uneven spot Jack had
stumbled on.

"I don't have any relatives," Jack said.

"I mean your grandfather. Wouldn't he have said
something?"

"My grandfather?" Jack said, and he sounded confused for a moment as he paused in front of a small gap
in the stairway. Jill was already out of sight around the
next switchback. Jack took a step back and then hopped
over the opening.

Wren followed, stopping on the other side to make
sure Simon didn't try to walk across it with his nose
buried in his notebook. When he had joined them, she
turned to Jack. "Yeah, your grandfather. Maybe that's
why he's such a conspiracy theorist. Maybe he knows
something."

"Oh, right," Jack said. "Grandpa. He knew stuff all
right, but not about Fiddling being genetic." He took a
deep breath. "Hey, look, we're nearly at the top!"

The uppermost stairway ended with a rickety old
ladder that dumped them out onto a grassy hilltop.

Jill was waiting for them, and Wren plopped on the grass next to her to catch her breath. From where they sat, a knee-tingling view of the entire valley spread below them. Peering down, Wren couldn't make out the exterior entrances to the Crooked House, but she could see the falcon mews way below.

Above, the first stars began to twinkle in the dusky twilight. Wren strained her eyes to see if she could recognize any of the constellations, but they all looked strange. Thin streaks of aqua played near the horizon, the first faint glow of the aurora that had become an everyday sight to her now.

Jill sighed and got to her feet, picking up the bucket of cleaning supplies and interrupting the stillness of the moment. "Break's over. Time to get to work."

The old observatory looked like it belonged in a collection of historical monuments. The crumbling limestone foundation, chipped and worn by many years on the cliff top, stretched up into a faded cylindrical tower that was topped with a glass dome. Even from where Wren stood, she saw places where the windows were cracked and broken. A stone balcony protruded from one side, with a stand that held a monstrous old telescope.

Wren felt glad Elsa didn't know how much she loved astronomy. Otherwise, there was no way she would have given her a punishment that actually felt like a prize.

"I can't wait to see what's up there," she said as Jill wrestled open the warped door. "I bet there's all sorts of ancient equipment from—well, how long has the Crooked House been around, anyway?"

"No one really knows," Jill said, leading them up a narrow stairway. "The Crooked House has expanded over the years, of course, but the main part—the summoning room and Opal Sea—it's always been here. Ever since the Crooked Man built it. Or that's what legend says, anyway."

"The Crooked Man?" Wren said, but forgot what she was going to ask when she followed Jill into the glass enclosed room, where a giant gyroscope perched in the center.

"Amazing," Jack said, sliding onto the tottering stool in front of it and reaching up to spin the frame. "It's still functional, even."

"And there's an armillary sphere." Wren pushed past Simon, who was sketching the equipment in his notebook, to examine something that looked like a globe balanced inside of a star. "Astronomers in medieval times used these to make models of the heavens."

"*Sapiens dominabitur astris.*" Jack poked his head out from behind the gyroscope. "'A wise man can rule the stars.'" He brushed the hair back from his forehead. "Maybe they did."

"We really should start cleaning," Jill said, nudging Simon, who was now copying down the markings on a huge compass. "Elsa won't be happy if she doesn't find us working. Here." She shoved a can of wood polish and an old rag at Jack and a bottle of glass cleaner at Wren. "Clean while you look. I stuck my neck out for you, and whatever else happens, Elsa has to find this room spotless."

"Right." Wren grabbed a rag out of Jill's bucket and began wiping things down. At first, she tried to hurry through the cleaning so she would have extra time to explore, but then she found that she could do both at once. She squirted some of the cleaner on a leaded-glass bookcase where someone had cataloged astronomical tools.

Wren wiped the moisture off, examining each item as it came into view. She'd seen some of the equipment before, at amateur astronomy meetings back home.

Some, she'd seen online or in journal articles. And some, she'd never seen at all.

"Check this out," she said to no one in particular. "They have a backstaff." She leaned closer. "And a celestial globe. This is amazing." The cabinet was locked, but she could see gyroscopes and sundials and something that looked like a cross between a candelabra and a microscope. Brass scales and a stone mortar and pestle. "No wonder people used to think Fiddlers were magicians." She read the little placards that talked about ways the equipment was used by early astronomers. A few items were unlabeled, their white cards blank but for an estimated date and the italicized words *No known use.* That and the flame of the Magicians.

"Look at this!" Wren called Simon over to show him the markings.

Simon lowered his voice. "I think we should ask Jill about the star map."

Wren glanced over at Jill, who was vigorously polishing glass lenses on a large telescope. "Why? How would she know anything about the Magicians?"

"Why would an apprentice not want to talk about her family?" Simon said.

Wren shrugged. "Tons of reasons. They could be

mean or dead or something."

"Or something," Simon said. "Or Magicians." He leaned closer, his cloth making a little squeaking noise on the glass as he worked. "Why do you think everyone is always talking about her and whispering? Why doesn't she have any friends?" He stopped scrubbing. "There has to be some reason she's stuck with Elsa as a mentor."

Wren chewed on her lip. Simon could be right. "Do you really think we can trust her?"

"Are you kidding?" Simon said. "She's confided her escape plan to us. She's probably the only person in the Crooked House besides Mary, Baxter, and Liza who we *can* trust. Besides that, we are wasting time cleaning up here, and for what? To wait for Elsa to come punish us?" He gave Wren a rare direct look. "You know we should be trying to find Mary. If we tell Jill, maybe she can help."

Wren looked back at the display of alchemist tools. It wasn't that she had forgotten what they had found earlier; it was just that it was nicer to not think about it for a few moments. Climbing the Crooked House had given her a break from worrying about how she was going to tell Mary about Boggen's lab without everyone thinking she was in league with the Magicians.

"I suppose it's worth the risk," she said, holding out her hand for Simon's notebook. "Besides, we have a bargaining tool. Imagine what Elsa would do if we blabbed that Jill wanted to escape." She flipped to the map she had copied earlier and walked straight over to Jill. "Any chance you can see these stars through that scope?"

"This Fiddler must have witnessed a gamma-ray burst." Jill bent close, one chewed-down nail running along the rumpled edge of the notebook. "Someone has marked a new star here."

Wren told her about her discovery in Boggen's lab. "We think whoever made this wasn't simply identifying stars but was navigating a route through them." She took a deep breath. "We think they might have made a gateway."

Jill flipped back and forth between the pages. "Wren, this is unbelievable." She peered closer, gathering her bushy hair to one shoulder so she could see the paper unhindered. She paused at the same spot that Wren had deliberated over in Boggen's lab. "Travel at the speed of light?"

"Yup." Wren could barely keep the grin off her face.

This was big. Bigger than finding out she was a Fiddler. Bigger than flying through an aurora on a falcon. Bigger than the biggest thing she had seen stardust do. Fiddlers didn't just fly through the night sky. They flew through the universe.

"What if the Magicians are out there right now?" Jack walked over and looked out the large glass window at the front of the room. "What if there are Magicians looking at us from a galaxy far, far away?"

It was a clear night, and the Milky Way had never appeared more beautiful to Wren. "What do you think about that theory, Jill? Do you know anything about gateways? Or the Magicians?"

"I don't know anything about the Ms," Jill said too quickly, and Wren exchanged glances with Simon. Perhaps he had been right about Jill's family.

"You mean the Magicians?" Simon asked with a frown.

"Stop saying the *M*-word," Jill said, glancing over her shoulder like she expected one to pop out and flog her right then.

"Call them something else, then," Wren pressed. "But tell us what you know."

"So much of Fiddler lore was lost after the Civil

War," Jill continued. "The worst part of the Ms leaving is that we've lost all their knowledge." She kept her gaze fixed on the map. "Or most of it. Elsa's studied it some, and when she's asleep, I sometimes read her notes. The odd thing is, lately she's been researching stuff about gateways, too." She gave a little gasp of discovery. "That's why she sent me hunting for candles, so she could see the star map." It came out like a whisper, and then she looked up at Wren, blinking, as though she'd just remembered the others were there too. "I mean, space travel—" She cut off midsentence. "Amazing."

Wren exchanged a glance with Simon.

"*Elsa's* studied the Magicians?" he said just as Wren said, "You need candles to see a star map?" The one she had found in Boggen's lab now felt heavy in her pocket.

Jill glanced over her shoulder as though a spy might spring from the forgotten observatory cupboards. "I shouldn't have said anything."

Wren laid a hand on Jill's arm. "We're on your side, Jill. But we need to know what sort of things she's studied." She squeezed Jill's arm. "Anything about Boggen?"

"I've seen his name," Jill said slowly. "It's mostly just history. How Boggen was killing people and animals to make living stardust." She fidgeted with her shirt collar. "I got nightmares the night I read that bit." She gave Wren a guilty look. "I mean, it's not forbidden to learn about Boggen. Or the Ms. It doesn't mean I care about them." Her cheeks were very red. "Or that I even want to know anything about them." She peered at both Simon's and Wren's faces. "That's what you think, isn't it? That Elsa and I are somehow connected to the M—" She stumbled over the word. "Magicians? That we've been doing dark magic?"

"Mary told us the Council thinks someone's been in contact with the Magicians. That they might even be trying to help Boggen," Wren said, hurrying on when she saw Jill was about to protest. "I don't think it's you, Jill. But could it be Elsa?"

"Whoa." Jill's eyes grew wide. "That *is* big news. Is that what that summoning was about when you first arrived? No wonder the Council has been in secret meetings ever since." She shook her head. "But I think you're wrong. I don't think even Elsa would do that."

"Why not?" Wren pressed, and then gave a little laugh. "She seems pretty interested in sucking the life out of apprentices to me."

"Don't joke, Wren," Jill said. "Elsa's family died in the Civil War." She stood and folded her arms across her chest. "All of them. Why else do you think she hates Mary?"

"Oh," Wren said as pieces of the puzzle fell into place. "Because Mary was Boggen's mentor, and he's the one who turned on everyone."

"Are you going on about your dreams again, Wren?" Jack poked his head out from behind the gyroscope. "Come *on* you guys, history is b-o-r-i-n-g. Have a look at the stars instead."

"Do you know why all the Magicians followed Boggen?" Wren asked, ignoring Jack.

"Well, he was part of the Council, I know that," Jill said, screwing her face up as though she was trying to remember. "I think the other Ms thought that Fiddlers should run the world, that it was stupid the Fiddlers were trying to help ordinary people who kept messing everything up. In apprentice lessons, they always tell us the Alchemists would've won for sure, but I suppose we'll never know, because the Ms all just disappeared."

"Through the gateway," Simon finished for her.

Jill leaned in close. "If what you say is true, I bet I

know why Elsa's studying all this stuff. She wouldn't be communicating with the Ms to help them, but to get her revenge."

Wren leaned back against a stool. No wonder Elsa hated her. If she couldn't get revenge on the Magicians, would Elsa settle for taking it out on Wren, the infamous Weather Changer who everyone was sure was connected with Boggen? She felt sick to her stomach. And the funny thing was, she wouldn't blame Elsa a bit. Everything pointed to Wren being Boggen's pawn. The strange dreams with their messages. The way the wings had led her to his old lab. Even the fact that she knew how to read a star map.

"What would it take to have a look at Elsa's notes?" Simon was asking Jill as Jack came over to join them.

"Are they still going on about this?" Jack pushed himself up to sit on the table. "Magicians. Alchemists. Who cares about the difference? We can use stardust to *travel through space!*" He waved his hands wildly around the room. "Look. You can see Jupiter through that telescope. If we can figure out what those Magicians knew, maybe we could see Jupiter *up close.*"

"If we could figure out what the Magicians knew, we could do a lot of things," Wren said.

Jill had flipped through Simon's notebook, and now they both were bent over the sketch of the mysterious evaporating fungi, debating its healing properties.

"Well," Jack said, "we know some of what they knew. Maybe we should go back and search Boggen's lab again. See if there's something we missed. Get a closer look at that star map. This is what stardust is all about! New discoveries! New adventures!" He leaned in close, his eyes shining with excitement. "Space travel, Wren."

Jack's energy was contagious. The worry she'd been feeling about what the Council would say paled in comparison to the significance of their discovery. She got to her feet, feeling a bit reckless. Jack's talk about the room they had found had given her an idea. Before she told the Council and they locked her up forever, or whatever it was Fiddlers did to punish apprentices they thought were traitors, she wanted to see it for herself.

"I did find something else down there." Wren pulled out one of the candles from her pocket. "Jill said the candles have something to do with the star map."

Jack raised an eyebrow. "There's a rooftop balcony." He pointed to a door in the corner. "I saw it from outside. Let's light it there."

★ ★ ★

Wren set the midnight purple candle on the widest area of the balcony, sending crumbles of wax down into an ashy circle.

Jack bent, and the starlamp he'd made flared with energy the closer it got to the candle. "All set?"

Wren felt like it was the Fourth of July, with Jack lighting the first firework. "Get ready to run," she said, pressing back a few steps.

But when Jack lit the candle, there was no explosion. No sudden shooting off of sparks. No burst of light. Instead, a thin trickle of stardust smoke trailed up and out into the twilit sky. The evening's first constellations were visible, and soon the wisps of stardust dissipated in the midst of them.

"It smells nice," Jack said, noting the incense-y aroma coming from the candle. "Maybe Fiddlers used it like perfume."

"More like deodorant. People back then stunk," Wren said with a bitter smile. She didn't know what she expected the candle to do, but *absolutely nothing* was a huge disappointment. Maybe they needed to light it back in Boggen's lab.

"Looking at the stars is like looking back in time."

Jack leaned back on his palms, tilting his head to take in the expanse of the heavens. "Didn't Einstein or somebody say that?"

Wren joined him, letting her gaze soak up the myriad stars. Because the Crooked House was out in the middle of nowhere, no neon lights muddied the view. She felt her face relax, and the knot of nerves in her chest loosened a tiny bit. She'd been so busy learning about stardust and fighting off dreams and worrying about what the Council thought about her that she'd forgotten how lovely it was to just be. How calming it was to see the infinite expanse of outer space and realize that she was spinning along in the middle of it, part of a whole that was more complex than she could possibly imagine.

One distant star pulsed, outshining its neighbors, and Wren watched it for a while. Perhaps it was worth taking a closer look. When would she get another chance to use an ancient telescope? She rose, deciding that it was probably best to blow out the candle, which was now nearly melted into a flat puddle of purple, but she froze halfway to her feet. Because she'd been looking in the opposite direction, she'd nearly missed it. The steady stream of stardust smoke hadn't dissipated after all. Either that or she was seeing things. She squinted her eyes, and it was clearer now: a spiraling web of the darkest stardust radiating up and out from the candle like a silver pathway in the purpling sky.

One star near the end of the pathway shone blindingly bright, blurring her vision, and the next moment she was back in the black-and-white dream world. She stood on the edge of a quarry, with hundreds of small shapes bent low to chip away at the earth. Mostly young children, it seemed, though some appeared to be closer to Wren's age, or even teenagers.

One after another they raised their faces, a chorus of oohs and ahhs as they pointed beyond Wren to the night sky above. Wren looked up and saw a tumultuous funnel, spinning out in a Milky Way–like swirl that took on a diamond shape. A loud cheer erupted from the children in front of her, their hands raised high, ragged clothes fluttering in the wind.

A little girl near the front spied Wren. "Look at her!" she exclaimed, eyes wide. A taller form drew near—the younger girl's sister, perhaps?—and placed a protective arm around her shoulder. The second girl looked up at Wren, and despite her dirt-smudged face, Wren recognized her. *The shepherdess from the first vision.*

"Dreamer!" the shepherdess shouted, but her voice was soon lost in the cheers of the others, who one by one were staring up at the strange phenomenon in the stars. "Dreamer! Tell them to find the out—" Her words were cut off. The scene flared blindingly white and then Wren was back on the astronomy rooftop with Jill, who was yanking hard on Wren's shirt sleeve.

"Do you want us to leave you behind?" Jill pulled Wren back into the observatory. "Now you *have* to leave, and you *have* to take me with you." Jill sprang across the room, Wren stumbling after, the hope on the shepherdess's face flashing through her mind. What was it the girl was saying? Something about finding something outside, maybe? Something Wren should tell someone. But what? And to whom?

Simon was waiting for them at the bottom of the stairwell.

"Not through the Crooked House," Jill gasped, herding them over to the cliff face. "All those questions about Elsa and the Ms, like you didn't know." She gave Wren a wild-eyed look. "And then you go and write their name across the sky?"

"What?" Wren tried to get Jill to stop, so that she could make sense of what she was saying, but Jill scrambled over the precarious-looking ladder hidden in the bushes. "What are you talking about? And where's Jack?"

Just then, Jack came puffing up, his cloak bunched up in his arms. "Almost forgot this in the tower." He scuttled past Wren and down the ladder after Jill.

Wren turned to Simon. "What's going on?"

"Nothing good," Simon said, preparing to back down the ladder. "Jack told us you lit one of Boggen's candles. That pathway it made? Look at it now."

Wren didn't have to search long. The silvery web arched across the sky, and there at the top of it, where the pulsing star used to be, was the glowing, unmistakable mark of the Magicians.

Wren had little energy for further conversation as she slipped and slid her way down the cliff face. Whenever they passed close to the green doors, she could hear the sound of the summoning gong, the reminder that she hadn't just said the *M*-word, she'd written it across the sky. She wondered fleetingly what would happen to Mary now or where Liza and Baxter were, but it took all her concentration not to fall off the mountainside. She would have to figure out how to find them later.

They raced past the door they had first exited what felt like ages before and sprinted down the narrow path. It was in worse repair here, and the places where it was in good condition, where a stone stairway curved down, were soon outnumbered by spots that had been left untended, some so badly crumbling that Jack began muttering that he thought they should brave the inside of the Crooked House.

They reached one such gap and Jill came to a full stop. The rock had eroded so much that there was a wide gap across to the other side.

"We can go back up to the next level," Jill said. "It's near the greenhouse, and I think I could bluff our way through. From there we could go straight down to the laundry. The apprentices there are usually the last to hear what's going on, and even if they have heard, they won't think it's us that lit the pathway."

"Too risky," Wren said, thinking of how Elsa's spies were everywhere. "We should jump."

Simon made it across easily. He barely needed a running start. Wren stood at the edge of the gap, pressing one side up against the solid wall of the mountain. Now that it was her turn, it looked awfully far to jump. Her knees tingled at the shadowy blackness of the ground far below.

"C'mon, Wren," Simon said, one foot braced down the edge and his hand outstretched. "Jump."

Wren took a deep breath and sprang forward, her heart throbbing through the breathless moment, and then she was toppling into Simon and sending him stumbling backward. Jack and Jill followed right behind. Wren's knees ached with the pounding descent. She and Simon were near the bottom when she heard Jack's cry of alarm from behind. He'd misstepped, or rather the mountain was giving way, or there was a rockslide. It was hard to tell, but a billowing cloud of dust mixed with the sound of falling gravel, and when Wren could next see, Jack and Jill were gone, and the cliffside was smooth.

"Jack!" Wren cried, sprinting past Simon down the final feet of their descent. Together they circled around to the site of the rockslide. Dust filled the air, and Wren pulled the front of her shirt up over her nose so she wouldn't have to breathe it in. "Jill? Are you okay?"

"Over here." Jill's answering groan led them to her. Jill was sitting up, flexing one ankle, her face smudged with dust. "I think I sprained it," she said.

"Jack!" Wren bent down over the still form. He was still breathing, but the large gash near his temple had started to bleed.

"Can you hear us, Jack?" Simon bent low. "Don't move your neck."

"Ohhhh," Jack groaned. "That was . . . not good." He opened his eyes, and the whites were bright against his dirt-covered face. Bracing his hands under him, he sat up. "What happened?"

"You slid down the last bit of the Crooked House," Wren said, pulling Jill up to a standing position. She limped forward, her mouth twisted in pain.

Simon braced his arm under Jack and helped him to his feet. Together they made their way across the valley floor to what, for the first time in her life, Wren found to be a happy sight: the falcon mews.

TWENTY-ONE

Row, row, row your boat,
Gently down a stream.
Merrily, merrily, merrily, merrily
Life is but a dream.

The falcon mews were empty except for the ancient Fiddler who worked there, and he squinted at them as though he had poor eyesight.

"It's the falcons you're wanting, is it?" He got to his feet, and Wren wondered if it was humanly possible for a person to move any slower. He reached for a lantern hanging on an old nail.

"We don't need the light," Wren said. "We're kind of in a hurry."

"Hasty, hasty," the old Fiddler said. "You young ones are always in a rush. The birds don't like it." He lit the lantern and then inched his way forward, Wren and the others crowded on his heels, until they were finally inside, where the falcons were roosting for the night.

It didn't take Simon long to spot his bird. The falcon hopped up onto his gauntleted forearm and rode smoothly out to the mews yard. Jill followed, intently watching Simon's every move as though she was memorizing the rhyme. Even Jack, as hurt as he was, began to quickly make his falcon grow, leaving Wren alone in the mews, where she tried to find her bird and instead managed to shoo away all the others.

"Having some trouble?" The old Fiddler came up behind her, ruffling the head feathers of the falcon perched on his shoulder.

"I'm fine," Wren lied. She clenched her fist to hide her trembling hands.

Simon's falcon was almost fully grown, and Wren willed herself not to panic. This was the worst possible time to screw up the flying thing. Who knew how long before Elsa and the others would think to check the falcon mews?

"Now would you look at that?" The old Fiddler pointed up at the sky, staring slack-jawed at the swirling gateway. "It's been many years since I've seen the

like." He squinted at Wren shrewdly. "You wouldn't
know anything about that, would you?"

"I know they're ringing the summoning bell inside
the Crooked House." Wren dodged his question. "All
full Fiddlers must attend, but we apprentices have an
urgent errand." With any luck, he would believe her
and leave them alone in the mews.

"A summoning?" The Fiddler frowned down at her.
"Well, hurry up and find your falcon. I don't want to
be late."

Wren didn't bother telling him that wasn't likely.
The man still moved with excruciating slowness as he
handed saddles to the boys. And then Wren heard it.
The awful hissing-squawking sound that her falcon
made when it was especially angry.

The old Fiddler laughed. "Such a feisty she-falcon. I
rather think it says something about you."

"Thanks a lot."

"Wren." Jack had grown his bird now, too, and both
he and Jill were watching Wren. And waiting. "C'mon.
Let's go."

Wren eased her way over to the falcon, holding one
hand out, cupped into a small bowl filled with a pinch
of the stardust. The falcon shifted on its claws, flicking

a twitching wing in her direction, but it stayed put. Wren crept closer. *Nearly there.* If she could just get within reach—and then the floor creaked under her, sending the falcon soaring into the sky with a final insulting screech.

The air around Wren grew thick with humidity. She stomped one foot, fighting the pounding headache, trying to remember what she'd learned about controlling her thoughts, but it wasn't helping very much. A distant rumble of thunder hinted at a storm to come. Wren tried breathing deeply. If the Fiddler Council wasn't already hunting for her, there was no need to remind them she was a Weather Changer.

"Wren? Remember what Liza said." Simon's voice was cautionary, as though he thought she'd forgotten about the weird weather thing. "If you don't control it, it will control you."

Wren ground her teeth. "Just a minute." She counted her breaths. If she could slow her heart down and clear the heat from her face, maybe then she could avoid the storm.

"Identify your response to the stardust, and then you can channel it appropriately." The old Fiddler's hand rested on her shoulder.

Wren's response told her that she wanted to swat his hand away. "I'm angry," she said through clenched teeth.

"Good," the Fiddler said as though he were a therapist. "What does your anger look like?"

Wren shut her eyes. "A hot ball of light." It burned in her chest, the same feeling that made her want to sprint off in the other direction.

"Use the stardust," the Fiddler said, and Wren felt the warm embrace of the magic as the Fiddler tossed some into the air above her. "Make the ball."

Wren tightened her jaw, focusing on the searing heat inside, channeling her frustration and anger, and cupped her hands to catch the stardust. She made the movements Baxter had taught them, the one for the starlamp. The words for the rhyme came out stiff, as though she was forcing them out, and the next moment her anger was gone, replaced by the brightest, roundest, most brilliant starlamp of all.

"Excellent," the Fiddler said. "I could tell you were a feisty one."

The air returned to normal, the heaviness gone, and the humidity evaporated. Wren took a deep breath. She felt relaxed, as though her bird flying off at the worst possible moment could be a ridiculous joke.

"We'll have to ride double," Jack said, pulling Jill up onto his falcon. "Until your bird is in a better mood, that is."

"Building trust is a crucial piece of the Fiddler-bird relationship," the old Fiddler said, reaching down to adjust the strap on Simon's saddle.

"I've heard." Wren pulled herself up and flung one leg over the falcon. "But how do you teach a psycho bird to trust someone?"

"Oh," the Fiddler said, tottering back toward the mews as Simon's bird began his preflight run. "I wasn't talking about your falcon."

The falcons needed little guidance, but even if they had, Simon had also taken detailed notes about the route on their first trip, so they arrived back at Pippen Hill without incident. Wren held tight to Simon's waist as his falcon dipped down and landed in the clearing in the middle of the wood. It was earlier in the day here, the golden light of afternoon sending leaf shadows playing on the grassy field. Simon immediately unsaddled his falcon and led it to food and water, but Wren gave it a wide berth. She'd had enough of falcons for one day. Besides, the relaxed feeling from earlier was gone, and now the question of what they should do next loomed overhead. Would the Fiddlers follow them here?

From overhead came a most unwelcome and familiar squawking sound. A normal-sized falcon swooped in front of Wren, dipping low enough to peck her between the shoulder blades, before soaring off.

"Why, you little"—Wren shouted at the red tail feathers of her bird—"I'm not happy to see you either!" Her falcon landed on a gnarled old bush, settling its wings with what looked to Wren like an unmistakably triumphant expression.

"Fine. You win," Wren said, stomping around to join the others.

"They'll check the apprentice quarters first, I imagine," Jill said.

"Mary will know." Simon hung up his saddle on the peg by the door.

"But will she tell the others?" Jack reached down to splash water from the trough over his face.

"You look awful," Wren told him. Some of the blood from the cut was gone, but his skin was very pale, revealing dark circles under his eyes.

"I feel awful," Jack said. "I could really use an ice pack or something."

Jill's cheeks grew rosy. "I'm pretty good at healing. I could give it a try."

"Like with stardust?" Jack raised an eyebrow. "I don't know about that."

"Well, Mary does have that herb room at Pippen Hill," Simon said. "If anyone knows which is which, we could use that."

"Forget the herbs," Wren said. Being in the Crooked House for so long had them all thinking like Fiddlers. They had other options now. "Jack and Jill, you guys stay here and get cleaned up. Simon, come with me." Wren wanted to press pause on all the Fiddler craziness. She wanted to forget about the fact that she had royally screwed things up by lighting the Magicians' gateway. To forget about the horrible dreams and Cole's unblinking stare and Elsa's endless spies, and the way everyone there seemed to think she was helping Boggen. She wanted pizza. And sci-fi movies. And her old boring life. "We're going to my house."

"Hello? Who's there?" Wren's dad called out from his home office when she let herself in the front door with her key. It seemed like she hadn't been home in years.

"It's me!" she shouted, and fought to blink back the tears that threatened to spill over.

"Wren!" Her dad was beaming, and she ran over to give him a hug. "Are you okay?" he asked when she didn't let go. "What's wrong?"

"I've missed you, that's all." Wren scrubbed a hand across her eyes. "Is Mom home?"

"She's upstairs. Come into the kitchen and I'll tell her you're here."

"Simon's with me." Wren pointed back to the front door. "Okay if he comes in, too?"

"Of course!" her dad said, but Wren could see the curiosity in his eyes as he looked past her to the front door. Which was when Wren realized how they must appear. Simon's apprentice cloak was streaked with dirt from the slide down the mountain. Glancing at her front, she saw that hers was hardly better. Several buttons had popped off and one sleeve hung at an angle. She slipped it off with an uneasy smile.

"Falcons are messy animals." She waved Simon in, hoping her dad wouldn't look too closely. Once everyone was done hugging and oohing and ahhing over how much they had missed Wren and why hadn't she

called and how quiet things were without her, they all
sat at the kitchen table. Her mom poured both Wren
and Simon a big glass of milk. "So how is the urban
farm experiment going? Your texts are so short I hardly
know what to make of it."

"Busy," Wren said. As happy as she was to be home,
it was going to be hard to juggle the truth. "And
interesting."

"How are the falcons?" her dad asked, bringing a
plate of cookies to the table.

"Hard," Wren said, happy to be completely honest
about something. "We don't get along so well, but I'm
hoping that will improve."

"That's somewhat of an understatement," Simon
said matter-of-factly.

"How is the play?" Wren knew she should hurry.
That Jack was waiting and the Fiddlers might be coming, but she wanted to savor the moment, to pretend for
a minute that everything was normal. She took a bite
of her cookie, which tasted better than anything she'd
eaten in the Crooked House, even Baxter's baking.

"Great! We started rehearsals a few days ago, and
I think we're in for some rave reviews." Her mom
gushed about how rich the Mother Goose rhymes were

for drama. "A reporter from the town newspaper even wrote an article about the origin of the Mother Goose rhymes. Did you know that some people think they are connected to historical events?" she asked. "Like Old King Cole might have been King Henry VIII. Or one guy thought the Land of Nod might have stood for the New World. Pretty crazy stuff."

"Yeah, I might have heard something like that." Wren felt a wild desire to giggle. If her mom only knew.

"I spent days researching it all down at the theater. The hardest thing was setting aside all those notes to actually write the darn play. What I think is the most interesting part is that many of these rhymes are so unknown. I'd never read some of them before." She refilled her coffee cup. "There are all these conspiracy theories. Like this one rhyme that's about the corruption in Parliament. And another is supposed to be a hidden treasure map. And there's a door that only opens with a forgotten key, and the goose that lays the golden egg, of course. And the best is the idea that Little Jack Horner is a call to rebellion against the monarch. The plum pie is supposed to be the crown. It's all too perfect." She scooped some sugar into her coffee and stirred. "Could you have ever imagined 'The Three

Little Kittens' as a coded message?" She took a sip of coffee and smiled at Wren. "You used to ask me to sing that to you over and over again."

"I remember," Wren said, rolling her eyes.

"I always wondered if you would be a poet or a writer or something." She shook her head and set her cup down. "And look at you! Learning falconry instead. Life is full of funny things."

"That's for sure." Wren brushed the last of the cookie crumbs from her fingers. It seemed that even here, far from the Crooked House, she couldn't escape being a Fiddler.

She excused herself to go the bathroom and left Simon to answer all her parents' questions about falconry. She found the Tylenol easily and grabbed some antibiotic ointment and bandages while she was at it. She tucked them into her hoodie pocket and stood for a moment at the bathroom mirror. Her hair was windblown, and her face was smudged with dirt on her chin. She ran some water and washed it off. She shouldn't look any different than before she left, but somehow the face looking back at her seemed more than just tired. Wren looked older. Like she knew things. She peered closer—were those wrinkles around her eyes? Then the wrinkles grew to ripples, like water in a pond, as the mirror shimmered and changed, until Wren found herself staring into the reflection of an entirely different room.

It appeared to be a storeroom of some kind, dusty and cloaked in shadows. A long table with a few stacks of paper was shoved against one wall that had thick metal pipes running in different directions. Pinned over the top of them was a canvas covered with scribbled equations. A bed that looked recently slept in stood next to a metal pan holding glowing coals. A book lay open on the nearby table, and even though some of the words were misspelled, Wren could still read the rhyme.

King and Queen of Cantelon
How many miles to Babylon?
Eight and eight, and other eight.
Will I get there by candlelight?
If your horse be good and your spurs be bright.
How many men have ye?
Mae nor ye daur come and see.

"Dreamer." The shepherdess crouched near one wall, casting glances toward the doorway as though she didn't belong there either. "The rhyme worked. I was hoping you'd come."

"Who are you?" Wren said. "And what do you mean *the rhyme worked*?"

The shepherdess pointed at the lit coals on the pan. "It brought you here, didn't it? Are you an Alchemist?" the girl asked breathlessly. "You've got to be. Say you're an Alchemist."

"I guess so," Wren said, pulling back as the girl reached for her hands. "I'm an apprentice."

The shepherdess glanced over her shoulder so often that Wren felt even jumpier than she did before.

"You've got to tell the other Alchemists that we need their help." She shook Wren's hands, her anxiety written plainly on her face. "Tell them Boggen is coming back to Earth."

"Boggen," Wren whispered. "When?"

"Very soon!" the girl hissed. "The Great Experiment failed. He's destroyed the Land of Nod with his magic, and now he wants Earth for himself." The shepherdess's grip was fierce, her nails cutting into the skin of Wren's palms. "He's already used the key to unlock the gateway on Nod's side, and someone on Earth has been helping him to find the key for your side," the girl went on. "We are running out of time. The gateway is lit. Perhaps even now the one with the key flies to open it. You Alchemists are our only hope." She opened her eyes wide, pleading for Wren to understand. "Do you hear what I'm saying? Nod has already fallen to his evil ways. Earth is next."

"Robin!" The voice that shouted from outside stopped Wren's breath cold. She knew that voice, the one from her dreams. The bent old man. The strong tall one in his black-and-white room. Both voices were one and the same. The voice of Boggen. The mark on her neck burned at the sound.

"Robin! Where are you?" Boggen's angry words sounded like stone scraping stone. "Why have you left the device's furnace untended?"

"You must go now." Robin hurried over to the fiery metal pan and doused the coals with water. "There's no time to explain. Tell the others before it's too late."

The entire scene disappeared in a puff of smoke, leaving Wren standing in her own bathroom at home, heart pounding and mouth dry.

Boggen is coming. Wren thought of Robin's panicked face and realized that the Council had been right. Someone *was* helping Boggen to open the gateway. She replayed what Robin had told her. All of it confirmed what they had suspected, except for one piece of new information: where Boggen was now. *The Land of Nod.* Something about that name tugged at her memory. She had heard it before, sometime recently, but she couldn't place it. She bent down and scooped cold water over her face. It had been a nice thirty minutes at home. A nice half hour of pretending things could go back to the way they were. But they wouldn't. She was a Fiddler now, and there was no pretending that away.

TWENTY-TWO

Star light, star bright,
First star I see tonight;
I wish I may, I wish I might,
Find the thing I need tonight.

As soon as she entered Pippen Hill, Wren heard the rumble of a conversation.

". . . about the Land of Nod," Jill was saying. "It could be anywhere."

Wren's throat tightened. She thought of what Robin had told her. That Boggen had ruined the Land of Nod. And now Boggen was working with someone here to try and ruin Earth. Wren's breath sounded loud in her ears. How well did she know Jill anyway?

Wren put a staying hand on Simon's arm. "Wait," she whispered.

Simon poked a thumb toward the closed door leading to the kitchen. "Why? It's just Jack and Jill."

"Shh!" Wren moved closer. "They're talking again."

"Well, there are other parts to it," Jill's voice was
quiet. "The idea of dreams, for instance," and her voice
dropped even lower so Wren couldn't hear what she
was saying.

"Really," Jack whistled. "That's interesting. How
do you know all this?"

"Elsa's done a lot of research," Jill said, and Wren
thought of how Jill had admitted she had read Elsa's
notes about Boggen. Maybe Jill was using that information to figure out how to help Boggen open the
gateway. "Though most people would rather not talk
about it. The thing is, there hasn't been a Weather
Changer since before the Civil War."

Wren held her breath. *Weather Changer?*

"Does Wren know?" Jack said, and then was quiet.
No moving. No speaking. Just quiet. Until the silence
was broken by the scrape of a chair.

"How about some tea? I'll just get it from this cupboard over here." Jill's voice was unnaturally loud.

Wren looked over at Simon, who was studying the
door thoughtfully, and pressed closer so that her ear

was almost up against it. She was so busy straining to hear what they were saying that she wasn't prepared for it to swing open. She sucked in a gasp as she, with Simon behind her, tumbled into the kitchen.

"Stop! Don't! It's Wren!" Jack held one hand out to where Jill stood with a frying pan raised above her head.

"What are you guys doing sneaking up on us like that?" he continued, his face the angriest Wren had ever seen it.

"I thought you were Elsa," Jill whispered, sinking back against the kitchen table.

"And you were going to whap her with this?" Simon plucked the frying pan from her hands and set it on the stove.

Jill shrugged. "Getting knocked on the head will hurt a Fiddler just as much as an ordinary person. Stardust won't help when you're unconscious."

"I suppose that makes sense." Simon moved to the fridge and started pulling out sandwich makings. A loaf of bread. Mustard and mayonnaise. Some sliced cheese.

Behind him, Jack stood near the table, feeding dried meat to his falcon. He hadn't wanted to leave it at the mews, and Wren didn't blame him. If the Fiddler Council showed up, a speedy getaway could be lifesaving, and if her falcon didn't despise her, Wren would keep it close, too.

"So what were you saying about the Land of Nod?" Wren asked, watching Jill's face carefully, but she seemed superfocused on spreading mustard on her piece of bread.

"Nod?" she said, reaching for the cheese. "What's with all the sudden interest in—"

There was a clumping sound from the pantry and then a groan. "Ooooh." Jack came out rubbing his head. "How did I miss seeing that shelf in there?"

"You are in rough shape," Wren said, dumping the contents of her pocket onto the counter. "How are you feeling?"

"Better." Jack squeezed some of the ointment onto his finger and rubbed it on his forehead. "Except for the what-do-we-do-now part."

"Right," Wren said, grabbing a piece of bread and eating it plain. "So. What do we do now?"

"As I see it, we have three options." Simon folded some cheese into his sandwich. "One, we return to the Crooked House and talk to the Council about what we know. Or at least talk to Mary, Liza, or Baxter."

"No way," Jill said. "We go back there and Elsa

will have us locked in the dungeons for a century. Besides"—she folded her arms across her chest—"now that Wren lit the M's candle, the Council will never let her out of their sight. They need her."

"Need me for what? I didn't even mean to do anything!"

"Doesn't matter." Jill shrugged. "You think they'll believe that you—the first Weather Changer to appear in hundreds of years—*accidentally* opened a gateway with the M's mark on it?" She took a bite and talked around it. "They'll have you under lock and key until they figure out what they want to do with you."

Wren slid onto a bar stool and leaned her elbows on the counter. "I wonder if we could send word to Mary without actually going back to the Crooked House. How long do you think it will take her to figure out we came here?"

"Who knows?" Simon ran his hands through his hair and shrugged. "I haven't seen her at all since that day she sent us to the repository."

"Yeah," Jack said. "Nice how Mary's always abandoning us. It would have been great for her to stick around for two seconds before she left us on our own in the Crooked House."

"Mary's our friend," Wren shot at him, not bothering to hide the irritation she felt at discovering Jack talking to Jill about her behind her back. She took a deep breath. It wasn't Jack's fault she had a no-win situation to deal with. Either Wren risked being trapped at the Crooked House for a lifetime or she waited for Mary to come home and had no way of acting on Robin's warning.

"We've got to think," Wren said, propping her chin up in her hands. "What does this all mean? Mary, Baxter, and Liza are there, but we've no way of contacting them without getting trapped by Elsa. I need to talk to Mary, or at least somebody does. She needs to know that we found the star map and candles in Boggen's lab. We need to tell her she was right—Boggen probably is working with someone here to find the key." Wren didn't want to tell them about her latest dream—not with Jill standing right there—which would confirm for them all that there was no *probably* about it.

"What key?" Jill said.

"We're not exactly sure." Wren watched Jill's face carefully to see how she would react. "He would have had to hide it before they all passed through the gateway. It won't be hard for him to open the gateway on

Nod's side, but he needs someone here to find the key to unlock this side."

Jill looked genuinely puzzled, like this was all new information for her. Either she was a very good actor or she really knew nothing about the key.

Wren folded her arms and laid her head down on them. "Maybe the rest of you could tell the Council. They might not be so interested in you since it was me who lit up the gateway."

"Fat chance. On what planet do you think they'd believe we all weren't involved?" Jack said, his falcon underscoring his words with a squawk. "There's no way I'm going back to the Council until I can prove I'm on the right side."

"That's a brilliant idea, Jack!" Wren gasped. "All we need to do is prove we aren't involved. If we can reveal who's really been communicating with Boggen, they'll know it wasn't us."

"And how exactly do we do that?" Simon said.

"Unless you hand deliver the person who's found the golden key or whatever, I'd say you're stuck." Jill popped the last bite of her sandwich into her mouth.

"Of course!" Wren said, latching on to the idea. Even better than delivering the culprit, she could bring the Council the key itself, and they could destroy it or do whatever they needed to do to stop Boggen. If she did that, surely they'd know she wasn't on Boggen's side. "What about your grandpa, Jack? He helped you find the message stone, right? Maybe he has something else about the key in all his conspiracy stuff."

Jack's face looked uncertain. "I don't think so. I've looked through it all already. Besides, Grandpa wouldn't like to, um, see me like this." He shook his head and gave a little moan, wincing. "Can you give me a hand, Jill?" Jack tossed Jill the bandage, and she began to wrap it carefully around his head.

"What about the rhyme?" Jack said. "If we found the rhyme Boggen made for the gateway, that might be enough to prove which side we're on. Any ideas about that?"

"So that's what they were after," Jill said meditatively. She secured the final length of the bandage behind Jack's ear. "Ever since the summoning, all the Fiddlers have ordered their apprentices to look for old rhymes, ones that the Ms modified. They did that, you know, changed the rhymes to make them do what they wanted. Elsa even had me skip a couple of workdays to hunt." She chewed her lip. "If there was a rhyme like that in the Crooked House, someone would have found it."

"That's it!" Wren stood up, knocking over her glass of water in her haste. "The rhyme isn't in the Crooked House!"

TWENTY-THREE

The strangest things are there for me,
Both things to eat and things to see,
And many frightening sights abroad
Till morning in the Land of Nod.

A policewoman was setting out traffic cones to block off reserved spaces when they arrived at the town park. SPRINGFEST CENTER STAGE, a sign proclaimed, MOTHER GOOSE RETOLD. Wren could see the main performance area and the temporary shelter that served as the theater's backstage. When she knocked on the makeshift door, a woman dressed in a pink flowery dress and blue cape opened it. She was holding an oversized wooden cane. "May I help you?"

"I'm Suzette Matthews's daughter," Wren said. "And these are my friends." She nodded to Simon, Jill, and Jack, who stood a little behind her. Jack had used stardust to cloak his falcon, so even though it fluttered its wings and resettled onto Jack's shoulder, the lady in front of them didn't blink an eye.

"You must be Wren!" The woman's stage makeup creased into a huge smile. "So you're the one we have to thank for the Mother Goose theme!" She grinned. "Your mom's not here yet, but you can wait for her if you want. Our last dress rehearsal starts soon."

"That sounds good." Wren peered behind her at the bustling theater. "I wouldn't mind having a peek backstage anyway."

As they followed the woman, they could see a man wearing a flannel shirt teetering on a ladder and fidgeting with lights that hung from the two-by-fours serving as scaffolding.

"That's too bright," an actor who was standing in the center of the stage and wearing some sort of poufy trousers and green tights said. "And it's off center. Angle it more to the left."

Behind him, two women were rehearsing their scenes. Something about three blind mice and how nameless corporations were going to cut off all their tails.

"So it's an interpretation of the rhymes, I guess," Simon said, and their guide nodded.

"Yep. Irony is the main selling point. The tame nursery rhymes set against corporate greed and how it's destroying our environment. Your mom's a genius, Wren." She pointed to her dress. "My character, for instance. I've lost my sheep, because they don't have clean grazing land anymore." She waved her crook up at the ceiling. "Take that, Monsanto!"

"So does my mom have an office here or something?" Wren felt the urgency of their search twitch between her shoulder blades. Who knew how long it would take to go through her mom's play notes?

"You could call it that," Bo-Peep said as they skirted some actors wearing hazardous waste suits. They pushed past a rack of costumes to find the chaotic backstage area.

"Stop moving around," said a woman kneeling to adjust the hem of an actor's ball gown. "Your costume doesn't need to be perfect. I'd settle for it not falling off, but if you keep squirming, you're going to have neither."

There were volunteers moving props into place and others using paint to touch up set pieces.

"One hour until go-time." A stage manager dressed all in black swooped through with a clipboard, and the volume of the frenzied activity tripled.

"Over there." Bo-Peep pointed to a curtained-off area in the very back. "Y'all can be here if you keep quiet, but you'll have to leave before curtain call." She turned to go.

"Thanks," Wren said, pushing aside the fabric and spying the familiar sight of her mom's coffee thermos on an old folding table in the corner. The surface was covered with three-ring binders and file folders wedged neatly between bookends.

"Thank goodness my mom is a neat freak," Wren said, handing several binders to Simon and a file to Jill. Little Post-its stuck out to catalog things by theme. "The rhyme we're looking for will be in a section on mysteries or historical basis for the rhymes. Something like that. Or she could have a section on conspiracy theories." She shoved a folder at Jack. "You should be good at looking for those."

Wren flipped through the pages. She found rhymes about porridge and others about hens. Blackbirds and sheep and cows. Butchers and bakers and candlestick makers, but no keys. She wasn't misremembering, was she? Her mom had distinctly said "forgotten key" when she was talking about the goose that laid golden eggs. That had to be it.

The stage manager was calling for quiet. They were getting closer to go-time.

"Hurry," Wren told the others. "We'll have to leave before they start performing." Jill sat cross-legged with her back up against the wall, Simon next to her. Jack was pacing back and forth, his falcon twitching nervously on his shoulder. Wren wondered what all the theater people would say if they could see it. Her eye caught the back of an actor carrying a chicken under her arm. With all the craziness, they might not even notice.

Wren skimmed her mom's loopy handwritten notes, wondering how many rhymes she had actually transcribed. Most were labeled, a few flagged for use in the play. At first, it seemed that her mom had organized them by subject, but then she found a folder where they were cataloged by rhyme. There were only a few notes here. *The King and Queen of Hearts. The Old Woman from France.* And Wren's gaze stopped fast on the last one: *The Land of Nod.*

She ran her finger down the page.

From breakfast on through all the day
At home among my friends I stay,
But every night, I go abroad
Afar into the Land of Nod.

All by myself I have to go
With none to tell me what to do—
All alone beside the streams
And up the mountainsides of dreams.

The strangest things are there for me,
Both things to eat and things to see,
And many frightening sights abroad
Till morning in the Land of Nod.

Try as I like to find the way,
I never can get back by day.
Nor can remember plain and clear
The curious music that I hear.

Wren's heartbeat quickened. This rhyme explained what she'd experienced with the weird visions. Seen in that light, what Robin had told her made more sense. Perhaps she wasn't getting messages in her dreams.

Perhaps she was actually seeing what was happening on Nod. What else had her mom found about Nod? Something about Boggen? She flipped through the pages. She had to be getting closer. She read a different poem about three old witches, mainly because they were sleeping in it, but it referenced nothing remotely close to keys—and then she found it.

"Guys, I think this is it," Wren said in a shaky voice. Jill stopped reading and looked up at her, and Simon reached for his own notebook, pencil ready to write down whatever Wren was about to say. Jack was over at her shoulder in an instant.

"You found the rhyme?" he said, his eyes wide with excitement. "Lemme see."

"Listen to this," Wren said, running her fingers along the words as she read the rhyme aloud:

I had a little treasure tree,
Nothing would it bear,
But a silver lockbox,
And a golden key;
The King of Nod's daughter
came to visit me,
And all for the sake of my little treasure tree.
So I danced over water

I hopped by the bay
Forty laps of moonlight
Will open up the way.

"I wonder what the forty laps of moonlight means," Wren said, skimming the poem again. "It's got to be tied in to the amount of stardust used somehow. What do you guys think?" she asked, but no one answered. In that moment, Wren realized that the room had gone eerily quiet, too quiet even for the minutes before a performance, and that she no longer heard the familiar scratching of Simon's pencil. She glanced over to see him fast asleep on the floor, one arm curved protectively around his note-book. Jill slumped down next to him, snoring softly.

"Simon?" Wren said, taking one step forward before the room began to spin around her. She reached for the table to balance herself, but managed to catch only the edge of the folding chair, sending it crashing down as she stumbled to the floor, right before everything went black.

Wren woke to find herself standing in a silent hallway. The air hummed with the sound of a million wings. What had just happened? Was she having another vision of Nod?

She moved down the hall, and she could hear voices, the man's and woman's, the same ones she heard in her very first dream. This time, the woman sounded terrified. Her tone was shrill, and every word came out sharp. "We have to hurry!" she said. "What will we do if we run out of time?"

Wren quickened her pace. She needed to find them, ask them about Boggen and what was happening on Nod.

The man's voice was a low rumble, but even he sounded frightened. "You worry too much, Elsbeth. We have to do what we have to do."

"He has Robin," the woman nearly shrieked. "There's no more time for her. Or the rest of Nod."

What had happened to Robin? How were these people connected to her? Wren sped her steps toward a door. The voices were coming from behind there. She had to find out what Boggen was planning to do. If someone at the Crooked House was working to help him come back to Earth, the worst possible thing would be to deliver the rhyme into the wrong hands. She had to know who was helping Boggen. The urgency of her need took hold, and she felt the same shifting sensation, the one that took her different places in the dream world, and the voices were gone.

She pushed open the door, but the owners of the voices weren't behind it. The sound of their argument cut off into silence, and instead, she was faced with a long hall, glowing on either side with blue fire and marked with the rows of U-shaped lines bent in on each other, matched up to look like pairs of wings. Her heart thumped loud. She was getting closer at last. She began to run, hurrying around the twists and turns, each footstep taking her closer to where she felt she was supposed to go.

She trailed her hands along the walls, the rough edges of the pattern marking her skin. The humming sound grew louder, urging her on with a pulsing intensity. Up ahead, she could see a glow of brighter blue, and she was a few steps away when it snuffed out like a candle, and she was alone in a dark passageway.

She felt empty inside, as though all hope had drained away, and her body refused to move. She wondered if she would stay planted there forever. She reached out a hand to touch the wall next to her. Perhaps she could still feel the carvings. She instinctively knew they would take her where she needed to go.

But the walls were smooth, damp to the touch.

Besides, the humming was gone. In its place, Wren heard a strange rough sound, like someone sawing on a piece of wood.

It was coming from behind her, and Wren retraced her steps. Nothing was the same: no tunnel, no glowing walls, no sound of the man and woman talking. She was in a stairwell. An old building, she'd wager, with a pipe-lined ceiling above and weathered stone beneath her feet.

The sawing sound was coming from a room up ahead. Wren could see the gilding around a green door, but there was a landing in front of it, a wide-open space that she would have to cross.

For the first time, Wren felt uncertain. Should she find the cause of the noise? Or stay in the shadows? A humming sound drifted toward her from somewhere up ahead, like the low thrum of an engine. The ever-present sawing noise barely drowned it out. A factory, perhaps.

Wren tiptoed toward the perimeter of light, peering into a scene that looked like it had come straight from a history book.

Gas-lit lamps lined the walls and these, along with a blazing hearth fire, lit up the crowded room. Women in drab corseted dresses and men in worn clothes leaned over worktables filled with strange apparatuses. Some reminded Wren of old-fashioned sewing machines, with foot pedals that workers pumped to set the gears spinning. Others looked like giant printing presses, with rollers and cogs maneuvered by small children who operated levers on the side.

Whatever they were doing, it seemed to charge the air with energy. Overhead, a tangled ball of stardust shot jagged sparks down to the machines, but the workers didn't seem to notice. Scurrying servants dressed in ragged clothes bobbed between them, delivering glass bottles full of brightly colored liquids and removing empty trays as the workers continued on. Wren couldn't tell if they were creating the stardust or using it for their frenetic activity, but she needn't have worried that they would notice her. Their attention was completely fixed on their work, as though they couldn't stop for a moment, and Wren thought she knew why. In the center of it all stood a giant statue, a figure holding a large hourglass, the bottom of which was filled with iridescent stones. The top half was nearly empty but for one final stone, tottering on the edge of the funnel. Whoever had made the timepiece had a strange sense of artistry, for as Wren peered closer she saw that the statue was actually a skeleton, its hollow skull leering at the dwindling time as though to give a morbid warning. She drew back with a shiver.

No one in the room seemed to notice how loud the sawing noise had gotten. Or if they did, they didn't care. Wren edged her way out from her hiding spot. She was having difficulty thinking clearly with the awful sawing sound. Back and forth. Back and forth. *I have to find the source.* She was in the middle of the landing now, and no one was looking in her direction. She hurried across to the gilded door. It was cracked open, and now she knew for sure. The sawing noise was definitely coming from in there.

She reached for the handle and waited a heartbeat. She felt a strange reluctance to leave the landing, as though she belonged in the middle of all that work below. She forced herself to turn her back to it, instead nudging the door in front of her open a fraction of an inch. She instantly wished she had stayed away. Her stomach roiled, and she staggered, reaching to the wall for support.

An enormous table filled most of the space inside the room. A solitary individual bent over its surface, gnawing back and forth at the carcass of a giant bird. It wasn't a sawing sound that Wren had been hearing. It was crunching. With every bite, the crunching grew louder.

A pile of bones lay underneath the table, and half the surface was crowded high with more birds. Dozens of them, Wren guessed. And all of them as black as night.

"Don't linger in doorways, Jack," Boggen said, not even looking up from his horrifying meal. "It's very rude."

"I'm not Jack," Wren said, and her mouth grew dry as she realized what it meant.

Jack. She stumbled backward. Boggen was expecting Jack. She felt behind her for the door. If she could just get away, escape onto the balcony, return to the tunnel, she could sort this all out.

"Wake up, Wren," she told herself. "Wake up before it's too late."

But it already was too late.

Boggen looked at her, causing the mark on her neck to flare, and Wren's stomach twisted, forcing her to swallow hard not to be sick.

Boggen's mouth was smeared red with blood. His forehead glistened with sweat. And his eyes. Ice-cold blue eyes looked at Wren with a piercing glare, her own surprise mirrored in his gaze.

"The Weather Changer." He dropped the bird carcass. "I must thank you for your assistance, however unwittingly given. Without you, that idiot boy would never have found the key to the gateway. Or the rhyme." He picked at his bloodstained teeth with a bone. "I am nearly ready to fly. I will thank you in person."

Wren staggered to the doorway, shaking her head back and forth, willing all of this to go away. Jack couldn't be helping Boggen. That would mean he'd been lying to all of them.

She rushed past the workroom, not bothering to hide herself, and she heard cries of alarm and surprise.

"A Dreamer!" someone shouted, and the whirring sound of the assembly line stopped.

"She was in with Boggen!" another cried.

"Quick!" A man's voice this time. "Catch her!"

But they were too slow. Wren hurried into her passageway, hoping that every footstep took her closer to waking up. She heard the commotion behind her, and she was running, running as fast as she could, the wooden floor pounding against her feet.

She heard the voices behind her, screaming for the Dreamer, and the noise of the crowd, growing louder into a nightmarish chant. "Get her! A Dreamer! Get the Dreamer!"

Their voices became drumbeats for Wren's strange flight. She had to get back. She had to warn the others. Figure out a way to stop Jack. The desperation grew inside, until she felt like she might explode. She must have outpaced them, or the dream was changing again, because soon all she could hear was the pounding of her own heart. She kept running anyway, wondering how long the dream could possibly last, when the tunnel abruptly ended, shooting her out into a valley.

Her breathing slowed, and her heart regained its normal rhythm. The valley was calm and nearly silent. Every rustle of wind against the grass felt loud to her ears. She half expected some woodland animal to arrive and start chiding her for being a Dreamer when she heard the humming again, the wings that called to her like no other. She retraced the way she'd come, but no glow lit her way, no familiar etching of wings.

She whirled in a great circle, waiting for a sign, any sign, to tell her which way to go.

"What now?" she screamed into the glorious blue

sky. "What am I supposed to do now?"

But Wren's voice only echoed with the harmony of the beating wings, and she was falling, falling down to the ground, down to the wet grass beneath her palms, falling into sleep, falling awake.

She shot up from where she'd been slouched on the cold floor of the theater. Her clothes clung damply with sweat, and her throat was so dry it hurt. She tried to force down a swallow, pinching herself to make sure she was really awake. No strange voices came from the room beyond. No odd symbols hummed at her. No vision. She was out of the dream.

Instead, she saw Simon right where she'd left him, his head thrown back and mouth open, snoring softly. Jill was dozing next to him, but Jack was nowhere to be seen.

From the stage area, Wren could hear that the play had started. The sound of projected voices built until the actors and actresses were chanting a rhythmic rendition of "Little Boy Blue."

"Simon!" Wren crawled over to him, shaking him roughly on the shoulder. "Simon, wake up!"

"Wha—" He made little smacking sounds with his mouth, his eyelids fluttering open.

"It's Jack, Simon." Wren shook him harder. "It's been Jack all along. He's the one who's been helping Boggen. We've got to stop him! He's been lying to us. About everything."

"What?" Simon was wide awake now.

"Boggen's coming." Wren's thoughts were racing faster than she could get the words out as she told him what she had seen in the dream world. "He said he was getting ready to fly. We've got to stop Jack from opening the gateway before it's too late."

"You dreamed about Boggen?" Jill pushed up to a seated position. "I don't understand."

Wren told her what she'd seen, how her dreams somehow took her to Nod. "He was expecting Jack, because Jack's been visiting him through his dreams." Wren felt jittery inside. Like she would jump out of her skin if they sat there wasting more time talking. "I don't know if Nod is in trouble because of what Jack's doing or for some other reason, but everything's about to get a whole lot worse. Jack's got the rhyme now. And Boggen said that Jack had already found the key." She left out the part where Boggen had credited her for helping him.

"And once he opens the gateway . . ." Jill sprang up.

Wren yanked Simon to his feet. "That's what I've been trying to tell you. Come on! Jack can't have gone far."

From the stage, Wren could hear someone reciting a very different, very angry version of "Mary Had a Little Lamb."

Suddenly, the rhythm of the actors' lines was cut off by a too-authentic scream and the unmistakable sound of a falcon's screech.

Wren tore through the curtain in time to see Jack in the final step of growing his falcon. Jack hadn't bothered to hide his bird, and the backstage workers were all in a fright. One had passed out cold, another stood gaping openmouthed, and the rest cowered, trying to avoid the set pieces that crashed down as Jack's bird hopped and jolted, trying to get room to maneuver. There was yelling and shoving and the stage manager was in the middle of it all, shouting into her headset. "We need to stop the rehearsal. I repeat. Stop the rehearsal."

"Jack!" Wren screamed. "Don't do this!"

"Too late, Wren. You picked your side, and I picked mine. I'm on the right one," Jack said, pulling himself up onto his bird. "Nice knowing you, but I'm off to

Nod." He gave Wren a cold smile. "And don't worry about your pesky falcon. I'll take care of her." His bird backed up, knocking a rack of clothes into Little Miss Muffet's spider, and then Jack was aloft, soaring out of sight.

The actors on the other side of the curtain let out a collective gasp, and then a wild cheer as if Jack's flight was somehow part of the show.

The few backstage workers still on their feet gaped at Wren, Simon, and Jill as though they were aliens from another planet.

"Sorry," Wren mumbled. From the other side of the curtain, her mom's voice bellowed, "What in the world was that? What is going on back there?"

"Run!" Wren said, tearing toward the exit. It was as she passed her mom's office that she saw it, a slim blue book that she had seen once before.

"Jack's notes! He left them!" Wren scooped up the tattered log, dodging and ducking her way through the backstage chaos until finally they were at the door, through it, and back outside. It wasn't until they were at the edge of the park, hidden under the cover of a thicket of trees, that she told the others to stop.

"I saw Jack with this," she panted. "That day we

were cleaning the repository." Simon made a star-lamp so they could see, and Jill crowded close as Wren flipped through it. Long lists of equations, followed by notes that proved he had been hunting for the rhyme all along. Pages torn from a book with detailed information about the capabilities of Weather Changers. A drawing of Boggen's lab they had found underneath the waterfall. Tables where Jack had calculated the amount of stardust required for interplanetary flight, where he'd scribbled rhymes about scraping cobwebs from the moon and riding the paths of the stars. The last part had drawings of instruments Wren had seen in the old Crooked House observatory and, below them, a rhyme:

Sing a song of Fiddlers,
A pocket full of pow'r;
Four-and-twenty blackbirds
Eaten in the tower.

The skies your voice will open
The stars begin to sing.
Light the darkest candle
Through the heavens you will wing.

Wren's stomach flip-flopped. What had Jack meant when he said he would take care of her falcon? An image of Boggen feasting on the birds flashed through her mind. What exactly had he said? That he was almost ready to fly. "Come on!" Wren shouted as she sprinted toward Pippen Hill. "We've got to save the falcons."

TWENTY-FOUR

A little cock-sparrow sat on a green tree,
And he chirruped, he chirruped, so merry was he;
A naughty boy came with his wee bow and arrow
Determined to shoot this little cock-sparrow.

The falcon mews at Pippen Hill echoed Wren's dream of Boggen eating blackbirds. They had run there as fast as they could, but Jack, flying on his falcon, was much faster. By the time they arrived, Jack had done his damage. The forest clearing was littered with clumps of matted feathers, and the iron smell of blood filled the air. As Wren, Simon, and Jill reached the door, a cluster of flies buzzed up and off a pile of something dark. Wren couldn't bring herself to look any closer.

"We're too late," Simon said, his voice grave. "Jack's already gone."

"How could he have done this?" Wren's throat clenched, and she gagged. "He killed them all."

"He didn't just kill them." Jill's mouth twisted down into an ugly, hard shape. "He consumed them." Her face was very pale, with two little spots of color in her cheeks. "This is forbidden magic. The kind the Magicians used to do. Consuming the energy from another living thing." She covered her mouth with both hands and ran toward the nearest tree. "I'm going to be sick."

Simon was silently making his way around the clearing. He paused by each clump, nudging the pile of feathers with the toe of his shoe and peering at it as if it was an observation for a science experiment. Wren wondered if he had found his bird yet.

Every time the thought of her own bird crept in, Wren shoved it out of her mind. She wouldn't wish Jack's awful magic on any living creature. The air felt heavy around her, as though its humidity was pressing in on her like a suffocating blanket. She moved over to the door of the outbuilding, averting her eyes from the red smear on the exterior. What had Boggen done to Jack? How had he convinced him to do this?

Her tears burned hot, and Wren couldn't hold them in anymore. She scrubbed a fist across her eyes. It wasn't as if she even *liked* her falcon. She was so stubborn. And, well, *mean*. Wren tried to steady her breathing, but it was coming out in strange, ragged sobs. She hadn't wanted her falcon to be killed.

"Wren?" Simon's voice sounded distracted. "Are you okay?"

Wren wanted to laugh at him. To tell him that no one is okay when they've seen slaughter. She wanted to ask him why the fact that their friend had murdered their animals wasn't driving him crazy. She wanted to yell and stomp and howl. But she looked into Simon's calm brown eyes, which swam with tears, and she knew that all those things wouldn't change what had happened. It wouldn't bring the falcons back, and it wouldn't stop Jack.

A wet wind began to blow, the kind that happens right before a storm, sending the twisted branches of the nearest bush rattling. One of the shadows reminded Wren of her falcon, how she would roost there, pretending to be asleep. How she would make Wren climb through that stupid bramble bush, as though she had to pass some ridiculous test just to be able to talk to her bird.

"Stubborn thing," Wren said with a half laugh, half

sob. She wondered if her falcon had fought Jack at the end, if her contrariness could have somehow made things easier for her. "Rest in peace." Wren whispered it like a benediction, as though she could make up for the horror of Jack's betrayal.

"Jack's made sure none of us could follow him," Wren said, purposely working to relax her jaw. "Why didn't we see this coming?" She turned and kicked the fencepost closest to her. "I *told* him what I saw in my dreams. I even found the star map for him. And then I just handed him the rhyme. How could I have been so stupid?"

"You're not stupid, Wren," Simon said, coming up next to her. "You are the smartest person I know." He said it so bluntly, as if it was a provable fact. At another time, his words would have been sweet. Now they simply added to the guilt.

"I should've seen it coming." Wren's chest tightened as she thought of Jack's slimy grin, how he had tricked them all. She wanted to scream and throw things. She reached over and grabbed the nearest branch with both hands and shook hard. A chill whistled through the wind, stirring up dust and a flurry of old feathers.

"Wren," Simon said, and his voiced sounded like it

was coming from far away. "Wren, you've got to focus. The weather. It's changing."

Wren knew he was right, but she didn't care. She wanted to lose control. She wanted to rip the bush out by its roots. She wondered if she could make a wind strong enough to do that. Or maybe she could change the weather enough to make it impossible for Jack to fly. Her hair whipped around her face, the ends of it stinging her cheeks. She could hunt Jack down and throw the bush at his sneaky, grinning face.

The next moment, Wren was gasping. Something freezing cold splashed down her shoulders, and her breath came in short choked spurts. Simon stood in front of her holding the now-empty trough of water in both hands. Wren was too surprised to be furious. She spluttered, her shirt cold and wet against her shoulders.

"I'm tired of controlling it," she spit out. "Breathing carefully and relaxing. Not getting worked up. I can't do it anymore." She rubbed her palms over her face. "I didn't ask for this, you know." She realized she was shouting, and that it made no sense to be shouting at Simon. She hadn't even known she felt this way, but as she spoke the words she knew it was true. Some of the strain in her chest eased. The wind itself had disappeared, along with the heavy humidity, leaving behind an ordinary night sky, starlight winking out from behind the puffy clouds.

"I didn't say to control it," Simon said. "I said you have to focus. Save it for Jack."

"I think I know where's Jack's gone." Jill came up to them, wiping a shaking hand across her very pale forehead. "Those instruments were still in the observatory when we left the Crooked House." She grabbed Jack's blue book from Wren, flipped to the final pages, and pointed to the sketches. "If he needs them to unlock the gateway, he'll have to go back for them."

"You're right," Wren said. "We just have to figure out how to get to the Crooked House ourselves." She looked up at the calm sky. "If I get angry again, I could make another wind. Or maybe even a tornado." The ideas were coming so fast she knew she wasn't being coherent. "Jack can't fly if there's a hurricane or whatever, and if it could somehow reach him and stop him, that would buy us some time. We can find some new birds and catch up to him." Wren knew even as she said it that it was impossible. Where were they going to find falcons? And Jack was probably already miles away. But she continued on anyway. "Surely Mary will come back soon, and then we can—"

"We don't need Mary," Simon cut her off. "Or new falcons." He pointed beyond the girls to the twisted old bush. There, perched in the spot where the two uppermost branches made a *Y*, was Wren's falcon.

"You're alive!" Wren raced over to the bush, and the falcon gave her a familiar warning screech. Wren didn't care. "I should've known you'd be too clever for Jack!" She beckoned to the bird with her palm, but nothing happened. The falcon only watched the humans with her unblinking depthless eyes. Wren knew it was ridiculous to expect that the falcon would have a celebratory welcome for her, but she had at least expected a lessening of hostility. She was wrong.

The bird still made Wren climb through the thornbush. She still glared down at her with one judgmental eye. She still hissed and ruffled her feathers when Wren used the stardust to make her grow. But the falcon didn't recoil from Wren's touch. Instead, she bent her neck the way Wren had seen Simon's falcon do and offered Wren her back. Whether this was because Wren had finally made peace with her falcon or because her falcon was furious with Jack, Wren couldn't be sure.

"Good bird," Wren said, happy tears filling her eyes.

"But will she carry all three of us?" Simon sounded doubtful.

"Only one way to find out. Quick, before we can give her time to fly off." Wren hoisted herself up onto her falcon's bare back, steadying the bird as Jill climbed up after. The falcon danced under her, unfurling her long wings. "Simon," Wren called, "I can't stop her!" just as Jill squealed, "She's going to fly!" The falcon ran forward a few paces, the same jerky steps that always preceded takeoff, and then Wren saw something at her side. It was Simon, loping alongside the bird. In one easy movement, he swung himself up onto the falcon behind Jill. Wren's blood coursed with the thought that she'd finally done it; she had worked with her bird. She didn't pause to savor the moment, though. Jack was somewhere up ahead. And they had to stop him. She kicked hard into the falcon's flanks and leaned low over her neck. "Hold on!" she yelled to the others, tugging on the lead feathers as her falcon took to the sky.

TWENTY-FIVE

The skies your voice will open.
The stars begin to sing.
Light the darkest candle,
Through the heavens you will wing.

Aren't you ones for timing?" the old Fiddler in the Crooked House falcon mews told Wren, Jill, and Simon when they arrived, Wren's falcon's sides heaving with the effort. "You leave in the kerfuffle over the Magician's gateway and return when the old observatory tower's been destroyed." Wren craned her neck to exchange desperate looks with the others.

"Destroyed?"

"Burnt to a crisp," the Fiddler said, pointing to a cloud of smoke over the mountain that Wren could barely make out in the dark night sky. "Happened not more than an hour ago, and the Council is in an uproar."

"It has to be Jack, but why? And where has he gone?" Wren said as though asking the question could give her an answer. She pulled out Jack's blue book and began flipping through the final pages for a clue. If he had gotten the equipment from the observatory, he must have everything he needed now. She scanned the sky. No sign of a gateway.

"Now what's that you have there? That looks to me like the mark of the Magicians."

Wren moved her hand to cover Jack's sketch. She hadn't noticed the Fiddler coming near to feed her falcon a handful of dried meat.

"What have you three young ones been up to?" he said. "That's dark magic, that is."

Wren sighed. "You have no idea." Maybe it was because it felt like they had done everything they could and still come to a dead end. Maybe it was because Wren couldn't imagine walking in to the Fiddler Council and telling them that, yes, she had in fact helped Boggen to return, even if she didn't mean to. Or maybe it was because the Fiddler's green eyes reminded her of her father's. Maybe it was all those things combined. She slid off the falcon, Jill and Simon following. "I hope you can help us."

The old Fiddler stood in thoughtful silence after they spilled their breathless story. He gently patted Wren's falcon's side. "Now that's a tale for the apprentice books, isn't it?" he finally murmured. "But it will be better once we know the ending."

"Do you know where Jack could have gone?" Wren asked in a last desperate attempt. "Somewhere that might've been important to the Magicians?"

"Aye," the Fiddler said. "But I'm not sure I ought to tell you three. Might be better for the Fiddler Council."

"We don't have time!" Wren leaped to her feet. "It could take another hour to meet with the Council, and Jack's already on his way to Nod! Where do we go? Tell us, I'm begging you!"

The old Fiddler's gaze seemed to weigh her, and whatever he concluded, he must not have found her wanting. "The Archway to Heaven. That's where Boggen and the others were last seen. Where we thought they died." He told them how to get there, leaning close to whisper instructions to the falcon as well.

Wren didn't have time to wonder if they could trust the wrinkled old Fiddler or not. They didn't have a choice. She grabbed Jill by the shoulders. "Find Mary and the others. Tell the Council what happened and where we've gone. They might actually listen to you since you've been an apprentice here forever."

Jill reluctantly agreed, but Wren couldn't tell if that was because Jill would rather come with them to find Jack, or if it was because Jill had to tell the Council such unwelcome news. Either way, Wren was glad Jill agreed to go. If they were lucky, the Fiddler Council would not waste time arguing about things but would come help.

Wren hoisted herself back onto the falcon. For a moment, she thought about taking off then and there. She had created this mess; she should clean it up alone. She should be the one to deal with Jack. But she couldn't have gotten this far without Simon, and she wouldn't be able to make it farther on her own. From somewhere that felt like a lifetime ago, Wren could hear her mother telling her *no girl is an island*.

"Simon?" Wren leaned down, extending a hand. "Will you help me?" Without hesitating, Simon pulled himself up onto the falcon and soon they were out in the wide-open field. Wren hoped the old Fiddler was right about the Archway. She gripped her falcon with

her knees. If they wasted time flying up to the Archway and Jack wasn't there . . . She shoved the thought
out of her mind. They were doing the right thing.
They had to be.

Despite what Wren told herself, the weather was
beginning to reflect her unease. The sky was clear, but
bursts of rain fell, a strange mixture of starlight and
showers. Every so often a gust of wind pushed hard
against them, and Wren's falcon flapped her wings
extra-vehemently to stay the course. Wren suspected
that the bird's stubbornness was matched only by her
rage.

The wind picked up, the raindrops falling hard and
stinging her skin. They sped past the Crooked House
and over the broad marshy plains. The colors of the
aurora glowed in front of them, blue and green and
orange light blazing across the horizon with unearthly
fire. They skimmed the edge of the ocean and then
skirted a hidden valley, the landscape speeding by
below them in a jumble of layered shadows. Off in the
distance, thunder rumbled, signaling the oncoming
storm. Wren felt tight inside, like her anger and frustration were simmering in a perfect stew of emotion. The
discovery at her mom's play seemed ages ago. Wren

couldn't tell how long they had been flying. One hour? Maybe two? They soared over a sprawling marshland and dipped past a dark canyon, and then Wren saw it.

Ahead of them, a mountain ridge sloped down toward the ocean. The land ended offshore, waves lapping at the great stone pillar that made up its foundation. Beaten down by the passage of time and the harsh elements, some of the stone had eroded, creating a natural archway that curved up and over the water to a second stone pillar planted right in the middle of the sea. At the farthermost end, a flat outcropping that was silhouetted against the impending storm jutted out into nothing.

The sky wore a thick ominous cloak of black and gray. Near the horizon, the colors were lighter, blue and yellow sketching the magic of the aurora. It was breathtaking. And completely empty. Jack wasn't there. The wind quickened as the awful realization struck. They had no Plan B. They had bet everything on the old Fiddler's memory. And they had lost. Jack could be miles away, with no chance of their catching up to him. Lightning struck in the distance, followed by a roll of thunder. Wren's falcon dropped a sudden twenty feet.

"Wren!" Simon groaned from behind her. "Pull it

together or I'm going to barf all over you."

The bird cut a hard right and regained the lost ground, letting out a chiding screech. They were close now, and all the falcon's attention seemed to be fixed on rising high enough to land on the outcropping.

"What do we when we get there?" Simon yelled. Wren clenched her jaw. Once the bird stopped, she'd be able to think. They'd come up with a new plan. She shifted sideways to tell Simon as much when she saw that it was too late for conversation.

Swooping in from somewhere behind them was the lean dark shape of a falcon. And riding on its back was Jack.

He must have been lying in wait for them, hiding to take them by surprise. "He's here!" Wren screamed at Simon. "Get down!"

Simon shifted behind her as Wren lurched forward as low as she could go without falling off her falcon. Twin bolts of lightning flashed above the water, followed closely by a boom of thunder. She felt the rush of cold air and the thump of wings as Jack's falcon swept through where they had been just moments before.

Fear and anger battled inside Wren, matching the weather with their intensity and sending a torrent of rain to heighten the buffeting winds. Wren's falcon dropped down again, the air pressure sending her spiraling toward the ocean, so close that Wren could see the ripples on the water, but the falcon pulled out of it, circling over the water's surface and gaining altitude. The bird's muscles flexed powerfully as she moved up, battling the increasing wind and driving rain.

"Nice job, bird," Wren whispered, smoothing her neck feathers as she'd once seen Simon do. "It's a good thing you're so powerful." Wren felt rather than saw the falcon respond. It was as though Wren's words gave her extra strength, and the falcon quickly recovered the lost ground. Could it really be that simple? Had flying been such a struggle for Wren because she'd never said nice things to her bird?

"You are doing great, falcon," Wren sputtered. "Keep it up!" She felt silly, like she was pretending to be a cheerleader, but she didn't stop. "That's the way. Good job, bird!"

"Get closer," Simon yelled. "I'm going to try something."

Wren's falcon obeyed, veering to the right and into the wind. The falcon was flying strong, but she still had Jack's bird to contend with. Its wing slashed the air in front of Wren's falcon and threw her off course.

"Oh no!" Simon's shout was nearly overcome by the rush of wind. "My stardust!" Something whipped by Wren's face. She reached for it, but she was too late, and she watched Simon's leather pouch of stardust fall down into the sea.

The rain turned to hail, beating hard against Wren's numb hands. She fumbled around her neck, relieved to feel her own pouch of stardust secure on its cord. The hail pelted against her face, and she squinted her eyes to see through the increasing gale. Below them, the waves whipped into a white-tipped frenzy. "He's circling back around!" Wren yelled. "Stay low."

Jack's falcon cut right, and they narrowly missed being torn by its talons.

Whenever Jack's bird came too close, Wren could hear his voice, singing:

Sing a song of Fiddlers,
A pocket full of pow'r;
Four-and-twenty blackbirds
Eaten in the tower.

After each phrase, Jack let loose a peal of laughter that sounded nothing less than insane. Wren stared at

him through the sheet of rain. Jack was doing something with stardust, his hair plastered down on his
forehead by the rain. The air between his palms was
illuminated, and Wren could see the energy dancing.

Her falcon swooped left in a neat maneuver that
completely outwitted Jack's bird.

"Nice one!" Wren shouted, and felt the answering
wing beats. Without the falcon, they would surely be
lost. And that's when Wren got her idea. She didn't
know what Jack was doing with the stardust, but she
knew one thing for sure. There was no way they were
going to best him in a flying match. Or somehow figure out how to defeat him with magic. A tiny sliver of
hope cut through her thoughts like a ray of luminescent stardust. There might be a way. She'd only have
one shot at it. It would have to be a surprise. And it
would have to be good.

"Great flying, falcon." Wren leaned down close to
the bird's head. "Do you think you can get us up above
them?" The falcon began to ascend, and Wren took
that for a yes.

"Do it fast, okay?" Wren whispered. "Without him
noticing, if you can." What was it Simon had said at
Pippen Hill? *If you don't control it, it will control you.* Wren
didn't know if he was talking about the weather or her

emotions, but now was her chance to see if she could control both and maybe, just maybe, have a chance at beating Jack. "Hold on," she hissed back to Simon.

Jack's voice carried over the air, saying something about eating *all* the blackbirds in a pie, when Wren's falcon made her move. In one powerful thrust, she was nearly vertical, driving hard through the storm, and Wren squeezed with her knees. The sudden rush of adrenaline unleashed Wren's simmering cauldron of emotion. Anger and fear. Outrage at injustice and death. Frustration at her powerlessness to see through Jack's lies. She pressed past the warning dip she usually got, the panicky feeling that told her it was time to calm down. Wren didn't practice the special breathing technique. Instead, she let it build, her heart beating faster and faster until Wren wondered if it would crash out of her chest, and she reached for her pouch.

The stardust didn't feel warm and luminous. It was burning like the sun's fire in Wren's taut fingers, pulsing with the heat of her anger. Wren didn't stop to think about what she was doing. She raised her arms in the Fiddler pose, willing her nature to do its work.

She sang the starlamp rhyme, modifying it slightly. "As your bright and tiny spark"—Wren felt the heat build—"saves the traveler in the dark." The mass in her palm was sparking, drawing together in bristling jagged ropes that looked like comic-book drawings of lightning. Comic book or not, Wren was going with it. She raised one hand high and threw the lightning bolt as hard as she could.

Wren didn't know if Jack saw it coming or not, but she knew when the bolt hit its mark. Jack's falcon gave a terrible screeching cry, and Wren could see her glowing dagger sticking out of its eye. Jack's bird's wings were faltering. It spun down and down, slamming against the rock face with several sickening lurches.

A wave of nausea swept over Wren, knocking out any sense of relief and evaporating all the anger and fear it had taken to form the weather weapon. She felt faint, like she might fall off the bird into the ocean below, when Simon's arms wrapped firmly about her waist.

"Hang on a little longer, Wren," he said. "We're nearly to the top."

Wren's falcon glided to the flat ledge on the Archway and touched the ground with the familiar choppy jerks. She pulled up short, stopping just shy of the mountain wall, and Wren slowly released hold of her feathers.

Another wave of exhaustion hit, and Wren's muscles started shaking, like her whole body would never be warm again. Her skin was clammy with sweat, and her ears echoed with a tinny ringing noise.

"I don't feel so well," Wren managed as Simon helped her down off the falcon. The storm had disappeared with her fierce emotions, leaving the air calm and still, the clouds drifting away to reveal a thick carpet of stars sprawling across the velvety darkness.

"Side effect of the weather work, I'd say." Simon peered at Wren, and she half expected him to pull out his notebook to jot this all down for future study. Instead he gave the falcon a handful of dried meat. "That was well done, Wren."

"Thanks." She wiped her forehead with her sleeve.

"You thought it up all yourself?" Simon said, tossing the last handful of falcon feed on the ground for the bird to help herself.

Wren didn't know why she felt suddenly embarrassed. For once since discovering she was a Fiddler, she'd done something right, and *now* she felt all bad about it? She brushed at the muddy spots on her jeans. "I felt connected to the magic." She moved out toward the cliff's edge, stopping a few steps short. "Do you think Jack's gone?" she asked, because saying he was gone sounded better than saying he was dead.

Simon came up next to her, but neither of them could even see the bottom of the cliff. "Hard to imagine how someone could survive that."

"It's all so horrible," Wren sighed. "I wish things could have ended differently."

"I wish we had figured it out sooner. But at least we didn't let him get in there." Simon pointed behind them to the cliffside, where a man-made opening cut a perfectly smooth hole into the rock. The interior was black as a moonless night, without even a glimmer to indicate what lay beyond. In fact, it seemed to be so dark that it sucked up what little outside light shone on it.

Wren's falcon had settled down into a comfortable and well-deserved roost. Simon went over to her and let her know that they were going inside, and he politely asked if she'd mind waiting out here alone. Instead of standing to the side, Wren tried her own version of respect.

"Thank you, falcon," Wren said, and she meant it. "You really saved our lives out there."

Wren's falcon stared back at her with her mysterious eyes, but Wren thought she detected a slight loosening of her stiff neck muscles, as though the bird was deigning to acknowledge Wren's existence. It was a start.

Wren and Simon were halfway to the cave entrance when Wren heard the rushing of wings on the windless air. And not just a pair of wings but a whole host of them. Hundreds of them. Thousands of them. Wren whirled around to see a horde of blackbirds, normal-sized ones, hovering together near the cliff's edge. The sound grew louder, almost deafening as the birds climbed higher, flapping in formation, never deviating more than a few inches to each side. Wren instinctively drew close to Simon as the mass of birds grew until its shape was recognizable. There, beating the air viciously with a myriad of feathery wings, was a giant bird shape made up of thousands of individual birds, and hovering over the back was a very angry-looking Jack.

TWENTY-SIX

Away, birds, away!
Take a little and leave a little,
And do not come again;
For if you do, I will shoot you through,
And there will be an end of you.

Wren grabbed Simon's hand. "Inside the cave! Maybe we can outrun him." Her knees still shook, and the arrival of Jack chased the last bits of anger out of her, leaving only clammy terror behind.

Simon didn't move an inch. "Give me some stardust." A weird smirk crept across his face, and Wren wondered if he had bumped his head or something.

"Huh?" She tugged on his sleeve, but Simon's feet stayed firmly planted. He was stronger than he appeared. Wren's head grew dizzy, and she felt like she needed to sit down. "Simon. We've got to go."

"Stardust. Now, Wren." He tossed his notebook down at his feet, arms out in front in Fiddler posture.

"What are you talking about?' Wren screamed, the terror pressing hard against her heart. "Jack probably knows a hundred evil Magician rhymes that could kill you."

Across the way, Jack whipped the birds into a frenzy, his voice echoing on the mountain air. "Heigh-ho, the carrion crow," Jack chanted, casting webs of stardust over the bird horde. Their wings began to thrum in unison, as if flying to a sinister drumbeat.

With the sound, Wren's dread tripled. "Simon." She hooked her arm in his and yanked, pulling him backward a few steps. "There's no way we can beat Jack. We've got to run." She turned and bumped into her falcon, who was behind them, wings stretched out to make her appear twice her size, an all-too-familiar hostile look on her face.

"You, too?" Wren frowned. "Look. We can't defeat him."

"Clear your head, Wren." Simon shook free from her grasp. "The terror. The discouragement. It's all part of Jack's rhyme. He's using the stardust to manipulate the way you feel."

Wren dropped her hands. Could Simon be right? Was everything she was feeling—the animal-like need to run, the heady alertness—was it all a part of Jack's scheme? She grabbed the pouch from around her neck, cupping the comforting weight of stardust in her palm. She looked back at Jack's flock, beaks pointed in their direction as though they were a sheaf of arrows set to fly straight at them. Manipulation or not, it was terrifying.

Simon grabbed her wrist and pinched some stardust from the pouch, tossing it high. He blew a puff of air in the middle, sending little fireflies of magic swirling about his face.

Right then, Jack's voice rose in a triumphant crescendo, and the first of the birds came straight at them. It was like a scene out of an old black-and-white horror movie. A battalion of vicious, violent birds, headed straight for Wren and Simon, the only two humans on the lone treeless ledge.

"Start moving this way!" Wren said, diving to the ground and inching backward toward the blackness of the opening. "You can fiddle whatever you want from in there."

But Simon wasn't listening. It seemed as though he was frozen in the middle of a storm of stardust, and all Wren could see was a Simon-ish shape shrouded with incandescent pricks of light that he was throwing toward the oncoming threat. That, and the birds headed straight for him, beaks poised to gouge. And then Wren's falcon was there, leaping in front of Simon with a deathly squawk. The first volley of birds launched straight into her outstretched pinions.

"No!" Wren gasped as the falcon's body flipped backward with the weight of the attack. Wren crawled forward, knowing that for once her bird wouldn't be able to scare her off, but this time it was Simon who was lugging her toward the blackness.

"Get in there!" he shouted at Wren. "I'll take care of the birds."

"I can't just leave her to die." Wren pushed his hands off and moved toward the nearly motionless body of her falcon. A new host of birds was launching toward them, their shrill cries escalating as they attacked. Wren wracked her brain. What was the healing rhyme they had learned at the Crooked House? Wren began to sing, "Intery, mintery—"

"Go to her, and we all die." Simon pointed a sooty finger to Wren's left. "Jack's almost inside."

While Wren and Simon had been distracted by her falcon and the blackbird attack, Jack had made a run for it. Wren turned just in time to see Jack's figure disappearing into the cave's interior.

"Get ready to move," Simon said, his hands spinning faster than his words, stretching a thin veil of stardust around both of them. The blackbirds were stuck fast on the other side, unable to penetrate his shield. "When they retreat, that's when you go."

"And then what?" Wren asked. There were thousands of birds. Even if Simon could manage to hold off a few hundred, what would he do then? What about when he ran out of stardust?

But Simon didn't answer Wren. He turned back to face the cliff's edge and began to chant. His voice started out low, and Wren was surprised at how deep it sounded.

"Away, birds, away!" Simon chanted. "Take no more and leave at once, and do not come again."

The birds stopped their frantic pecking, hovering just out of reach of the shield.

Simon's voice grew louder. "Away, birds, away!" As he sang, the stardust swirled into little tendrils that reached out toward the birds, pushing them away and shaping a foggy tunnel that led straight toward the cave entrance.

There was no time to argue more. Simon was right. Their only chance now was for her to try to stop Jack. She grabbed a handful of stardust for herself and thrust the nearly empty pouch into Simon's hand. Maybe it would be enough to outlast the blackbirds.

Wren raced toward the dark opening, her muscles straining. Jack hadn't seen the last of her yet. She felt some of the clammy terror feeling lift, and then the mouth of the cave loomed up in front of her, and she was running inside, the thick darkness embracing her like cold water.

TWENTY-SEVEN

Hush-a-bye, baby, on the treetop!
When the wind blows the cradle will rock;
When the bough breaks the cradle will fall;
Down will come baby, cradle and all.

Even though Wren's eyes told her there was nothing in front of her, she could still feel resistance. She pushed forward into the cave like she was swimming in air, and then she was through, on the other side of whatever, the sound of the birds' flapping wings and Simon's chanting cutting off in an instant. The absolute silence of the cave pulsed loud in her ears.

Wren pinched the tiniest bit of stardust and blew it up into a miniature starlamp. She couldn't afford to waste much. The embers glowed bright in the heavy darkness, and it was as though Wren had switched on a hundred-watt bulb. She saw that she was in a great cavern, one that looked very much like the interior of the Crooked House, only the walls here pulsed a sickly yellowish green. Stalagmites pocked with something bronze glistened on either side of her, forming a menacing corridor. There was only one way to go: forward.

Wren let the stardust play above her upraised palm and hurried on, her blood pumping with the knowledge that Simon was still fighting the birds outside. Soon she was in another dense passageway, this one much longer. She swam hard, pushing on the unseen barrier, and felt her throat clench with claustrophobia. What if she couldn't make it through and was stuck forever in this invisible quicksand?

Her muscles grew tired from beating against the unknown, her legs stumbled, and she wondered what would happen if she stopped altogether. Panic gave way to a calm exhaustion. Everything would be much simpler if she just leaned back and went to sleep. Wren's eyelids grew heavy, and she wanted more than anything to shut them. She rested against the unseen barrier and let her hands fall to her sides. As she did, a streak of stardust caught her attention, winking at her as though it were the wet eye of her contrary falcon, and Wren's senses jolted into awareness.

Simon's and her falcon's lives depended on her. This was no time to sleep. She fought back at what must be more of Jack's mind games, kicking hard against the unseen presence, feeling her own will strengthened as she moved forward.

With one final push she was through, thrust out into another cavern as though reborn. This one blazed with blue light, and Wren raised her hands to shield her eyes from the sudden glare.

"So the little bird has made her way into my nest." Jack's mocking tones reverberated around the room.

Wren saw his familiar lean form on a raised platform. Behind him stood a gyroscope that was as tall as he was. Underneath it sat a book, its strange words alight with blue fire. Jack must have come here before, because an array of equipment was spread out on the round platform, paralleling the shape of the circular opening above that revealed the brilliant night sky.

Wren recognized one of the Alchemist's tools, the one that looked like a candelabra, stolen from the old observatory. Three of the candles were already lit, their smoky trails snaking up and out, tracing a familiar webbed path to the Magicians' mark written across the stars.

Wren rubbed the remainder of the stardust all over

her palms. She had to be prepared for anything. Every opportunity might be her last.

"You are a liar and a murderer." Wren spat the words out as though they were poison. She took a Fiddler's stance, every sense attuned to Jack, ready for any tricks he might pull.

"Tsk, tsk, Wren," Jack said, clicking his tongue at her like she was a small child. "It isn't nice to call people names." He was bending over a shallow bowl that rested on the center of the platform. "If you can't say anything nice, better not to say anything at all." His words were singsong, almost like he was reciting a rhyme.

Without looking up, he waved one arm, sending a puff of stardust racing toward her, and then an invisible hand clamped hard on Wren's jaw. Her tongue wouldn't work properly, and she couldn't open her mouth. She tried to scream, but all that came out was a muffled, "Mmmmmmph!"

Jack's laugh was low and sinister. "Now, that's better. How can I finish my calculations with you blabbing at me?"

Inside, Wren was yelling, but all that did was turn her silent throat hot and make her head feel like it might explode. Anger surged through her, but she couldn't see any changes in the cloudless night sky overhead. Even if she could channel the weather again, it wasn't like she could take Jack by surprise, or even say a rhyme. She looked down at her stardusty palms. They might as well have been covered with dirt.

Jack continued working, silently focused on the calculations in front of him. It was as if he had forgotten Wren altogether, as though she didn't exist. And then Wren realized that for him, she didn't. This wasn't like a movie, where the hero came across the bad guy at the last moment, and the villain divulged the whole secret plan. Jack didn't have a nefarious purpose for Wren. He didn't want to see her dead. He simply didn't care about her at all.

Jack pulled out a rolled piece of paper from his long apprentice cloak and held it up to the sky. Wren could see that it was a star chart, a copy of the one they'd found in Boggen's lab behind the waterfall, but this one had a certain route highlighted with stardust. Wren stopped squirming. Whether it was because he thought she wasn't a threat or because he was too preoccupied, Jack had made his first big mistake. He might have trapped Wren's tongue, but he hadn't trapped her body.

She crouched down to the wet cavern floor. She had been a Fiddler for less than a month, and she'd fallen for it, too. The dependence on stardust. The belief that rhymes were essential to any endeavor. Sure, they were helpful, but there was also a good old-fashioned punch in the face. After all, as Jill had said, stardust wouldn't do a Fiddler much good if he was unconscious. Wren crept toward the platform, scanning the ground in front of her for anything she could use as a weapon. There, over near the foot of it, was a stone about the size she could carry, maybe even big enough to knock Jack out.

Jack began to chant, a crooning rhyme that matched the slow dance of his stardust. "All night long their net they threw to the stars in the twinkling foam," he sang, the stardust trailing up from his fingers to take the shape of a giant cobwebby net. "T'was all so pretty a sail it seemed as if it could not be, and some folks thought t'was a dream they'd dreamed of sailing that beautiful sea."

As he sang, a single star from up above shone blindingly bright, and the wisps of the aurora began to tangle together, stretching upward toward the star.

Jack's voice grew louder, more frantic, as he repeated the words of his rhyme, and the round platform he was standing on began to tilt, as though it were a gigantic globe, swirling on an axis of stardust. The air around Wren grew heavy with the unseen thickness, and she had to push hard just to take a single step forward. She was almost there. Right next to the stone. She scooped it up, her muscles straining with the effort, the air a crushing weight around her, and Jack's voice crowed over all like the dark Magician he was.

Wren could see the platform tilting up, the stardust pulled taut as though it could launch Jack into the air to meet the single shining star, and Wren knew with a sudden insight that it was now or never. This was her chance to get on the platform.

She dropped the stone, pushing forward with all her might, a surge of exhausted strength that propelled her one last step, and she was stumbling up against the rock face, clawing at the platform edge, even as the stardust combined with the magic of the aurora to lift it skyward. Wren's fingers found a handhold, and she clung tight, her feet trailing along the ground, and then they were up, flying out and past the mountaintop, over the Archway to Heaven, and into the vast stretch of sky beyond. Wren swung her body, working the momentum so that her other hand could reach up, battling the numbing effect of the cold air. They were accelerating, and every second threatened to drop her into the gleaming water below.

Wren heard Jack's voice, echoing the same chant about sailing and nets and the foam of the stars. She felt the aurora before she saw the colors dancing around her, the bath of liquid warmth immediately dissolving the force of gravity that pulled her down. All her muscles tingled with energy, and she felt strong enough to do anything, strong enough to stop Jack once and for all. Wren flung herself up onto the platform to see that Jack, too, was lost in the sensation of the magic.

The net he'd woven was a masterpiece, a rainbow of color that shifted gracefully in the waves of the aurora, stretching out and covering the distance between the platform and the bright star. Jack's rhyme sounded eerily beautiful in that warm light. Wren flexed her hands. Perhaps she was strong enough to push Jack over the edge. But even as she considered it, Wren knew she couldn't. Whatever he was now, Jack had once been her friend. Besides, the aurora throbbed with the very current of all life, and she couldn't kill another living creature while swimming in it.

Jack saw her then, and his mouth made a little O of surprise. He must have been hindered by the aurora as well, because though Wren saw his fists clench at his sides, he didn't make a move toward her, nor did he begin to sing another rhyme. Instead, he returned to his navigation, adjusting something on the gyroscope dial in front of him, and looked anxiously up at the net as if to reassure himself that it was there.

They were hurtling through the air, the aurora's light wrapping them in a glow of strength and wind, but the atmosphere around them was changing, darkening somehow and becoming colder and more alien. Wren sat on the edge of the platform and peered over, watching as the ball that must be Earth shrank silently away below them.

In the light of the stardust, this made Wren want to laugh. They were flying through outer space. She looked up, out past the rainbow net that was sheltering them, and saw the bright glow of stars streaming past, their lights pale in the face of the one glowing fiercely in front of them. They'd left Earth far below, a ball of shadow with slight indentations to mark the continents. The stars tore by faster now, streaks of white light whistling past the net's glow. They spun, dancing through the stardust, deeper and deeper into the unknown.

And then something changed. Even from within

the protective stardust, Wren felt a sense of foreboding. Cold air whipped past her face, and she darted an anxious glance at Jack, who looked anything but worried. He rubbed his palms together in anticipation and reached greedy hands to adjust the newly woven net.

The streaks of friendly starlight grew sparser, the air crowding close, so that now even the rainbow net seemed like a pale flicker of fading light.

"What are you doing!" Wren screamed at Jack inside her head. "You're going to kill us!" Her breaths came shallower as the stardust's preserving glow waned. Jack must have felt it, too. His pale face had a blue tinge, especially around the mouth, but he opened his hands wide and cast his net ever onward.

Wren followed his feverish gaze, and that was when her breath was swept away altogether. The last of her sense of well-being flickered away with the final dying glow of the stardust.

Wren could sense the pulsing weight of the gateway somewhere up ahead. They were in deep blackness now, ten thousand times the invisible pressure she felt back on Earth. Her body was pressed to the platform, face crushed against the ancient stone surface. She crawled toward Jack, each inch forward an agonizing struggle.

Even if they could endure the weight without being torn apart, even if the stardust's magic could somehow shield them from the natural consequences, even if they could somehow survive, what then?

Wren saw Jack across the way, his form flat against the platform. His face looked different, older somehow and more angular. Her skin crawled at the thought of their shared conversations at the Crooked House, how she had laughed at his jokes, and she felt like a fool.

Jack was still, conserving his energy no doubt, but he had something cupped carefully between both hands. A round object coated with ashes that looked like a dirty stone. Wren's pulse quickened. She had seen something like it before, back in Boggen's lab when she had sorted through the forgotten chunks of coal. Beneath the dusky cover a light pulsed, transforming the dirty stone into a mysterious golden object. *The key to the gateway.* Jack was only a few feet away, but he might as well be miles. And then Wren knew it, as sure as she'd known anything. This was the moment to stop him. Now, before they arrived at the gateway door, before he had a chance to use the key and let Boggen through.

Jack's rhyming had dwindled to a whisper, a dying effort to control what had so clearly spiraled out of control. With one final lunge, Wren was at Jack's side, her hands around his shoulders, grappling hard with him, hoping that the weight of their struggle would be enough to push them near the edge. With luck, she could knock the key out of his hands and stop everything. She'd taken him off guard, she could see.

"Get back," Jack hissed at her, his skin taut with the force of gravity, the angles of his face making it look like his blue eyes were staring out of a skull. "Get back or die."

He raised his hand to deliver some deadly blow with stardust, but he didn't realize Wren had already decided to die. Before he could act, Wren grabbed for his neck, rolling forward, letting the crushing weight pull them over the edge of the platform and into the swirling blackness of outer space.

They fell together. For a heartbeat, Jack's gaunt countenance split wide in a scream of horror as the key to the gateway fell from his hands, dropping out of sight into the pulsing hole below them, and then they were apart, spiraling through the last protective sheen of the stardust. Wren's breath was gone, all oxygen snuffed out in the void. Her skin burned hot as her heart pumped a final searing burst of blood through her veins. Her senses were aflame with pain. Everything hurt as the intractable grip of the gateway began to crush the life out of her.

Wren's last thoughts were of home. Of her parents and how they would never know what became of her. Of Simon and his friendship. Of the warmth and life of Earth. And then she felt it. The whisper of wind against her cheek out in the eternal silence of space. A sensation of heat. Of well-being and hope. Something tugged hard on her shoulders. And then came the smell, the scent of spices and warmth and winter. And the rushing of wings. And the harmony of voices, before everything was blotted out in a brilliant flash of blue light.

TWENTY-EIGHT

Ring around the rosies,
Pocket full of posies.
Ashes, ashes, we all fall down.

When Wren opened her eyes she saw nothing but darkness, as though a black hole had swallowed her up. Then, as her sight adjusted, she saw glimmers of stardust nearby. She stood, ignoring the quaking of her knees, and moved closer to the wall that was covered with a glowing pattern. It was the winged shape, the one that she saw in her dreams, and this time it was alive. Papery wings sparkling with every shade of color fluttered like a butterfly's. With each movement, the soft sound ushered in the low notes of an antiphonal song. The sound didn't only reach Wren's ears, it thrummed through her chest. She stretched one hand toward the wall of winged creatures, and that was when she heard it. *Wren.* Woven into the music, someone was calling her name. More than calling. Commanding.

Wren moved slowly toward the voice. The luminescent wings all around her lit a path through the darkness, the rocky floor sloping to a gradual descent. Illogically, the air grew warmer the lower she went, and the heat awakened the pain of her struggle with Jack. Her hands burned where the stone cut into her flesh, her jaw ached from clenching it under Jack's spell, and her calves grew more sore with every step.

The winged creatures accompanied her as she drew near the music. The notes sounded first like woodwinds, but earthy, as though someone was playing the breeze in the tops of the firs. Next came a chorus of strings interwoven with the pattering of rainfall. Percussion blended with the rush of waves on the ocean shores. Flutes with birdsong. Violins with the sound of weeping.

Wren wanted it to stop, and she wanted it to go on forever. The compelling voice rose above the music, urging her onward. *Wren.* She felt it coursing through her, pounding with each beat of her heart. *Wren. Wren. Wren.* And then she was there. In front of her was the towering version of the wings. Two gigantic bird shapes, older and larger than Wren's full-grown falcon, stood stationed on either side of a doorway that throbbed with light.

Their wings were slicked back against their sides, the *U*-shape clear because of their size, feathery tips brushing against each other near the back. They weren't lit with the dusky light of stardust like their miniature counterparts were. Instead, they were the color of ashes, a blend of shadows the likes of which Wren had never seen. Beyond them was what seemed to be a fire that burned with blue flame instead of red. Opal-like stones ringed the blaze with cool light. In the center, pale green and turquoise and shimmering silver leaped and swirled in a mesmerizing dance. Above this hung something familiar. A giant pendulum, slowly tracing a smooth route over and among the unearthly flames.

Wren didn't know how long she stood there before she noticed that the music had stopped. A silence heavy with expectation filled the space, broken finally by the creatures in front of her. With the sound of entire flocks of birds in flight, they unfurled their wings, their length lit with a thousand tiny lights that peered out through a swirl of cloudy ash.

Wren. This time Wren knew the voice was coming from one of the creatures. The word reverberated inside her as the creatures' wings met in an arch that framed the pendulum. Wren peered closer into the swirling stardust and saw two figures fighting on a platform in the midst of a streaked aurora, Jack's unmistakable web spread over them.

"That's me," Wren breathed, as the images solidified. She watched them topple over the edge, outside the safety of the net, and then saw the swoop of a shadow, the outline of the giant creatures now in front of her plucking Wren out of the downward spiral.

"You saved me?" she asked.

We are the Ashes, the voice told her. *The Crooked Man appoints us to watch this gateway. We have been watching for a long time, yet you and the boy are the first to come.*

"Watching for what?" Wren asked, but the Ashes didn't reply. "The boy. Is he okay?" Wren wondered what more she should say. Had they rescued Jack as well? If so, where was he?

He lives. More of the silence. *But he is not well.*

Wren squinted at the dust that was moving faster, blotting out the image of her and the Ashes and forming the recognizable shape of Jack, kneeling on the floor.

Dark, ominous clouds whirled around him. "Where is he?" Wren asked.

Beyond. We warned him, and we warn you as well. Do not open the gateway. If you try, you will surely die.

"We can't open it," Wren said simply. "We lost the key when we fell."

The boy will not listen. He means to force it open, and he will do so regardless of the cost. The boy is in great peril. He always has been. Look.

The dark clouds cleared from around Jack's form. He looked like Jack, but younger, and he sat alone at the edge of a crowded cafeteria. Ordinary boys and girls moved around him, a few pointing and laughing, but most ignoring him altogether. And then the dust swirled, the scene shifting to show Jack sitting in a doctor's office.

"And what exactly is it that you claim to see?" the doctor was saying.

"Dust filled with lights of every color," Jack said, his eyes wide with wonder. "It's beautiful. Like magic." The stardust spun in the air between Jack's fingers, but it was obvious the doctor saw none of it.

The doctor frowned, making a note in Jack's chart. He reached into a sterile cupboard behind him for a bottle of pills, and the swirls of stardust faded as the doctor explained the medicine to Jack.

The next image was of Jack in a small white room all alone. He sat in a corner sobbing, but no one came to him. Wren's throat felt raw. What was she watching? Things that had happened to Jack? Or things that were about to? *Swirl.*

The next picture answered it for her. The Ashes showed her a scene from the dream world. The room with the black-and-white window. Boggen's room. And there was Jack, sitting across the table from Boggen, leaning in.

"You'll find the stone with my last message in the crypt," Boggen was saying. "I hid it there before we left for Nod. Show it to Mary, give it to her, sell it to her, I don't care—but do whatever it takes to gain entrance to the Crooked House." He patted Jack's head in a fatherly way. "They will lie to you. The Alchemists will tell you all sorts of horrible things about me. Don't believe them."

"How could I?" Jack looked up at Boggen with a glassy-eyed worshipful gaze. "You saved me. You found me in my dreams and saved me, and I got away from that awful place." He shivered. "I will find the key for you. And the rhyme."

Boggen's voice turned syrupy. "You have brilliant potential, Jack, and I doubt the Alchemists will see it. Why else do you think I'm going to all this trouble?" He patted Jack's head again. "It's for you, Jack. So that you can come be with us Magicians. You are special. You belong with us."

Jack was nodding vigorously, the sadness around his eyes replaced with determination. "I will find it," he said. "I'll do anything." *Swirl.*

It was Jack as Wren knew him now, dancing around the falcon mews at Pippen Hill. He held the gateway key in both hands, hugging it to his chest. "I found it! I found it! Boggen's going to make me a prince!" He skipped in a circle, his cloak streaming behind him, as he cast a stardust spell over the falcons.

Wren leaned closer, as though she could leap into the scene in front of her. So that was why Jack had done what he'd done. To escape whatever horrible thing had happened to him when he first tried to tell ordinary people about stardust. To go to Nod. To belong with the other Magicians. The scene began to grow dim, as though the light was fading, and then the swirling clouds of darkness and stardust returned, obscuring Wren's view. Soon, all sight of Jack was gone, leaving only the swinging pendulum and beyond that a slab of a door that looked like it had been fashioned from a giant opal. Swirls of color covered the surface, and from its depth came an icy clarity that reminded Wren of the aurora.

Now you see, the Ashes told her. *The boy will do anything for Boggen. He means to force the gateway open, and he will die if he does. You must go to him. You are the one who will save him. Use the rhyme.*

"What rhyme? Go to him how?" Wren took a step back looking up at the silent creatures. "And do what?"

The Ashes didn't answer. Instead, the melancholy music began again, this time joined with the Ashes' singing: *Ring around the rosies; pocket full of posies; ashes, ashes, we all fall down.* The third time through, the translucent door in front of her shuddered as a single crack thundered right through the center, dividing the mineral mass into two halves that fell backward into pieces. Wren felt the feather touch of wings against her skin, whispery ministrations that coated her with stardust. When her entire body was covered, they swept Wren past the jagged remainders of the door and into the space beyond.

As soon as Wren stepped through, the haunting song of the Ashes disappeared. She whirled around, and the pendulum and blue fire behind her were gone. In front of her was a cavern, and Wren could see Jack kneeling before a circular opening in the floor about two paces across. Beyond it was a doorway covered with thick reams of stardust, woven so tightly together it looked like a giant glimmering spiderweb. *The gateway.*

"I'm trying," Jack was saying to someone. "But there's nothing I can put in the lock. I told you I lost the key."

"Don't be a fool, boy," a voice said from beyond the stardust web, and Wren's blood went cold, sending icy chills of fear all over her body. *Boggen.*

"All along I thought you were the special one, Jack, that you were *different*. How you disappoint me. What a waste." Boggen's words dripped with scorn and disgust, and Wren saw Jack crouch lower, his shoulders crumpling with shame. "I should never have dreamt of you in the first place, never have thrown away my time teaching you."

"I can do better; just don't send me back." Jack sounded panicked, all hints of his usual easy humor gone. "Not to the hospital. Not there." Jack was babbling now, something about being stuffed with medicine and water dripping and night terrors. "They thought I was crazy. Said I was hallucinating. That none of it was real." A note of desperation entered his words. "You can't send me back now. Now that I know." He gave a little cry of pain and then stood, pacing in front of the cobwebbed opening. "I can find something to open it. A stone or stardust or something." He kept saying the same thing over and over, as though he were reciting a poem. Or a prayer. "You promised. You promised to give me a home. To teach me. You said the others would understand in the end." His voice cracked with a sob. "You said you'd be like a grandfather to me. You promised."

"Shut up!" Boggen's figure, a dark silhouette on the other side of the stardust web, pressed in. "And open the gateway." His words took on a wheedling note. "Be a good lad and open the gateway. If you can do that, perhaps you can still come and live with me on Nod."

"Don't do it, Jack. You'll die if you try," Wren said, moving into the room. "Don't open the gateway."

Jack's head darted up, fast as a snake's. He leapt to his feet, all trace of his sobbing gone, replaced by a smug smile on his face. He looked older and harder somehow. Less like the sobbing boy or the Jack Wren knew and more like the dark Fiddler he was becoming.

"Boggen's using you," Wren said in a low voice.

The shadow outside the door shifted. So much for Boggen not knowing she was there.

"The other Weather Changer," Boggen said in that same bewitching voice. "Both of you the most brilliant apprentices in centuries."

Wren couldn't see any stardust, couldn't see how Boggen could be working his magic, but he must be, because something in her wanted more than anything to believe him. The idea of being the most brilliant apprentice in centuries sounded good. Her lips formed a half smile in response before she remembered who she was. And where she was and why.

"Don't listen to him, Jack," Wren said, trying to lock her gaze on Jack's. "He's a liar. He's been lying to you all along. About the message. About the Magicians. About everything."

"What, are you jealous, Wren? Jealous that you might not be the only special Weather Changer Fiddler after all?" Jack sneered. "Who cares what you think? Besides"— Jack sprinkled some stardust over the hole in front of him—"you're too late."

"Don't!" Wren shouted as she realized what he was doing. A cloud of stardust blossomed up from the gateway lock, but it wasn't the usual harmony of colors. This was an array of unsettling hues: an eerie green, blinding red, and a ghastly brown color that sparked with black bolts of jagged energy. "I had a little treasure tree." Jack began to sing the rhyme that would open the gateway.

"Jack, you've got to stop!" She ran toward him. "Jack! No!" Wren was halfway across the room when the ball of tainted stardust exploded into streams of piercing black daggers. One shot toward the gateway opening, the other swarmed toward Jack, and one pelted straight toward Wren.

She hardly had time to think. She rubbed some of the stardust the Ashes had coated her with and swirled it up in the air, scrambling for the words to the rhyme Simon had used to ward off the birds. She saw the stardust forming the same barrier, felt the warmth of the magic, and the smoking black missiles evaporated into her shield. Beyond, Jack had not been so lucky. The cloud of tainted stardust filled the air around him, covering him in a suffocating blanket that pressed his form down against the hard floor and seeped over to the gateway.

From behind her shield, Wren could hear Boggen's cry of pain, could see his shadow on the other side of the gateway crumpling under the tainted stardust, the weapon of his own creation. Boggen fell to his knees, one hand stretched high in the cobwebbed door, as if to reach for help, and then his cry was cut off. For a moment, Wren thought the tainted stardust might yet pierce through, breaking open the gateway at last, despite all she had been through to stop it. But instead, it crept through the cracks, taking its sickly colors with it, seeping its poison onto the other side, and leaving the room empty except for Jack's lifeless form across the way.

"Jack!" Wren dropped the shield and ran over to him. Could he really be dead? His body lay crumpled, curved around what was now a burnt-out hole in the floor. The Ashes has been right. Jack had tried to force the gateway. Whatever he'd done, whatever dark rhyme he'd used, it hadn't worked.

Wren knelt by Jack's side, feeling his wrist and then neck for a pulse. *Nothing.* The skin on his face and hands was covered with countless cuts where the stardust had flayed him. She flipped him onto his back, racking her brain for what she had learned in that one CPR class she had taken for babysitting. Compressions, she thought, and then the breath of life. She pushed hard on Jack's chest. Wasn't there supposed to be some song you could count to? Some way of timing the compressions? Her mind went blank. She couldn't think of the song, any words at all, except the strange rhythm of the Ashes. She placed her hands on his chest, pushing down hard, willing his heart to keep beating. She waited. Listening for breath. She did it again. And again.

Wren didn't know how long she had been working on Jack, what she was waiting for. She might be keeping his heart beating, but if it couldn't start manually, he was beyond hope. It wasn't like someone was going to run and call 911 and then the ambulance would come and shock his heart back. No, she was alone. And the Ashes were wrong. She wasn't going to save him. *Ring around the rosies.* Two presses. *Pocket full of posies.* Breathe into his mouth. Wren felt the shock wearing off. The exhaustion and the unreality of what had just happened came crashing in. Jack. Dead? Hot tears flooded her eyes, and her throat clenched so that she could barely breathe. *Ashes, ashes.* The stupid Ashes. Showing her how Boggen had used her friend. Telling her she could save Jack with a rhyme? She choked back a sob, willing herself to hold it together just a little longer. Sending her here in just enough time to watch him die?

Wren's eyes grew wide. *Of course!* She had been going about this all wrong. *The rhyme.* She shook some of the stardust out of her hair, swirling it in the air above Jack's motionless form. Her addled brain had missed the whole point of the rhyme. She thought back to what she had learned at the Crooked House about healing, how the stardust had bathed the wounded tree and straightened it, righting it—how Mary had healed Jack's cut on that long-ago day with the falcons. She swirled her hands through the air, her shaky voice growing stronger as she said the words to the Ashes' rhyme. She watched the stardust form, flaring brightly with the intensity of her emotion, twisting and curling. Sweat beaded on her forehead, the exhaustion of the past hours threatening to undo her completely, but she set her mind fast, working the stardust until it fell into a white-hot stream of light.

Wren took a deep breath—*the Ashes had better be right*—and funneled all of it, the bright hot living stardust, straight at Jack's chest in one powerful jolt. The cavern around them blazed with heat. She saw Jack's body spasm and then through the blinding light saw the steady rise and fall of his chest. *He was breathing.* Wren sank back onto her heels, the last bit of her energy spent with the stardust. She felt dizzy. Her vision blurred. She reached out to steady herself on the floor but she was already laying down. Streaks of blue and white shot across Wren's vision, and Jack's voice weakly calling her name sounded like it was coming from the end of a long tunnel.

And there at the end of it was a familiar song, the rhythm of the Ashes singing, the low beautiful harmony of their eerie music tucking her in to a dreamless sleep.

TWENTY-NINE

Sleep, baby, sleep.
The Ashes guard the keep.
Another shakes the dreamland tree,
And from it fall sweet dreams for thee.
Sleep, baby, sleep.

The first time Wren opened her eyes she saw Liza sitting next to her bed. She was in an unfamiliar room, the starry night sky clear outside her window, and Baxter dozed nearby, slumped in the chair next to the fireplace. Wren wanted to call out to them, to shout for them to wake up and see her, but her mouth wouldn't work properly. Her eyelids felt heavy with sleep, and though she fought it, they shut, sending her back into dreamless slumber.

Next, it was Jill. Wren still couldn't speak, but Jill saw that she was awake.

"You must rest, Wren," Jill said, bathing Wren's forehead with a cool washcloth. "Wielding the amount of stardust you did"—she wrung out the cloth over a bowl on the nightstand—"is unheard of, even for a full Fiddler. Rest."

Wren struggled against it, but no matter how hard she tried, she couldn't stay awake. Each time she opened her eyes, someone else was there, soothing her, telling her to sleep, that she was going to be all right, that all was well, that she must rest.

Once, before she even opened her eyes, she heard Mary's voice, and then Cole's answering her. "The gateway remains closed," Cole had said definitively. "The Ashes confirmed it."

"And at what cost?" Mary sounded sad. "Two apprentices."

"Jack and Wren both still live," Cole had said. "Don't give up hope."

Wren wanted to comfort Mary, to tell her she was all right, but her mouth felt dry as dust, as though she might never speak again. She wanted to tell them that Nod must be okay, because for the first time in a long while she hadn't dreamed about it. She hoped that meant Robin was all right now. Wren pushed hard, fighting through the way her jaw felt wired shut, but to no avail. Sleep came unbidden, and Mary and Cole were gone.

Each time she woke, it was someone else. Once she even saw her parents, which she knew was impossible. Most of the time it was Jill or Liza. Sometimes they washed her forehead. Other times they held a spoonful of hot broth to her lips. But beyond that Wren couldn't speak, couldn't move, couldn't do more than blink at them. Until the time Simon came.

Wren opened her eyes, looking immediately to the chair where someone always sat. Instead of a person, though, she saw her falcon perched on it, and behind the chair stood Simon, looking down at her with his warm brown eyes.

Wren felt happy tears prickle at the back of hers, and her wooden mouth melted into the hint of a smile.

"Thank you," she managed through parched lips.

Simon's eyes grew wide, as though Wren had done something unimaginable. He disappeared from sight, and Wren moved her head weakly, watching Simon run to the door.

"She's awake!" he called out to the hallway. "And she spoke."

The next moment her room was filled with people.

Simon and Jill. Baxter and Liza and Mary and, next to her, Cole. Wren blinked. And beyond them, her parents. Wren's mother and father hovered behind the Fiddlers, eyeing them warily. Mary drew close, leaned over and felt Wren's forehead, peering into her eyes.

"The sickness is breaking. She'll recover," Mary said breathlessly. "She's going to be all right." She clasped Wren's hand in both of her own. "You're going to be just fine, Wren, you wonderful girl, you."

"And Jack?" Wren was surprised at how tiring it was to say the words. Like being awake for two minutes was running a marathon.

"Jack is here, too," Mary said, but she wouldn't meet Wren's eyes. She looked down at her hand. "But he hasn't woken. The Ashes brought you both back from the gateway."

Wren felt her eyelids beginning to close. She fought to keep them open. She had so many questions. She wanted to talk to the Ashes. To find out what the others knew. Did they hate Jack? Did they know how Boggen had tricked him? She worked her mouth, but no words came out.

"We're tiring her out. She must rest to regain her strength." Mary rose, shooing the others out of the room. "Suzette? Walter?" Wren wanted more than anything to sleep, but she saw her parents drawing near, and she willed her eyes open for a few more moments.

"Little Bird," her dad said, tears making his eyes all shiny. "We've missed you so much."

"We love you, sweetie." Wren's mom kissed her on her forehead. "We won't go anywhere. We'll be right here when you wake up."

Wren wondered if this was actually happening. Her parents? And the Fiddlers? The last thing she saw was them settling into the unoccupied chairs by her bedside, her mom and dad sharing a smile. Wren stopped fighting. She had done it. She had saved Jack and kept Boggen from opening the gateway. Mary's words echoed through her mind. She was going to be okay.

Wren let her eyes shut, succumbing to sleep, and, for the first time since the gateway, she dreamed of Nod.

ACKNOWLEDGMENTS

I am so very grateful for all those who have contributed to *A Sliver of Stardust* and feel indescribably fortunate to work with such amazing and talented people.

I want to especially thank my agent, Laura Langlie, for her support and insight into the story; Erica Sussman and Stephanie Stein for their brilliant and creative editorial notes; Jakob Eirich for his breathtaking artwork, and the entire team at HarperCollins Children's for their partnership and commitment to getting good books into the hands of readers. I know very little of the magic that turns the plain document I produce into the lovely book readers hold in their hands, but I deeply appreciate the contribution of all those who have made it possible.

Heartfelt thanks also to Joy McCullough-Carranza

for bravely reading a very early draft, to Casey Walton for sharing his mad brainstorming skills with me, to Christy Goodman for cheering me on through writerly angst, to Renee Weathers for the gift of her loyal and longstanding friendship, to Steve and Ron for their truthful and life-giving insights, and to the many kindred spirits at Advent for your encouraging words when the writing process was less than magical. I am so thankful I get to know you and share life with each of you.

A few lines on this page always feels too small to properly thank my husband, Aaron. But hopefully the gratitude I feel comes through loud despite its littleness: Without your love and partnership, I wouldn't be the person, or writer, that I am. Thank you. And to my boys, Griffin, Elijah, and Ransom: I'm so glad that you are you! You each are wonderful gifts, and I'm so happy to get to be your mom.

And, finally, to my readers: One of my favorite things about meeting other book lovers is the instant friendship that comes when I discover someone with whom I share a favorite story. As a writer, that feeling is magnified a thousand percent, and I am so happy to have shared this story-world with you. Thank you for reading.